Sherlock Holmes

Consulting Detective

Volume Fourteen

AIRSHIP 27 PRODUCTIONS

AN AIRSHIP 27 PRODUCTION ™

Sherlock Holmes: Consulting Detective, Volume 14

"The Adventure of the Frozen Irregular" © 2019 I.A. Watson
"The Ghost of Otis Maunder" & "The Adventure of the Apologetic Assassin" © 2019 David Friend
"The Case of the Singular Tragedy" © 2019 Raymond Louis James Lovato

Cover illustration © 2019 Ted Hammond
Interior illustrations © 2019 Rob Davis

Editor: Ron Fortier
Associate Editor: Fred Adams Jr.
Production and design by Rob Davis
Promotion and marketing by Michael Vance

Published by
Airship 27 Productions
www.airship27.com
www.airship27hangar.com

ISBN: 978-1-946183-68-2

Printed in the United States of America

10 9 8 7 6 5 4 3 2 1

Sherlock Holmes
Consulting Detective
Volume XIV
TABLE OF CONTENTS

Sherlock Holmes

in

"The Adventure of the Frozen Irregular"

By
I.A. Watson

𝕴 had met Sherlock Holmes' elder brother Mycroft on a number of occasions. Stout, red-faced, and jowly, he resembled a much-bloated version of my friend and companion, and shared that same acute deductive intellect. Holmes insisted that Mycroft's abilities were actually the stronger, except that the elder's lethargic nature and dislike for practical investigation hampered their application.[1]

Mr Mycroft Holmes claimed to be a functionary of the British government. He did indeed spend an hour or so three days a week in a Whitehall office. The remnant of his time was occupied behind the stately doors of the Diogenes Club, that eccentric establishment for gentleman of a solitary nature where all speech is banned, except in the Stranger's Room provided should communication with guests be required.[2] Somehow, from that fortress of solitude, the elder Holmes dispatched his duties and made his unseen but significant contribution the preservation of our Empirc.

I had never seen him look so concerned as he did when Holmes answered his urgent summons that bitter cold morning during the great snow of 1895. He had evinced less reaction when caught out by us in his Byzantine manipulations undertaken 'for the good of the Crown and nation'.[3] If I could read that corpulent face at all, then what I was seeing was surely fear.

Sherlock Holmes was a much more acute navigator of his brother's

1 In "The Adventure of the Greek Interpreter", *The Memoirs of Sherlock Holmes*, the detective says of his brother as Mycroft's introduction to the Canon, "If the art of the detective began and ended in reasoning from an arm-chair, my brother would be the greatest criminal agent that ever lived. But he has no ambition and no energy. He will not even go out of his way to verify his own solutions, and would rather be considered wrong than take the trouble to prove himself right. Again and again I have taken a problem to him, and have received an explanation which has afterwards proved to be the correct one. And yet he was absolutely incapable of working out the practical points..."

2 Holmes also describes the Diogenes Club and its function in "The Greek Interpreter": "There are many men in London, you know, who, some from shyness, some from misanthropy, have no wish for the company of their fellows. Yet they are not averse to comfortable chairs and the latest periodicals. It is for the convenience of these that the Diogenes Club was started, and it now contains the most unsociable and unclubbable men in town. No member is permitted to take the least notice of any other one. Save in the Stranger's Room, no talking is, under any circumstances, allowed, and three offences, if brought to the notice of the committee, render the talker liable to expulsion. My brother was one of the founders, and I have myself found it a very soothing atmosphere."

3 A reference to "The Clockwork Courtesan" by I.A. Watson in *Sherlock Holmes Consulting Detective* volume 4 and *Sherlock Holmes Mysteries* volume 1.

expressions. "You have something to tell me," he said at once. "No, something to confess. You are afraid that I will be angry with you."

Mycroft Holmes nodded, as if it was natural that his concerns should be understood by the clues of his appearance alone. His sibling had taken in the tiny details of his dress, of yesterday's collar still worn, of the faint splashes of three consecutive suppers eaten last night in haste under stress, of white spats that bore tell-tale signs of snow-splashing from twenty-four hours earlier and not since. The civil servant had not left his Club since the morning of the day before, which signified some singular crisis.

"You will recall that I mentioned when I gave my assent that I could not offer any special favour to him," Mycroft replied gnomically, assuming that Sherlock would know to whom he referred though I did not.

"I will require the details and circumstances, Mycroft."

"You are aware of the constraints. If you would agree…"

"I am content as a general consultant, brother. I have no intention of taking a position in Her Majesty's government. If that was your ploy…"

"A mere bagatelle, of no relevance to the present issue; but without such assurance of permanent allegiance there are matters in which you may not be included, and…"

"Your apology is somewhat lacking, Mycroft, since it comes hedged with so many caveats. I trust you will not compel me to set my talents to…"

"I advise you not to attempt such investigation, Sherlock. There are matters in which I would be required to thwart you."

"There are matters in which you would be required to attempt to thwart me. If the case in hand necessitates my discovery of things that you would prefer remained unknown then you had best afford me access to the relevant data in a civilised manner."

The exchange took place in rapid, clipped undertones, a fraternal shorthand as each leaped ahead of the other's words and understood his thoughts. Two intellectual giants tussled, raced.

Mycroft's red face suffused a darker crimson as his ire rose. "Sherlock, do not mistake me for some criminal meddler spidering away in the underworld. My resources are vast and established, reserved for dealing with threats to the British Empire. I advise you to not become one of them."

"Mycroft, do not imagine that your sheltered position insulates you from me, or offers you absolute advantage should our interests diverge. Whatever gifts you possess are strong in their milieu but cannot match the experience I have in applying my own in turn. Nor should you try to divert me from the matter in hand and your guilt in it by turning this into some schoolyard feud. Eschew these unworthy posturings and speak plainly!"

So alarmed was I to see these two fierce intelligences locking horns that I felt compelled to intervene. "Excuse me. I remain a little behind the two of you in knowing of what you speak and the cause for your concerns. Might I be enlightened as to the problem which is before you?"

The Holmes brothers stared at each other with identical gimlet gazes, but Sherlock turned back to me at last and said, "Wiggins is missing."

"Wiggins?" I frowned at the news. I retained a warm affection for the lad who had once been foremost amongst those street-Arab ragamuffins that ran errands and overheard gossip, Holmes' 'Baker Street Irregulars'. These days there was a new generation of troublemaking youngsters at my friend's beck and call for spying and trailing, but Wiggins had been there at the start. Wiggins had been there before me.[4]

"He was on an errand," Mycroft told me. "Sherlock spoke with me about finding the young man a position as a footman here at the Diogenes. He has proven to be an able and trustworthy messenger on several occasions."[5]

"You use the staff here as you use the premises, as an unofficial outpost of the British civil service," Holmes remarked. "There are advantages in possessing informal systems as supplement to affairs of state on record."

Mycroft sniffed. "Of course. You have your Irregulars and I have mine."

I had known, or suspected, that young Wiggins had found his place in that kind of employment. A smart lad who had apprenticed chasing Sherlock Holmes' quarries about the streets of London would be an ideal recruit for Mycroft Holmes' uncivil games of politics and national security. Wiggins had been discreet about confessing it, though. He had not even admitted his additional job description when I had spoken with him at his wedding.

"Wiggins missing?" My mind was catching up. "Then what about

---

4 "...the spokesman of the street Arabs, young Wiggins, introduced his insignificant and unsavoury person," to Dr Watson in *A Study in Scarlet*, where he and his fellows were already in Holmes' employ at the rate of one shilling per mission. The Irregulars also contributed to the investigations in *The Sign of Four* and "The Adventure of the Crooked Man" from *The Memoirs of Sherlock Holmes.*

5 The progression of Wiggins from barefoot street urchin to adult footman at the Diogenes Club is not mentioned in Canon but has been a favourite idea of subsequent Holmes fiction. It was popularised in Billy Wilder's film *The Private Life of Sherlock Holmes*. Wiggins actually starred in the 1983 children's TV series *The Baker Street Boys*.

Jenny? Mrs Wiggins, as she is now?"[6] Another thought. "Is she not in her second trimester of pregnancy?"

"She has not yet been informed of her husband's disappearance," Mycroft replied, somewhat indifferently. His emotional concern was not for the gravid wife nor even for his missing lackey but for his brother's ire, and possibly for Sherlock Holmes' interference.

"When did Wiggins disappear?" I demanded. "What has been done about it?"

Holmes evidently read Mycroft's intended response and interjected. "Do not consider withholding the basic facts. If there are security aspects to the situation that must be concealed then I shall respect them until I have reason not to. The remainder of the data must be laid out plainly. Indeed, they shall be, one way or another."

The fat man sighed and slumped further into the Stranger's Room armchair. The leather squeaked as he settled back. "Very well. Some facts. Appropriate facts."

Holmes took the seat opposite and gestured that his brother should continue.

Mycroft rested one balled fist into the palm of his other hand, scowling as if he was being tortured for information. "I am occasionally sent messages, delicate messages that cannot be delivered by telegram, postal service, or recognised courier. They come via a variety of means, but one of them is that a junior employee of this establishment will pass by some public place, brush against an apparent stranger, and a note will be exchanged. At other times they visit some quiet spot and retrieve a packet concealed there by an anonymous source."

"Wiggins was such a staff member," Holmes stated.

"Sometimes, yes. He was quite new in this establishment, still something of an unknown quantity, so he was seldom tasked with the most sensitive of assignments. However, yesterday there was urgent need for a contact and the weather somewhat limited my choices."

Mycroft indicated the window through which I was staring. All of St James's[7] and London beyond was a white snowscape, the streets deep with

---

6 Jenny Wheeler, formerly "In service... at the household of Mr Crosby the tailor," was rescued in dramatic circumstances by her beau Wiggins in "The Abominable Merridew", by I.A. Watson in *Sherlock Holmes Consulting Detective* volume 5 and *Sherlock Holmes Mysteries* volume 1. Our present account is Dr Watson's first indication that things have progressed for the young couple over the three years since then.

7 The Canon never specifies a location for the Diogenes Club but it is generally assumed that it would be established in the exclusive 'clubland' around St James's Street, and possibly in the heart of that area in one of the former luxury mews houses of St James's Square itself. On St James's Street it would be neighbour to such clubs as Boodle's, Brooks's

drifts. It was that bitterly cold January of 1895, the worst snowstorms in living memory.[8] Even the main thoroughfares of the capital were hard to traverse dug-out tracks. Travel was restricted and commerce and industry were at a virtual standstill. It would require a young, vigorous man to venture to some rendezvous in such weather conditions.

"You sent Wiggins to a meeting or to collect a hidden message?" Holmes asked his brother, matching him dispassion for dispassion. I had the sense that some long fraternal contest was continuing even as we conversed.

"A meeting," Mycroft clarified. "My regular man is of somewhat advanced years, with a trick hip. The circumstances required a different courier."

"How would he be known to his contact?"

"A rolled up copy of the *Morning Standard* in his left hand and a merchant navy pin on his right lapel. The walk-past was set for ten a.m. yesterday, by the statue of Achilles in Hyde Park."

"That was the last that was seen of Wiggins?" I ventured, only to be censured by two frowns at interjecting so obvious a comment.

"Wiggins left the Diogenes at nine forty so as to be certain of making the journey in a timely manner," Mycroft continued, as if I had not interrupted. That would have given the lad plenty of time even in such weather as we now suffered; the near corner of Hyde Park is much less than ten minutes' brisk walk from St James's Square. "He did not wear his uniform, of course, but rather nondescript clothing appropriate to the weather and to a man of the inferior working class: long boots of worn

---

(sic), the Royal Ocean Racing Club, White's, Arthur's, the Conservative Club, the New University Club (strictly for graduates of Oxford or Cambridge), and the Primrose, not counting the many other clubs on adjacent and intersecting streets. In St James's Square it would be placed beside the Caledonian Club, the Den Norske Klub, and the Sports Club; other clubs moved into proximity after the date of our present story.

A modern reader without an intimate knowledge of London may not recognise the geographical significance of 'clubland'. St James's Street. along and around which these extensive, expensive townhouses were situated, descends to St James's Palace and the Mall, proximate to Buckingham Palace and a short walk across St James's Park to the most senior offices of British Government including the Treasury, the Admiralty, the War Office, and Downing Street itself. The richest and most exclusive personal homes of central London were within easy walking distance. St James's was therefore the quiet exclusive home of elite society, adjacent to the administration of the most powerful empire on Earth.

8 Watson is not quite accurate in his assertion. The winter of 1894/5 was actually the coldest in London since 1881/2 and was unmatched again until 1940/1. Many climatologists mark 1894/5 as the last great event of the "Little Ice Age" that had affected Europe since the 13th century. January 1895 was also notable for the appearance of thundersnow over Britain, a rare form of lightning storm in which snow or sleet not rain pelts from the sky. The coldest London winter of the 19th century, before Watson's "living memory", would have been the long snows of 1814, when the Thames last froze entirely and hosted the last of the Frost Fairs on the ice.

brown leather, dark grey britches, a thick Aran sweater of dark green, a long dark blue double-breasted ship's coat with buttoned epaulettes, and a Balaclava helmet."[9]

"His instruction?" Holmes prompted.

"He was to receive the package, an envelope of documents that would be slipped into his outer clothing as he passed by, then proceed on a perambulation as far as the Italian Gardens,[10] along the bank of the Serpentine, and then to return along Rotten Row."[11]

"That precaution would assist in detecting anyone in trail," Holmes judged. "Wiggins has been familiar with such methods since boyhood."

"One reason for which he was assigned the duty. He was due to return through a circuitous route by eleven fifteen at the latest. He did not."

"Whereupon you initiated investigation. What? How?"

Mycroft reached for a handful of the jellied fruits in a side-dish beside him, crammed then down to steady himself, and outlined in precise detail how staff had been dispatched in a thorough and sensible search pattern. The park had been scoured, as had adjacent roads on the eastern side, and the connecting Green Park and Kensington Gardens.[12]

---

9 The item is sometimes referred to now as a ski mask, but was originally named after its use at Balaclava during the 1854 Crimean War, when a generous public sent thousands of home-knitted hats of this pattern to ill-equipped British troops that were freezing to death.

10 The Italian Gardens were added to Hyde Park after Prince Albert saw a similar water garden at Osborne House on the Isle of Wight. In 1860, James Pennethorne was commissioned to create a pleasant layout of large raised terraces, fountains, urns and geometric flower beds, extending Kensington Gardens at the north-west perimeter of the park where the Serpentine begins. The fountains discharge into the Long Water, the northern half of the Serpentine. The Pump House that once operated the fountains actually contained a steam engine with its chimney disguised as an ornate masonry pillar.

11 Rotten Row is a wide track running almost a mile along the southern edge of Hyde Park. Originally established by King William III as a safe route between Kensington Palace and St James's Palace through the then-robber haunted park, in 1690 it became the first artificially-lit highway in Britain. By the 18th century, the Route de Roi was known by its corrupted name, Rotten Row, and it and the adjacent South Carriage Drive had become the fashionable place for noble and wealthy Londoners and handsome military officers to ride, to see and be seen.
    The two most senior regiments of the British Army, the Life Guards and the Blues and Royals (Royal Horse Guards and 1st Dragoons) were and are headquartered at Hyde Park (Knightsbridge) Barracks by the eastern end of Rotten Row; together these regiments are the Household Cavalry, the monarch's official bodyguard.
    To facilitate Rotten Row's popular use, in 1876 the road was converted into a 'modern' bridleway with a brick base covered in sand. Its popularity as an elite social venue continued well into the 20th century, and Rotten Row remains open to the public to ride their horses along even today.

12 The heart of London contains four remarkable parks, linked in a chain. St James's Park is easternmost, reaching almost to Downing Street, bordered to the south by Birdcage Walk and to the north by The Mall that leads to Buckingham Palace. Where St James's

Holmes required detail. We learned that first other staff from the Diogenes Club, then junior personnel from some of the ministries, and finally a specialist force that Mycroft would not describe had been employed in the hunt. The first, least organised check had been made before noon yesterday. A more through and better-manned search had taken place between two and four. The one that finally convinced Mycroft that Wiggins was not in the park lost, injured, or dead began at four and continued late into the night.

"There was only one possible sighting," Holmes' brother reported, dabbing his jowls with a silk napkin. "At ten past ten or so, at Speaker's Corner, a gentleman was holding forth on the subject of the French army captain Alfred Dreyfus who has lately been convicted of passing secret documents to the German military and is deported to Devil's Island. You are familiar with the case?"

Holmes nodded assent. "The evidence, if honest, is robust; but there is doubt regarding the veracity of certain testimony. There is a whiff of anti-Semitism."

"More than a faint odour," Mycroft confirmed. "Doubtless there will be more heard on the matter in due course. But it is not my duty to correct the French government in their shambling judicial blunders."[13]

"I am surprised there was anyone at Speakers Corner in weather such as this," I admitted. "Was it not snowing, if not blizzarding, at that hour yesterday? Would anyone dare such conditions to stand on a soap-box and shout at a non-existent crowd?"[14]

Park reaches the perimeter of the Palace it touches with Green Park, which is divided from the private gardens of Buckingham Palace by Constitution Hill. The western tip of Green Park meets Hyde Park Corner. From there Hyde Park spreads north and west, up to Speaker's Corner, famous as an open-air space for public speaking - and heckling. The Serpentine lake and adjoining Long Water form the boundary to Kensington Gardens, which features the Round Pond, the Albert Memorial (facing the Royal Albert Hall) and terminating at Kensington Palace.

Other famous green spaces such as Regent's Park and Hampstead Heath are some distance separate to the north.

13 Mycroft Holmes, with his special interest in political affairs and with appropriate international sources to support his opinion, may have been one of the first to discern irregularities in what later became known as "The Dreyfus Affair". Between the time of French Jewish officer Captain Dreyfus' false conviction in 1894 and his final exoneration in 1906, the affair and its several cover-ups divided French society and politics, inspired Emile Zola's strong defence of the wronged soldier, *J'Accuse...*, led to the coining of the term 'intellectual', and stoked anti-Semitic feelings and even riots that left a long and unpleasant shadow over Europe.

14 After riots in Hyde Park in 1855 over the *Sunday Trading Bill* and later protests there by the Chartists and the Reform League, the *Parks Regulation Act* 1872 allowed for the park authorities rather than government officials to grant permission for public meetings there. Although sometimes seen as a mandate guaranteeing free speech, such licence is custom rather than law. The area of Hyde Park beyond the former site of the Reform

"If there was an earthquake during a hurricane you would find some-one stood there on a soap box, Dr Watson," Mycroft assured me. "On this occasion, the gentleman held forth to no less than three supporters, despite the ambient conditions. All of them report that a passing young man of Wiggins' description halted to shout heckling comments at the speaker in 'ignorant common parlance' before hurrying towards Marble Arch."

"Why would Wiggins stop to do such a thing?" I puzzled.

"To draw attention to himself," Holmes replied promptly. "To be noticed."

Mycroft nodded as if it were self-evident. "The boy thought himself in danger, or at least that he was pursued. He made certain that we could ascertain his passage, away from the course through the park that he was instructed to follow."

I mentally drew up a map of the park's layout. Achilles' statue is in the southwest corner of the park, nearest to the Diogenes Club. There were two reasonable paths that Wiggins might have taken northwest to the Italian Gardens. One of them would pass through the intersection where lie the Old Magazine, Police House, and Rangers' Lodge. If the young man suspected trouble he might have found refuge there. But he had not.

Sherlock Holmes read my chain of reasoning from my expression. "If Wiggins felt himself followed then he may have suspected danger lay along the paths he was due to take. He may have had cause to think that his routes back to St James's and the Diogenes Club were likewise compromised. Instead he struck due north, for Speaker's Corner and the Marble Arch."

"But why...?" I began, then answered my own question. "He intended to cross Oxford Street into Orchard Street, and then follow on... to Baker Street! If Wiggins required assistance and felt himself hemmed in by enemies, where else would he retreat but to the house of his first mentor and great idol?"

The Holmes brothers both nodded as if an unpromising student had finally reached a useful conclusion. "The Speaker's Corner sight-

---

Tree to Marble Arch is therefore available for anybody to gather, speak, or listen (and to heckle). Though not so popular in the internet age, Speaker's Corner has been used for political and social speechmaking by such luminaries as Karl Marx, Vladimir Lenin, George Orwell, C. L. R. James, Walter Rodney, Ben Tillett, Marcus Garvey, Kwame Nkrumah, and William Morris.

The spirit of the place was summed up by Lord Justice Sedley in his 1999 decision regarding *Redmond-Bate v Director of Public Prosecutions*, a case which established modern legal principals of freedom of speech in British law, wherein he described Speakers' Corner as demonstrating "the tolerance which is both extended by the law to opinion of every kind and expected by the law in the conduct of those who disagree, even strongly, with what they hear."

ing was when?" Sherlock checked with Mycroft. "Ten ten or so? Near to Cumberland Gate? Dare we assume then that the exchange had been made? That Wiggins was trying to escape with this packet that is so important to Her Majesty's government?"

"We cannot be certain," Mycroft admitted. "The courier who made the pass is also missing, although that may simply be protocol. He is instructed if suspicious of threat to simply disappear for several days."

"You will not inform me of his identity or general description?" Holmes asked.

"Nor of the nature of the communication he carried," the older sibling replied primly.

Sherlock Holmes glowered for a moment, like a stubborn child denied a desired toy. "You have questioned the regular courier who was unable to make the meeting, and the other staff who were aware of the rendezvous?" he asked at last, expecting an affirmative. "You are confident that such a meeting was not betrayed by any of your people? You have sent to Scotland Yard, and to those shadowy agents of your own who keep watch upon foreign nations with suspicious business in our capital?"

"Naturally. I have also set watch upon Wiggins' lodging house."

"But not informed his wife of his disappearance!" I objected.

"My brother admits the possibility that Wiggins has disappeared of his own accord for nefarious purposes. A man of limited means, due to become a father, is sometimes vulnerable to bribery or coercion."

"Not Wiggins," I insisted. "His wife must be informed. He did not go home last night."

"He was due to sleep over as a night-footman here," Mycroft answered indifferently. "His absence will not be noted by his family until his due return home this afternoon."

"We shall inform her," I insisted. "A woman who is with child must not be left alone in uncertainty and distress. If she has no other support she shall come to Baker Street and Mrs Hudson's care!"

"A splendid suggestion, Watson," Holmes approved. His brilliance did not always extend to the personal requirements of humans that lacked his intellectual blessings. "It will be more convenient to interview her there."

He demanded a runner and I dispatched a note to our redoubtable landlady with instructions regarding the wellbeing of Mrs Wiggins.

"Is there any more of this affair that you intend to lay before me?" Holmes asked Mycroft.

"I have dispatched my duty in informing you of Wiggins' disappearance."

"You did so knowing that I would investigate."

"I did so hoping to confine your investigation to acceptable bounds."

"You realised that your hope was vain."

"I recognise that you are not very good at understanding constraints. You never have been. It is a significant fault."

"Many criminals have thought so. Detection, like truth, does not accept compromise."

"Ignorance can cause significant damage, however."

"Then those who should have amended ignorance must share the blame." Holmes turned aside, calling for his cape and hat. "We shall begin by reviewing the trail of our missing fellow, Watson," he told me. "The weather is poor but it will be good to get out into *fresh* air."

We walked up Piccadilly, picking our way along the thin path cleared in the banked snow. It was strange to see the road so empty of traffic at noon. A few stout horsemen ventured the street but we saw only one carriage-and-four struggling against the ruts in the embedded drifts. The light flurry would eventually render vain the work of the pavement-sweepers, but for now our progress was unhampered except by patches of dangerous black ice.

"Wiggins would probably have come this way," I suggested. "It is the logical route from St James's Street."

"He had shed his livery and was dressed unremarkably as a common working man," Holmes replied. "It is useless to ask any shopkeeper if they marked the passing of a fellow aiming to be unremarkable. His only distinguishing feature was his newspaper, and he would likely have kept that tucked under his coat in this weather until it was needed."

"It is hard to understand how anyone might simply go missing in the heart of London, even in conditions like these."

"On the contrary, it is remarkably simple. One needs only to walk up to a person, press a firearm to his torso, and instruct him to step into a waiting Brougham.[15] If anything the weather impedes such undertakings —and the Brougham."

"You believe Wiggins was abducted?"

"Belief is not relevant to our study, Watson. We shall review facts, test them against theories, and thus utilise the science of deduction to form an

---

15 A light four-wheeled two-door horse-drawn carriage with two interior seats, a common vehicle and the most prevalent model of cab in Victorian London.

ineluctable conclusion. You know my methods and have often recorded them."

"Of course," I agreed. "Yet I cannot help remembering that cheeky comic fellow in his scrubby shorts and scabby knees who first came to Baker Street bringing information for your investigations. Nor can I overlook that happy bride whose wedding I attended and the future that she and young Wiggins had promise of. You will pardon my anxiety."

"I would have you no other way, Watson. Be assured that we shall pursue this matter wherever it takes us, despite any obfuscation that may be placed in our path."

I did not comment on Holmes' dispute with his brother, but resolved then that this case would be placed into that dispatch-box file I set aside for publication only long after the principals are gone to dust.

We crossed a Park Road grown sombrely beautiful under its cold white blanket, its lines of trees covered in heavy deposits ready to release as pedestrians passed beneath. A lone policeman in a heavy greatcoat trudged past, his helmet and side-whiskers frosted with snow.

We passed Apsley House[16] and under the Hyde Park Screen.[17] A half-frozen newspaper vendor bravely plied his trade in the shelter of arch. He did not remember anything of one particular muffled traveller yesterday. This was the most popular entrance to the park. Even now there were idlers enough ignoring the weather to make it impossible to distinguish if any of them were searchers or observers aware of our business.

I took a paper. The front page was full of news about the appalling snows that wracked the nation. The Manchester Ship Canal was frozen over. Gas and water pipes had fractured across Britain; Northampton was entirely blacked out by the complete loss of its gas supply. The Thames estuary was impassable because of ice, with some floes on the Thames itself. Another five inquests had returned verdicts of death by exposure to extreme cold weather.[18] There was not yet any count for the number of victims due to pneumonia.

16 The home of the first Duke of Wellington is the most prominent building at the Hyde Park Corner junction of Park Lane, Piccadilly, Constitution Hill, Grosvenor Place, Grosvenor Crescent, and Knightsbridge. It is now the Wellington Museum.

17 The Hyde Park Screen (now known as the Ionic Screen) is a ceremonial entrance designed by Decimus Burton in the 1820s as one of two intended to line up as a formal approach to Buckingham Palace. Burton's complimentary Wellington Arch (or Constitution Arch) was shifted from its aligned position as a gate to Green Park due to traffic congestion and is now entirely surrounded by roads on the modern Hyde Park Corner traffic island.

18 Watson is conflating accounts of January and February 1895. The blackout at Northampton, for example, occurred in February of that year.

A newspaper vendor bravely plied his trade in the shelter of the arch.

And yet that had evidently not deterred visitors to Hyde Park. "'It is estimated that between 50,000 and 60,000 skated on the Serpentino yesterday,'" I read out to Holmes. "'The thickness of the ice averaged 6½ inches...' Remarkable."

"That tens of thousands of Londoners have conspired to cavort over any useful track or helpful marking?" my companion objected. Snowflakes settled on the bill of his cap as if to mock him.

It was true that the main walkways through the park had been brushed and what snow remained was stamped down by the passage of many feet, but beyond the popular roads the vast space was still drifted and hard to pass. Thick stands of trees were now shrouded in white, guarding their mysteries. It was sometimes hard to remember that this place had been a haunt of highwaymen and footpads a century ago, but as the snows reclaimed the lawns and woods and an odd silence fell upon the city such remembrance did not seem so far away.

Achilles[19] was deserted today, mantled in a cloak of snow, though tracks along the footpaths showed the passage of many Londoners undeterred by the weather and enjoying the unexpected holiday.

This was where our former Irregular was meant to receive his anonymous package. I imagined him stood there with his newspaper and lapel badge, perhaps stamping his feet to keep warm, breath steaming in the chilly air. He might look around as if waiting for an appointment to arrive, or pause to take a smoke in the lee of the heroic monument. In glancing about he would discern if he was being watched.

At some point a stranger might pass by and then the exchange would be made. Wiggins might feel the weight in his pocket where there was nothing before. He would pause until his unknown courier had time to move on and then begin his promenade towards the Italian Gardens.

Or had something already gone awry before then? Did the messenger arrive at all? Or had Mycroft's agent already been intercepted and was the man who came for Wiggins some enemy? What happened to cause so simple an exchange to go so wrong?

Holmes paused a moment by Achilles to refresh his memory of sight-

---

19 This 33 ton bronze statue by Sir Richard Westmacott was commissioned by the Ladies of England society in 1822 at a cost of £10,000 (about $1.3m dollars today) to commemorate the feats of Arthur Wellesley, 1st Duke of Wellington, and his troops against Napoleon. The 18-foot statue atop an 18-foot stone plinth is sited towards the south-eastern edge of the park near Hyde Park Corner. The metal came from cannon captured during Wellington's French campaign. The body is based on a Roman figure at Monte Cavallo in Italy, but Achilles' face resembles that of the Duke. The Ladies of England initially commissioned a statue that was entirely nude, but soon after its unveiling an outraged public required them to fit the conquering hero with a fig leaf.

lines along the trails of the park. "We are assisted, Watson, by the snow being so heavy here. Only certain of the paths are somewhat cleared, restricting Wiggins' choice of route from here to the Italian Gardens."

I reviewed the options. "He could have taken that way, along Serpentine Road, past the Rose Garden and Bandstand and Nannies Lawn to trace the edge of the Serpentine and Long Water. Alternatively, he would cut

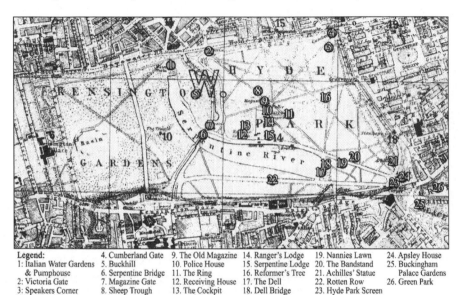

Legend:	4. Cumberland Gate	9. The Old Magazine	14. Ranger's Lodge	19. Nannies Lawn	24. Apsley House
1: Italian Water Gardens	5. Buckhill	10. Police House	15. Serpentine Lodge	20. The Bandstand	25. Buckingham
& Pumphouse	6. Serpentine Bridge	11. The Ring	16. Reformer's Tree	21. Achilles' Statue	Palace Gardens
2: Victoria Gate	7. Magazine Gate	12. Receiving House	17. The Dell	22. Rotten Row	26. Green Park
3: Speakers Corner	8. Sheep Trough	13. The Cockpit	18. Dell Bridge	23. Hyde Park Screen	

past the Ring and Sheep Trough, past the Police House and then along Policeman's Path to Serpentine Bridge and the Peacock Walk to the Italian Gardens."

"We can only assume that Wiggins attempted his ordered saunter around the park *if* he had acquired his package. The purpose of his sojourn was to obfuscate from whom he had received the message. If the meeting was aborted then he had no reason to walk in that direction."

"But if he did get the materials then he still did not proceed with his instructions. He had no time to walk to the water-gardens. Within ten minutes of the time of his appointment he was heading for Marble Arch, with or without Mycroft's documents."

Holmes nodded acceptance of the facts, then led on towards the police station that nestles in the park's mid-southern quarter. "We shall begin at the Hyde Park Police House," he told me. "Mycroft's people will have already made enquiries there, but they may not have asked the proper questions." He did not add that his brother might not have passed on the proper answers.

"The constables must be well-versed in hunting the park for missing children and the like," I considered.

"But not in such weather as this, for a man who has either placed himself where he does not wish to be found or may have been well concealed."

Holmes meant that Wiggins' corpse might be hidden somewhere amongst those snowy trees, obscured by the deep chill drifts. I shuddered and trudged with him to the Police House.

The quaint one-storied building with long veranda and neat lawn behind iron railings had once been a military guard-room, but now it displayed the familiar blue lamp that designated it a bastion of the Metropolitan Police.[20] We passed inside and Holmes made himself known to the duty sergeant in the Charge Room.

"Sir! 'Ow did you ever 'ear so fast?" the wondering policeman marvelled.

"Hear what?" Holmes demanded. His eyes took in the details of the station: the Inspector's door flung open and office abandoned, the lack of any of the other thirty or so officers based at the site, the evidence of a hasty and urgent relocation of men and equipment. "What is happening?"

"The body," the sergeant replied, confused now. "The bloke in the ice. On the pond?"

Holmes clarified by precise questioning what was occurring. At eleven fifty-four, some fifteen minutes before our arrival, a constable had returned with urgent news that skaters on the frozen Long Water believed that some unfortunate had fallen through the ice and was now entombed beneath. The inspector and officers had hastened out to break through and see if the unfortunate might yet be retrieved and revived.

Holmes and I hastened up past the Old Magazine to Serpentine Bridge,[21] where bobbies were holding back a growing crowd of curious onlookers. North on the Long Water and south on the Serpentine there must have been five thousand skaters taking advantage of the freeze. The section of ice immediately north of the first span of the bridge had been cleared of people and a small party of rescuers trod carefully on the ice in case it was weaker near the arches.

---

20 This house was replaced in 1902 with the larger courtyarded building that exists today. The descriptions of the former site come from *Hyde Park, Select Narratives, Annual Event, etc, during twenty years' Police Service in Hyde Park* (1906), written by Edward Owen, a former officer who served there.

21 Serpentine Bridge was erected by John Rennie in the 1820s to carry the then-new West Carriage Drive over the then-undivided Serpentine River. It is a handsome stone bridge of five wide water arches flanked by two smaller arches for foot traffic along the lakebank.

We climbed down to the footpath and identified ourselves to the inspector in charge, a relatively young chap by the name of Frome. "I'm gratified by your attention, sirs," he said in a tone between deference and resentment that his case might be interfered with. "I'm not sure as there is much mystery to be had, though. Some poor fellow has slipped through the ice and been caught there. We ought to post warning signs, but who will pay attention to them?"

Holmes shook his head. "You will note, Inspector, that although our view of the dead man is somewhat obscured by the ice, he is not wearing skates nor dressed for such an activity. Moreover it is clear from the solidity of the freeze beneath us that he did not fall in here. He entered the water elsewhere and was lost beneath the ice-sheet. Currents dragged him to this spot where the pillars of the bridge and the narrowing of the waterways caused the body to lodge."

I was more concerned by what I could see through the obscuring Long Water. The corpse was that of a young man, wearing a merchant navy style double-breasted coat of the type in which Wiggins had dressed. What other details of costume I could discern matched Mycroft Holmes' description exactly. My heart sank and I felt as cold as the frozen lake beneath me.

Sherlock Holmes was stern and sober too. "You were contacted yesterday about a missing man, I think, Inspector?"

"Well, yes. We and the Park Rangers made search for some fellow who… How do you know about this?"

"This is Sherlock Holmes. Every detail speaks volumes to him," I told the Inspector, by way of obscuring our interview with Mycroft.

Holmes did indeed read the troubled policeman. "You have orders not to bring the matter up, Inspector Frome? To whom have you already dispatched word of this discovery?"

"I have orders to report any such matter to the Chief Constable at once, and so I have," Frome answered with dignity, then answered with a touch of anxiety, "Do you think that this is him? The fellow who went missing?"

Holmes avoided answer. "You have men coming to take up the body, Inspector? Have them make cuts here and here. The dead man floated to this place where he lodged but the ice had since formed around his uppermost parts, locking him in place. Haul out any ice that has accreted round the corpse as a block entire. There may be evidence preserved by the freeze that must not be destroyed."

Inspector Frome winced. "The Park Rangers are coming, but we'll need to get more horses."

I adjudged that the safe breaking of hard ice and the necessary retrieval might take an hour or two.

"That will give us time to walk the perimeter of the lake," Holmes replied. "A day has been lost but snow is a great preserver. Unfortunately every idler in London has decided to holiday-make along the Serpentine, tramping with their skates and sledges."

I defended the populace of the city. "This is their water. It has been for a long time. Why, in olden days this was the main bathing-place – the only bathing place – for the poor of London. Thousands came every day to wash and swim.[22] That's how the Receiving House came to be built there."

I indicated the gracious neo-classical building behind the rescue boat-sheds on the Serpentine's north bank. The Royal Humane Society's emergency centre was established over a century ago to aid and revive members of the public who have difficulties in the water. It is an institution now, containing hot baths for men and women as well as the medical facilities and laboratory required for its original purpose.[23] The facility was occupied in those frozen days of 1895 with those who had injured themselves on the ice or had otherwise been overcome in the inclement weather.

Holmes was indifferent to our capital's history except where it pertained to his investigation. He likewise avoided the masses who frolicked on the edge of the lake, the squealing children hurling snowballs at each other, the opportunistic vendors offering roasted chestnuts or hot broth. We continued to trace the perimeter of the Long Water, disturbing miserable mute swans that had made nests for themselves in the snowdrifts, and

22 A parliamentary answer given in the House of Commons in 1859 about the use of the Serpentine for bathing indicated that "3,963,689 bathers" had used the facility in the last fifteen years – more than a quarter of a million visits a year. In that same period there had been 377 accidents to bathers in which 29 drowned, and 273 suicide attempts of which 88 ended fatally.

23 Established in 1774, 'The Institution for Affording Immediate Relief to Persons Apparently Dead from Drowning' soon became the Royal Humane Society. In 1792 they repurposed an old farmhouse on the Serpentine to become their 'Receiving House' where people who had drowned might be revived, with adjacent coracle wharf from which rescues might be effected. A Superintendent, a Deputy Superintendent and several Boatmen continuously manned the site "during bathing hours". Gold, silver, and bronze medals, and sometimes cash awards, were granted to members of the public who had saved lives on the water. The purpose-built replacement Receiving House designed by J.B. Bunning and indicated by Dr Watson in our present narrative was raised in 1835 and survived until bombed in the Blitz in 1940.

A full description of the Receiving House and two excellent engravings are offered in The Illustrated London News, August 31, 1844, p.144, reproduced online at http://www.londonancestor.com/iln/humane-society.htm

Holmes examined the bank for traces of catastrophe.

I was still trying to divert my thoughts from Wiggins' frozen corpse. "It must have been very insanitary, back when so many people used the Serpentine for their ablutions," I reflected. "In the old days this water was supplied from the River Westbourne.[24] When that river became a practical sewer[25] it was determined that the Serpentine would require another source."

"Hence the pumping house," Holmes replied distractedly. He gestured to the head of the Long Water, where the elegant Pump House at Prince Albert's Italian Garden now provided water from more wholesome sources.[26] He evidently read my need to converse, pointed down the bank, and added, in his own Holmesian manner, "Over there is the spot where Shelley's first wife drowned herself."[27]

I did not feel up to discussing the domestic tragedies of notorious poets, so returned to the cause of my distress. "Ice has covered the lake here for several weeks, ever since the snows began. It is considered strong enough for the great number of skaters that now whirl across it. How then could there be a weak-spot that allowed Wi... the dead man to end up under the surface?"

"An interesting point. You will notice that some safety-conscious soul has actually hammered iron rods into the ice? That is at once proof of the robustness of the surface and warning of its imminent failure should the

---

24 In 1772, Queen Caroline, King George II's wife, embarked upon a project of improving Kensington Palace and Gardens and the adjacent Hyde Park. She ordered eleven former monastic ponds to be joined into a single lake, defying the then-fashion for straight artificial watercourses and setting a much-copied precedent for 'naturalistic' water features; hence the Serpentine.
    The Westbourne, the original source of the Serpentine's water, is now one of London's 'lost rivers', covered like the Fleet and the Tyburn in the 19th century and eventually reduced to a sewer and storm drain.

25 1815 lobbying from the London water companies who wanted to promote plumbed water closets succeeded in revoking the by-law that had previously forbidden disposal of sewage in public rivers. The new Bayswater Road sewer cut the Serpentine off from a regular supply from the now-contaminated Westbourne River – thereafter also known as the Ranelagh Sewer – but a high water overflow weir still allowed occasional faecal contamination of London's primary bathing pool.

26 These inputs included a deep fresh-water borehole and the River Thames, itself a source of pollution. Nowadays the Serpentine is supplied by three boreholes, the most recent of which was added in 2011 in preparation for the Olympic Games.

27 Percy Bysshe Shelley's heavily-pregnant estranged first wife Harriet (née Westbrook) ended her life in the Serpentine on 10th December 1816, erroneously believing herself to have been abandoned by her lover Lieutenant Colonel Christopher Maxwell. Three weeks later Shelley married his lover Mary Wollstonecraft Godwin, future authoress of *Frankenstein: or, The Modern Prometheus.*

flags begin to tilt. Yet the corpse found its way under, what, six inches of solid ice? More?"

I saw that Holmes was leading us up towards the head of the water, where the outfall from the Italian Gardens now supplied the lake. A rise of steam from the disguised chimney of the Pumping House betrayed that even now the Long Water and Serpentine and were being supplied with fresh liquid.

"You are looking for where the water gardens void their water."

"Indeed, Watson. This is where we must look for a body to begin its journey."

The large shallow formal ponds of the Italian Garden were all frozen solid, but where the promenade walk abutted the top of Long Water there was still a flowing discharge. Three curved steps led down to a circular basin some ten or twelve feet wide, flanked by a pair of chilly-looking top-less stone nymphs holding cornucopia from which welled arcing streams. An ornate cherub-supported fountain bowl rose eight feet from the centre of the basin, filling the great carved cup and then escaping down through dozens of carved grooves to cascade into the head of the lake. Though the rest of the Long Water's surface was frozen thick, the turbulence within two yards of the fountain spays prevented ice from forming.

Holmes examined the location with a mixture of satisfaction and irritation. He clearly felt he had found the place he had sought, but here in this picturesque and popular spot the passage of many visitors had tramped down the snow to hard-packed slush and eradicated all useful evidence.

"Here we are, Watson," Holmes declared. "Observe the poles with red ribbons warning of unsafe ice where the confluence enters. The constant agitation of the waters here prevents the accretion of strong ice."

He regarded the view from the edge of the water garden. Only a semi-circle of waist-high iron railings sectioned off the fountain basin adjoining the Long Water. The long ornamental balcony beyond the nymphs was white stone and the ice came up to the wall.

I stamped my feet and looked at the frozen surface of the lake. Snow was now piling on the sheet ice, making it even more treacherous. "So the dead man most likely entered here, where the fountain prevents freezing and the pump house supplies water in a constant stream."

"Either here or along the parapet if the ice surface is thin and brittle below it. We shall now test it."

"You mean to break the ice and see if you can fall though?" It did not sound like a good plan.

"We shall acquire a boat-hook and make our attempt from the vantage point of the garden wall," my companion assured me.

The acquisition of an appropriate tool and the subsequent investigation took some time. It was clear even to me from the layout of garden and Long Water, though, that a dead or dying man might easily have been heaved over a low balcony to end up beneath the surface of the lake; or an injured or fleeing man could have fallen in himself with little effort.

During that hour the weather worsened again, with more chill easterly winds and a new flurry of sleet. Deteriorating conditions drove many of the people from the park and obscured our view of the rest. By the time Holmes had satisfied himself that a falling or thrown body might easily penetrate the gap in the ice at this juncture we were almost alone in the appalling blizzard.

Not quite alone, though. "Watson," Holmes said to me quietly as he withdrew the boat-hook from the broken ice pool, "In the stand of trees to the left. We are observed."

I covertly glanced through the rising snowstorm to the dark grove of frost-rimed silver maples on the eastern embankment. It took a moment to identify the well-concealed watcher who was covertly following our actions.

"One of Mycroft's chaps?" I ventured.

"Possibly, but I think not. I cannot be sure from this distance, but that fellow's boots look to be of European manufacture. Let us be certain."

Holmes swung about and marched towards the trees. The secret observer retreated into the blizzard, vanishing before we could reach the grove.

"Size ten and a half, hob-nailed, round toed," Holmes told me as he stared at the imprints the spy had left in the crisp new snow. "A chip in the right heel and some wear on the left. Our watcher has a very slight limp, Watson, from an old injury now mostly healed. As you can see, you leave a similar tread. Our sentinel weighed around eleven stone four and was trained well enough to not fidget at his post."

"The murderer?"

"Mere speculation; but I am convinced that the fellow did not watch us by accident or idle curiosity."

We followed the tracks until they vanished amidst the general trail of many footprints around Victoria Gate Lodge on the main path to Speaker's Corner.

I reflected on what we knew so far. "Wiggins made for his meeting at the statue. Soon after he was heading out of the park at Cumberland Gate, towards Baker Street. Or else that was his intention and he got diverted. Later, his… a body fell into the head of the Long Water and was washed down to lodge under the Serpentine Bridge."

There was nothing more to do here. We turned back to check on how Frome fared in recovering the dead man.

Constables had pushed back the gruesome onlookers that had found the proceedings more interesting than the inclement weather. Holmes examined the line of gawkers carefully, doubtless drawing conclusions about each of them, sifting the spectators for one whose interest was more than morbid curiosity.

None of them resembled the lurker from the stand of maples on Buckhill, but that did not mean there was no other interested party.

We approached the underside of the first water arch. The footpath on that side of the lake was closed off by the police and planks had been laid out across the ice. Drills and saws had cut away great chunks of the surface, pulling out frozen lumps the size of paving stones. The accretion of ice under the bridge must have been almost a foot deep.

"It always grows thicker at the edge of the bridge," the senior Park Ranger explained helpfully. "Something to do with the interruption of the currents and suchlike. But thinner under the middle spans."

That was how the body had come to lodge here, of course. I wondered what would have become of it had it not been washed from the course of the waterway.

"Well that depends," the Ranger replied, sighing from knowing of the four or five suicides a year whose retrieval he oversaw. "The flow of the Serpentine is not consistent but rather depends upon the rainfall and ground water levels of the last few days, and how full the pumps above the Italian Gardens are working. During heavy rains the flow is appreciable but in high summer there is almost none, and without artificial pumping the whole lake can become stagnant, despite it covering forty acres."[28]

I observed that the mechanism that drew water up must be working now. Holmes and I had seen the steam from the pump house chimney.

"The current comes from that end, of course," the Ranger noted. "Most of the bodies, if you'll pardon my coarseness, wash up on the north-east-

---

28 The Serpentine and Long Water cover 40 acres (16ha), roughly the same area as sixteen football fields. For comparison, New York Central Park's biggest lake, now named the Jackie Kennedy Onassis Reservoir, covers 106 acres (43ha). Hyde Park was 370 acres (150 ha) in Holmes' time (now reduced by 20 acres (8.1 ha) by modern road improvements) and adjacent Kensington Gardens covers 275 acres (111 ha). Central Park (a mere new-comer established only in 1857) occupies 672 acres (292 ha) excluding the Reservoir.

ern bank of the Serpentine. That is probably one of the reasons that the Receiving House was put there, although I understand that originally there was a farmhouse on that spot that was conscripted for the purpose. Anyhow, by planning or fortune that's where dead men wash up most often. Some are even drawn from the water and revived."

"And if not there," I persisted. "What becomes of the water when it leaves the lake? There must be an outflow."

"And so there is," the park man agreed. "At the far end is a dam and weir, at Dell Bridge, and these days the water tumbles into a cut from there and joins up with the modern sewer system to discharge in the lower Thames.[29] If a corpse is not washed to the bank before that it will catch on the weir."

"It could not be lost over the weir?" Holmes interrogated the Ranger.

"That would not be possible, even were not the outflow stacked with ice at present. And if somehow so large an… an *object* went over the fall, it would be caught by the railing that protects the culvert entrance."

"Then there is no way to easily dispose of a body in the Serpentine," my friend decided.

"How deep is the lake?" I wondered. Bodies sink or float during different phases of decomposition in water.

"Sources vary on that," confessed the Park Ranger. "By my experience I'd say no more than eight or nine yards at the middle, but my predecessor would have sworn forty feet in some places. It might be as the old monks' ponds that were flooded to make the Serpentine were considerably deeper than the rest. We're on shale and London clay here and that tends to sinkholes and other oddities."

The man could make no sense of Holmes' enquiry but I wondered whether the detective was calculating how far down and unfindable a body might be if loaded with bricks or stones and deposited in the right part of the lake.

"There is no other inlet to this lake?" Holmes persisted.

"There's a lot of small runoff flows in. And it might be there's still a

---

29 Before the creation of the park and the diversion of waters from the then-aboveground River Westbourne, the Dell was site of Westminster Abbey's conduit house (managing water supplies to the monastic foundation) and supplied a pair of gravel pit ponds known as the Great Lake. Substantial changes made before 1844 erased the last of this landscape and created a discharge channel and culvert through Albert Gate. By the time of our present story, 1895, a sub-tropical garden had been created around the dam outfall from the Serpentine and the water was disposed into the now-buried remnant drainage channels that had once been the Westbourne River.

The Royal Parks' *Hyde Park Management Plan* 2006-16 includes an intention to investigate exposing again some of the buried and lost watercourses below the park, including possibly recovering parts of the Tyburn Brook and restoring some portion of the Great Lake.

"By my experience I'd say no more than eight or nine yards deep at the middle..."

channel somewhere near the Dell from the old Tyburn Brook-as-was, but if so it's under the surface and lost now."

"The Tyburn?" I echoed. That was another of London's notorious 'lost' rivers, but the Ranger had dealt with this confusion before.

"Tyburn Brook, sir. Nothing to do with Tyburn River. That used to run through St James Park, and it outflowed into Thames by Whitehall Stairs. At one time it made Westminster Abbey an island, Thorney Island. Now Tyburn Brook, *she* fed into the old Westbourne but never touched the river of the same name as her. She ran through this very park once a long time ago. She's on all the old maps."[30] He smiled shyly and apologetically. "They're both named from *Teo Bourne*, you see, sir, the old words for 'boundary stream'."

Holmes sighed impatiently, but the Head Ranger was not now to be contained. "The village of Tyburn took its name from *our* brook, not *their* river," he explained in partisan fervour. "That's why the gallows was first set up there in olden times, for to hang the thieves that preyed on travellers in this wood as it was then."[31]

A shout came up from the constables and labourers at the ice-hole. A foreman called to a lad who held a pair of dray horses on the bank. The team trotted on, up the path from the riverside walk to the bridge, dragging a harness-rope after them, and by that device the body under the ice was dredged to the surface. Policemen in oilskins reached down to ease the frozen corpse out of the water.

"Easy. Easy!" Holmes commanded them urgently, desperate to pre-

---

30 A good example is *Cary's New and Accurate Plan of London and Westminster 1795*, which is available online at http://mapco.net/cary1795/cary10.htm Although not named on the map, the Tyburn Brook is seen feeding the "Serpentine River" from the middle top of the plan. This map is one of the first to call the improved and gentrified Park Lane by its modern name, replacing the older nomenclature Tiburn Street. Also of interest is the old arrangement of the Serpentine's outflow, into the drainage ponds that originally gave The Dell its name and then through open channels (the Westbourne River or Ranelagh Brook) southwards, parallel to Sloane Street.

31 The Ranger is reporting history as it was commonly held in his time. The earliest recorded execution at Tyburn was of revolutionary William Fitz Osbert in 1196. In 1571 the famous "triple tree" was erected where the Marble Arch now stands at the northeast corner of Hyde Park, a triangle-topped tripod from which multiple felons could be hanged at the same time, allowing as many as 24 prisoners to be disposed of on the same day. The notorious site inspired several euphemisms for execution, such as "dancing the Tyburn jig," or "being made lord of the manor of Tyburn," or simply "going west" (from Newgate Prison). The last execution there took place in 1783 when highwayman John Austin met his end. It was bungled and the prisoner slowly asphyxiated. After that time executions were moved to take place outside Newgate Prison, and later inside.

The London district of Marylebone, which includes Baker Street, also takes its name from the humble Tyburn Brook, being a corruption of the original parish name St Mary's le Bourne; a bourne is a small stream, in this case the Tyburn Brook that once wound its open way along the streets there.

serve what evidence he might. So eager was he to inspect the body that I feared he might plunge into the icy hole himself to guide it safe to land, or else slide in by overbalancing too close to the fragile edge of the gap.

It occurred to me that perhaps even Sherlock Holmes might suffer a little anxiety that our dead man was his messenger Wiggins; but we did not discuss it.

The corpse was frosted over. Crystals of ice obscured his features. Even his hair was solid under a black Balaclava. My heart fell as I recognised with certainty the clothing that Mycroft Holmes had described: 'a long dark blue double-breasted ship's coat with buttoned epaulettes.' There on the right lapel was a merchant navy pin, a wide copper oval cast like a knotted rope enclosing the letters MN, topped by a crown imprinted with two masts and a shield.

The whole front of the corpse was obscured, rimed with ice. The body had lain in the water on its back and the sheet had formed around his face.

A canvas tarpaulin lay ready to receive the remains but Holmes did not allow the corpse to be wrapped or moved from the lake's frozen surface without an initial examination. I saw him check hands, neck, and mouth, frowning. He gestured to Inspector Frome. "Turn him on his side – gently."

When careful hands rolled the body, all of us could see the slit in the back of the sailor's coat where a blade had penetrated. Most of the blood had been washed off but the incision through cloth and flesh was quite obvious.

"It was murder," Frome announced, his fears confirmed. "This was no accidental falling-in. This was foul murder!" His brow furrowed; he would need to send off another report.

I scrambled down to examine the corpse's countenance, determined to ease away the layer of accreted ice.

"It is not him," Holmes told me.

"Not Wiggins? But... his outfit!"

"It is Wiggins' clothing," Sherlock Holmes observed with a gleam of interest. "But it is not Wiggins wearing it."

The body was transported not to the Police House but to the Humane Society's lodge. The Receiving House was better equipped for medical situations and was long used to working with the police on the matter of bodies drawn from the Serpentine.

"I am not qualified to pronounce on a cause of death," the junior doctor on duty there warned us as we shook the snow from our clothes and watched the cadaver be laid in the laboratory. "You will need a police surgeon, and that will take some time in this weather."

"Dr Watson is quite sufficient for that," Holmes assured the perturbed young man. "He is quite experienced in such matters and his word is good across the metropolis and the entire Home Counties."

"I have no objection," Frome assented.

"You'd better observe and make notes," I told the junior. "Let's see. We have a male of perhaps thirty, of medium stature in apparent good health, except of course for a stab wound. Put down that the trauma is located on the right side of the back, 21 inches below the top of the head and 5 inches from the front of the body. It is vertically oriented and after approximation of the edges it measures 5/8th of an inch in length."

Holmes added his deductions. "Left handed, a sea-farer used to rough work who also did a good deal of writing or book-keeping; habitually tanned but only on face and hands; old injuries consistent with an adventurous life; recently shaved off a beard and moustache, only a matter of days ago; a smoker of cheap tobacco in cigarette form judging from the discolouration on his fingers."

"He is thawing out," Frome observed. "Can we get those clothes off him?"

"One moment. Observe the bloodstain on the coat's right sleeve. There is a further slash at the upper arm and a significant mark of staining that the water has not sufficiently erased."

"He took a lesser injury before his fatal one," the junior doctor suggested.

"Perhaps. He was also in a fight, I see. Regard his knuckles, those grazes there. But that was some hours before his death. The scabs had time to form. And he was a canny fighter. There are no blemishes on his face, or bruises where he was hit." Holmes checked the man's hands further. "There are some small scrapes on his fingertips, abrasions that have not had time to heal pre-mortem, and here a tiny residue of blood crusted under the fingernails that his swim has not quite erased. He got his hands bloody, and not clutching at his own wound."

We carefully cut away his garments so that I could do a more thorough inspection of the dead man's injuries. I was cautious not to intrude upon evidence best left for an autopsy but was able to offer a little more detail. "The pathway of the lethal wound is through the skin and subcutaneous tissue, then brushing the right seventh rib. Thereafter it enters the right pleural cavity, which probably contains blood that is presently frozen. Estimated length of the total wound path is four inches and the direction is right to left and back to front with no other measurable angulation. The intrusion caused perforation of the right lung and a hemothorax."

Frome looked to Holmes for assistance with my medical notation. "A sharp object, probably a knife, was plunged into the victim from behind," the detective translated. "The wound penetrated a lung and flooded the interior cavity with blood."

"Death was then inevitable," I added. "The strike was either fortunate or expert."

"The killer avoided the rib that might have mitigated his attack," Holmes agreed. "But the injury was not instantly lethal. Consider his clothing – or rather the clothing he wore. The blood has been somewhat rinsed out by long immersion under water but there was considerable effusion. The heart was still pumping and the man was on his feet, or vertical anyway."

"He was wounded and staggered away," I suggested. "Did he then simply tumble into the lake? Or was he disposed of deliberately?" My eyes were drawn to the slashed remnants of the dead man's wardrobe. "And how did he come to be in Wiggins' garments?"

Holmes advanced no theory ahead of his data. "You have not yet inspected the arm where coat and shirt were gashed, Watson."

I examined the right shoulder and upper arm. The dead man bore no injuries there. The damage to the jacket and the blood it had absorbed had happened before this man had worn it. "Wiggins was hurt."

"Unless this outfit had a third wearer, I fear we must assume as much. You see the shirt has a long stain running along the sleeve to the cuff. Wiggins was wounded but not too severely. He was upright for some time after, for the blood trickled vertically down his arm. A gash, judging by the cut in the fabric of his jacket, from right to left diagonally downward, rendered by a man between five-feet ten and six foot, facing on his right flank."

I tried to reassure myself that our old ally had survived the attack. If he had fallen over then Holmes would be reading a different pattern of stains.

I looked back to our present corpse; there were more formalities for me to undertake to make a proper record. Holmes examined his fingernails and palms again, the soles of his feet and the underside of his boots. He even went so far as to sniff the leather.

I noted a tattoo on the dead man's chest and some old marks on the corpse's flesh, signs of previous injuries long-since healed. As a military doctor I was all too familiar with what old stitched cuts and a bullet wound looked like. I bore similar marks myself.

Holmes returned to the garments which the dead man had last worn. "There are rust marks on the trousers," he noted. "This man or Wiggins brushed against old wet iron. Brushed against it vertically. Climbing or descending? And some small catches on trousers, coat, and jumper. Brambles, I would say. Scrambling through bushes."

The coat's pockets contained little. There was two shillings and ninepence in small coins, a box of seaman's matches with only one stick remaining, a cheap dented fob compass, and a soaked tobacco pouch with rolling papers. Holmes fell upon the tobacco and instantly identified it. "A French regionally-cut blend, derived from dark Syrian and Turkish weed. Commonplace along the western Gallic ports. Cheap and inferior, but much used by sailors."

"You said he was a sea-farer," Frome remembered.

"Yes. His hands and other callosities clearly read 'seaman', but a literate one given to the record-keeping of an officer. The cut of his hair suggests military Navy discipline at some time, though perhaps not recently. The contents of his pockets support it. But what sailor – or smoker - ever travelled without a pocketknife? It may have been lost in his struggles, buried in the snow or fallen in the water."

"The… the murder weapon," the on-duty humanitarian ventured.

"Wrong size and blade type," Holmes dismissed the theory. "Pocket knife wounds are thinner and shallower. Quite distinctive."

"Ah. Of course," the junior doctor agreed feebly. I felt sorry for the chap. I had been there.

Holmes ran his fingers along seams, cuffs, and collar of the jacket before some other detail caught his attention. "There is a light coating of sludge at the bottom of this naval coat's right hand side-pocket. None in the left pocket or elsewhere on the garment. Something was placed in there that was either muddy or slimy."

To my dismay he touched some grains to his tongue. "Salt," he reported. "Sea-salt in this mud, if I am not mistaken, and a scatter of sand. There are also several granules of a different composition." He took care to scrape away the wet brown stain onto a trio of specimen slides, looking pleased at his discovery.

"Can we speak to time of death, Dr Watson?" Inspector Frome enquired.

"The ice makes such an estimate very unreliable," I admitted. "However, you may have discerned from our remarks that we expected this corpse to be that of the missing young man who entered Hyde Park dressed exactly like this at or just before ten o'clock yesterday. I cannot imagine how his clothes came to be on this fellow but clearly our victim was wearing them when he died; which places his death sometime after ten yesterday." Since the policeman looked disconsolate at my answer, I also ventured, "I doubt he bled for long before entering the water. I'd hazard he was in the lake no more than a minute after he took his injury. Whether he was dead before or after he fell below the ice at the Italian Gardens inflow I could not say without autopsy."

Holmes snorted, as he often did when disconcerted by what to him seemed appalling ignorance of those about him. "You have other observations?" I ventured.

"Several, doctor. The fellow was alive when he took the plunge. Examine his fingertips, the scratches taken as he scrambled over the parapet of the water garden – injuries of a living man. He was dying and he did not want to be taken by his enemy; that is, he did not want his killer to have his corpse. Look at the abrasions on his trousers. Not the rust or brambles, which were before that, but the other signs. He climbed over the edge and hurled himself where he knew the ice would be thinnest, hoping with some justification that he might plunge through and be lost."

"Why would he do such a thing?" Frome challenged. "Why not just call for help?"

"He recognised his mortal wound and perhaps did not trust that it was aid that his shout might summon. A naval officer might retain some tactical perception even at such last dire circumstance."

"Certainly a navy man? A captain?"

"Nothing so senior, but possibly a first or second mate aboard a small merchantman where everyone must pitch in, and a junior officer in his younger career."

"His tattoo," I realised. "It depicts a knot."

"An alpine butterfly knot," Holmes supplied, "to form a secure loop in the middle of a length of rope. The work is Oriental, probably from Shanghai or thereabout judging by the pigment and technique, and of about twelve years' vintage – a young ensign's rite of passage, I fancy. His present light tanning on hands, neck, and face indicate some time in tropical latitudes up to perhaps a month ago, not for leisure and 'sun-bathing' which would offer a wider scope of flesh to the sun's rays, but rather in a work capacity. The purchase of French west coast tobacco suggests a trip from equatorial climes then up via the Atlantic coast and through the English Channel to London."

"I can send a description to the Admiralty," Frome offered. "If he is a serving officer then he would be missed."

"An enquiry of the vessels in the Basin and along the river might also be useful," I added.

Holmes had not yet finished his corrections. "Nor has he exchanged clothing completely with Master Wiggins," the detective continued. "You will note that his underclothing and boots are his own. Exchanging foot-wear was impossible, of course, since he is a size and a half larger than Wiggins. His underwear is of cheap foreign make and style, without labels, but I would place its origins somewhere in the Guianas[32] - the right lati-tudes to achieve his tan."

As usual when Holmes reels off his observations I was left in reluc-tant admiration, mixed with chagrin at my own slowness to reach what were now self-evident conclusions. "I should have got that far myself," I declared.

"Of more interest, Watson, is what is *not* here. The pockets of his jacket are almost empty, as are his trousers. What sailor, what man, would ven-ture out with so little upon his person? No sailor's identification papers to verify his station? Not a scrap of correspondence or any clue as to whom he was!"

"If he has Wiggins' clothes, might not Wiggins have his? Could the things he carried still be in those pockets?" I did not say in front of Frome that Mycroft's disguised footman might well have been instructed to carry no sign of his origins or identity on his secret sojourn.

"We cannot yet know the circumstances of this remarkable wardrobe change, but it is unlikely to have been non-consensual on this fellow's part. Even if accomplished in haste there might have been chance to snatch some valuable or keepsake from his previous ensemble."

Unless this man too had come with no intention of being identified, I reasoned. Did that make him the courier with whom Wiggins was to meet, or some other actor that had led the former Baker Street Irregular to deviate from the script?

"For that matter, Holmes, where on earth might two men exchange clothes in a snowstorm? They could hardly have stripped down and changed garments in Hyde Park in view of the general public—even in

---

32 That is the north-eastern coastal countries of South America, called at the time of our story British Guiana, Dutch Guiana, and French Guiana and neighboured by Venezuela and Brazil.

such bad weather. If the park was as populated yesterday as today…"

Holmes made a noise of frustration. "There are too many leads, too much that must be done at once! I need to avail myself of this laboratory and examine that mud. I must also survey the park, especially the area of Buckhill and the Water Gardens, to find bloodstains of the murderous attack. I must question that fellow protesting about the Dreyfuss case at Speaker's Corner yesterday. And I need to put in hand some enquiries about my brother's business that will doubtless cause him to issue further futile warnings. Each of them requires my first attention!"

"Perhaps you will trust me with trudging the ground about the Italian Gardens?" I offered. "Day-old blood splashes may now be covered by this new snow, but count on me to find what I may."

Holmes nodded. He contented himself with dispatching a dozen or more telegrams and instructing Frome on a co-ordinated series of searches and investigations, including questions to be put to the witnesses of Wiggins' heckling - "If indeed that was Wiggins!" Finally he took his prized slides and jealously annexed the Receiving House laboratory for his studies.

I braved the blizzard to hunt for bloodstains.

The search was long, cold, and frustrating. Borrowed constables with me discovered some traces of smeared blood around the Italian Gardens balcony at the Hyde Park side, but nothing to show exactly where our mystery naval man might have fallen. We swept the ice as best we could but found no definite sign of where the sheet may have been broken. Likely the body entered where the nymphs and fountain kept a gap open but there was no proof such as Holmes might like.

As the day progressed the snowfall dwindled but the winds increased. Such flurries as battered our searchers now were whipped up by Arctic zephyrs.

There was too much ground to cover and the combination of foul weather and many passers-by was a fatal combination for detection. Holmes had been right in his concern. I briefly toyed with sending for some scent-hound like the lop-eared Spaniel Lurcher Toby[33] but realised

---

33 Toby, whom Holmes attests he would "rather have… than the whole detective force of London" appears in *The Sign of Four*, property of the taxidermist Sherman. Watson might think much of the dog since Toby helped him to a wife, Miss Mary Morstan.

that the many visitors and thick snow would mask any useful trail.

In that long, icy, and tedious clue-hunt the only bright spot was the gradual appearance of numerous of the past and present lads who brought data to Holmes at Baker Street. I do not know how word was passed that Wiggins was missing, but as the news spread our hunt across Hyde Park was supplemented by many eager urchins and former urchins, those Baker Street Irregulars who had once counted Wiggins amongst their number. I was touched at their devotion and I knew that Jenny Wiggins would be too when she heard of it.

It was those unconventional searchers who turned up the missing pocketknife far from the area where we had concentrated our hunt. Simpson[34] led me to the spot, a hundred yards or so west of where the Reformer's Tree once stood and is still remembered.[35]

34 Simpson's only named appearance in the Canon is in "The Adventure of the Crooked Man", which took place around six years before our present story. Wiggins does not attend with the Irregulars on that occasion, which is unsurprising since eight years had then passed since his debut and he could scarcely be described as an urchin any more; instead it is Simpson who fronts the youngsters.
    This character should not be confused with the bookmaker Fitzroy Simpson who appears in "The Adventure of Silver Blaze" in *The Memoirs of Sherlock Holmes*.

35 There is mystery around the Reformer's Tree. A handsome mosaic dedicated in 2000 by Tony Benn MP at the junction of nine paths just west of the Parade Grounds includes an inscription to commemorate the venerable assembly tree that supposedly burned during the Reform League riots of 1866. The charred stump became a notice board for political demonstration and a gathering point for Reform League meetings about universal male enfranchisement. This memorial explicitly mentions a new tree planted by Prime Minister James Callahan in 1977 to replace the original in the same spot where it once grew – which is clearly not where the mosaic lies. The identity of the actual replacement tree is now a matter of speculation.
    The demonstration at Hyde Park on 23rd July 1866 was a turning point in British political history. Home Secretary Walpole proclaimed the Reformer's League meeting illegal and the park gates were chained and guarded by more than 1,600 constables on foot and horseback. The wealthy of London came in carriages to further block the reformers' way. However, 200,000 people marched in protest, overwhelming the police, breaking the park gates and railings, and reaching the Reformer's Tree gathering place. The Horse Guards Blues, sent to quell the riots, were instead cheered by the commoners who assumed their support; the soldiers actually held back and did no more than manoeuvre while the police commissioner was pelted with stones.
    Rioting went on for three days and is well documented. No contemporary account mentions the burning of the Reformer's Tree, though many later histories repeat the story. *The Reform Act* 1867 finally gave the vote to working class urban males in England and Wales for the first time.
    Ex-police sergeant Edward Owen gave a different, first hand account of the Reformer Tree's end. In his *Select Narratives, Annual Events, etc., during twenty years' Police Service in Hyde Park* he described how "the 'original' stood [in 1875]; I believe an elm like its neighbours [not the oak referred to in the modern mosaic], but not a vestige of green or anything to indicate that species simply a stark, blasted-looking old trunk, dead as a doornail, whether from lightning or old age, it had fallen into such a state..." A well-attended "well-ordered" trade dispute meeting in 1875 ended with "mischievous boys" setting fire to the old stump. Eventually the park authorities removed the remains to prevent further arson.

Two younger street-wretches guarded the place, standing sentry in their rags, their feet wrapped in thick cloths and string for want of shoes. The girl wiped her nose on her sleeve and pointed to an excavation in the snow where a bloody knife had been discarded. "Is that wot you wanted?" she shrilled.

I tried to approach the scene as Holmes would. The pocketknife was hinged but fully open. There was blood crusted on the top two inches of it and splashes down one side of the hilt. It had dug deep into someone. And been left behind, embedded in a foe as its owner hastened away?

I looked closely around the discovery. If there were more stains they had been obscured by subsequent snowfall, but perhaps there was some other information I might usefully discern.

Simpson did the job for me. "We found it like this, see?" he explained, pointing to where the weapon's tip was embedded in the turf. "It were proper stuck in, like. We reckoned that some cove 'ad chucked it away as far as 'e might from the road, and it landed by chance this way up. We'd never 'ave spotted it else."

That made sense. If the blade had been discarded that way then this was nowhere near the attack. Either the man who had been hurt by the knife or some comrade had evidently decided it must be disposed off and hurled it far aside.

I instructed a constable to take over watch duties and to prevent the scene being disturbed, in the off-chance that Holmes might want to see the evidence *in situ*. I tipped Simpson and his companions a guinea between them and sent them off well-pleased with their work.

I walked the nearby footpaths despite the treacherous ice underfoot but found no sign of the place from which the knife might have been hurled away or of any disturbance where it could have drawn blood.

By four the light had failed. Though the gas-lamps along the main thoroughfares were lit, the vast majority of the great royal park was plunged into darkness. Further search became futile.

I thanked our searchers, official and unofficial, supplied the youngsters with funds for hot chestnuts from the retreating vendors, and returned along the lakeside path to find Holmes at the Receiving House. I spotted a fellow in the livery of the Diogenes Club hastening off and concluded that Holmes' brother had sent for an account of what was happening. A carriage and pair was also pulling from the iron gates of the rescue station,

---

Whichever version is correct (assuming either are), whatever the species and actual location of the old tree, the gathering for political discourse and speech-making at the Reform Tree migrated to the traditions of Speaker's Corner and the purpose, if not the details, of the original meeting point have not been forgotten.

bearing away a well-muffled elderly gentleman with old-fashioned mut-tonchop whiskers.

Holmes watched him go from the welcoming doorway of the Receiving House. "You have just missed the visit of Sir Hugh Ridgeward," he informed me.

"A pathologist?" I guessed.

"A botanist, Watson. He is a leading man in his field, one of the heirs of Gregor Mendel."[36]

I discerned that I had missed some discoveries while I had been developing frostbite in my extremities, and said as much. I also outlined the discovery of the knife.

"Dear chap, I appreciate your pains," Holmes assured me as he sent to have the evidence carefully taken up and brought to him. "It left me free to analyse and identify that mud residue in Wiggins' jacket pocket. Hence my calling upon my correspondent Sir Hugh and his special expertise. We are fortunate that the snows trapped him in London so he was on hand to advise."

"About... botany?" I ventured.

"About the specific components of the particles which became the sludge deposit I discovered," Holmes clarified. "You know that mud can be as distinctive as a signature, as good as a map. When it also contains sea-salt, seabed sand, fragments of fewmet, and alien pollen, then it only requires the right expert to read the evidence."

The cold had dulled my wits even more than usual. "Are you saying that Wiggins was carrying a pocket full of animal droppings?"

"Hardly a pocketful, but there was a definite residue, inside mud containing hematite, carbonaceous and amorphous substances, boehmite, kaolinite, and mica, in soil rich in phosphorous and nitrogen. There are also fragments of Pleistocene snails and modern tropical aquatic remains – all helpful indicators, as are the pollens of *Pentalinon luteum*, the shrub Hammock's Viper's-Tail, the endemic Puerto Rico applecactus *Harrisia portoricensis*, and a range of other zerophytic leguminous plants."

I nodded wisely. "Sir Hugh was able to guide you as to the origin of your mud."

"There is no doubt. The material in Wiggins' coat was from the Greater Antilles archipelago, midway between Puerto Rico and the Dominican Republic, most probably from the shallows of Isla Mona or the nearby rock of Monito. The geological evidence and the botanical material offer a

36 Augustinian friar and abbot of St. Thomas' Abbey, Moravia, Gregor Johann Mendel (1822-1884) was also a prominent botanist who gained posthumous recognition as the founder of the modern science of genetics.

most plausible address."

My brows shot up. "But why on Earth would Wiggins, or the fellow in his coat, have mud from the West Indies in his pocket?"

Holmes pressed his fingertips together and touched them to his mouth, a sign in him of intellectual pleasure. "Consider the naval pea-coat," he proclaimed, indicating the cut remnants of the garment from the corpse. "Mycroft selected this as a disguise for his agent not only because it is common and relatively anonymous but also because it has large square vertical pockets."

"For holding tropical slime…"

"For ease of slipping an envelope or parcel in *en passant*. The pea-jacket is ideally suited to the walk-past exchange. I am considering a monograph on the choice of apparel for nefarious and covert street enterprises, and I assure you the naval coat will appear prominently."

"Then Wiggins did perhaps receive his package – and it was muddy."

"More likely crusted with mud dried to dust. The small traces it left would be on the outside of any packet, flaked off to the bottom of the pocket.," Holmes assured me.

"To be soaked again when our victim entered the Serpentine!"

"Indeed. But we can do better than that. Sir Hugh Ridgeward has given us a locale. I can offer a little more. My examination of the sludge further uncovered a few tiny fibres of duck – not the quacking animal but the sailors' name for Dutch sailcloth, made of flax and hemp. *Doek* is the Dutch word for cloth."

"Sailcloth?"

"Think, perhaps, of a sailcloth bag; a waterproof canvas document case, say. Dropped onto soggy ground or in contact with ocean-floor it easily picks up traces of wet soil, enough to flake off when dried out and slotted into a coat-pocket."

I considered the implications. "Mycroft's message came from the a ship? A ship from the Caribbean?"

"The mud is indicative, but we cannot rely upon the botanist's evidence alone. The West Indies covers a good portion of our globe, Watson, and other men than seamen find uses for watertight pouches. It does not complete the chain of connection that might help us forward our case."

"A connection that leaves us with a dead sailor and a missing footman."

"And a mysterious observer who favours his right leg, Watson. Let us not overlook him."

I confessed to being at a loss as to how to proceed with the investigation. An early night had fallen on the frozen park. Perhaps it was better to

"Consider the naval pea-coat..."

return to Baker Street and comfort Wiggins' wife with assurances of our investigation tomorrow?

Holmes shook his head. "Time is not our friend on this case, Watson. I suspect that if Wiggins is at large then we are not the only ones hunting him. If he is captured and still alive he may be in a very unpleasant circumstance. In either case, losing even one night might be enough to lose him entirely."

Or he might be dead, of course, but neither Holmes nor I was ready to countenance that option.

"We shall head to the Police House and see if any word has come back from enquiries at the docks," Holmes declared. "I will also require their detailed maps of the park."

"Is there any likelihood that if we return to Mycroft with what we have discovered he may reveal more of what he knows?"

"None. Mycroft's priorities depart from ours on this venture. He serves the greater national good to the best of his definition. We shall pursue the immediate good of our absent colleague and let the greater good look after itself."

I thanked the junior doctor and other staff of the Royal Humane Society on Holmes' behalf and joined my friend on the short, chilly, slippery walk back to the Police House.

Our breaths steamed as we returned along Policeman's Path, past the snow-choked lawn and bowl of the old Cockpit. The gaslamps were very intermittent on this lesser route but we had a good storm-lantern borrowed from the Receiving House. Its yellow oil-light played upon the narrow section of the track still cleared and sanded ahead of us. My feet felt like two more lumps of ice; an afternoon of tramping had overcome my boots' waterproofing.

"Watson," Holmes breathed *sotto voce*. "We are followed again."

I wished I had my service revolver. All I possessed was a stout, bronze-handled walking stick. "The same fellow?" I murmured back.

"I am unsure. I suspect we are being flanked as well."

"An ambush?"

"If so, an unwise one." Holmes dug into the pocket of his Inverness cape, dug out a regulation steel police whistle, and let off three shrill blasts. The alarm echoed across the emptied park and he repeated it twice more.

If there were attackers lurking in the dark they melted away as a patrolman's lamp appeared ahead of us.

"This was undoubtedly the man who watched us earlier," Holmes assured a chilly and tired-looking Inspector Frome. "His tracks were unmistakable. The four other fellows that left fresh imprints to our flanks and ahead of us shared his taste for hob-studded footwear."

We reported our adventure in the hearth-warmed Inspector's Enquiry Office at the Police House. Frome looked unhappy and defeated as he received our account. We had heard from the duty sergeant that senior men from the Home Secretary's Office and a representative of the Chief Constable had called in the course of the last two hours; doubtless Mycroft Holmes was extending his interest, and perhaps not him alone.

"We will make further search, of course," Frome promised, "But now that darkness has come we have not enough officers, even with the dozen sent in from other stations to supplement the thirty usually on hand here, to thoroughly search areas away from the paths. Your pursuers could already have left the park by any of a score of ways."

That prompted Holmes to demand the large-scale Ordinance Survey maps[37] and grounds plans for Hyde Park and Kensington Gardens. He was mildly irritated to hear that a representative of the Ministry of War had been down earlier and made detailed photographic plates of all of them.

"Mycroft will already have studied these, then," my friend growled sullenly as the double-elephant[38] maps were laid out on the inspector's table.

The park was laid out before us in scale. It and Kensington Gardens form a rhomboid running east-west, intersected diagonally by the wide curve of the Serpentine. Frome was right about the choice of exits; on the Hyde Park side alone there were Marlborough Gate and Buck Hill Gate behind the Italian Gardens, then along Bayswater Road came the Victoria, Clarendon, and Albion Gates, to Cumberland Gate by Speaker's Corner and Marble Arch. Leading east to Park Lane were gates at Green Street, Brook Street, Grosvenor Street, and then the Hyde Park Screen through which we had entered weary hours earlier. Round the south edge parallel to Knightsbridge were the White Horse, Albert, and Park Passage Gates before Hyde Park Barracks and the Exhibition Grounds;[39] and that was

37 Ordinance Survey is the United Kingdom's national mapping agency. Formed to map Scotland after the Jacobite Uprising of 1745, originally based in the Tower of London, and urgently expanded to cover the whole British Isles with the threat of Napoleon, the Ordinance Survey became the pattern for national cartography programmes across the world. By Holmes' time the whole nation was mapped to 1:2500 scale, with urban areas mapped at 1:500. Restricted War Office versions of the maps contained additional detail.

38 In imperial paper measurements, double elephant is the proper name for a single sheet sized 26½ x 40 inches (67.3 x 101.6 cm), commonly used for older maps and charts.

39 Period maps refer to the present Westbourne Gate as Buck Hill Gate and omit the present Stanhope Place, Alford Street North and South, Curzon, and Achilles Gates. The

supposing that nobody had vaulted the tall railings that surrounded the rest of the perimeter or resorted to one of the many other ways out from adjacent Kensington Gardens.

"The question is why Wiggins, having received his package, did not avail himself of any of these exits," Holmes mused. "Young Wiggins knows the back ways and hidden passages of London as well as anyone alive. He might vanish into any neighbourhood and be hard to follow. If he had cause to believe he had been identified or was being pursued, why did he not summon assistance from any of the several places he might have sought aid? From this Police House, from the Rangers Lodge, from Cumberland Gate Lodge, from the Pump House at the Italian Gardens which was manned by burly boilermen? Why exchange outfits with our naval friend? Why...?"

He turned suddenly to Frome and called for the statement taken in a second interview with the Speaker's Corner agitator. "The heckler who interrupted his speech had a low London accent," Holmes noted. "Wiggins was quite adept at disguising his origins but spoke there in his native tones to indicate his authenticity. We may infer that it was Wiggins, not our sailor, who then wore that costume."

"He was seen leaving the park," I contributed. "Why would he then return?"

"He was seen heading to the exit," Holmes amended. "If he perceived some threat there then he might turn aside and seek a different route."

"If an enemy watched for Wiggins then covering the gates would be the best way of catching him. But so many exits must mean a significant search team."

"Which suggests prior information about the planned rendezvous! Did Wiggins shy from seeking help because he feared he had been betrayed? Had those to whom he might refer for help been infiltrated by his opponents? Was he under orders from Mycroft to avoid seeking such support?"

Holmes was becoming frustrated. I recognised the signs and asked him about the knife uncovered by the Irregulars.

"You and Simpson apprehended the key point. The blade was aban-

---

Green Street Gate and Grosvenor Street Gate and Lodge were erased by significant 20th century widening of Park Lane that removed 20 acres (8.1ha) from Hyde Park; not for nothing is Park Lane the second most expensive space on the original Monopoly board.

'The Exhibition Grounds' refers to the original site of the Crystal Palace created for the Great Exhibition of 1851, which occupied 990,000 sq. ft in the southernmost part of the park. 15,000 exhibitors from around the world attracted six million visitors. Three times the size of St Paul's Cathedral and always intended to be temporary, the structure was transplanted to Penge Peak in 1854 (that area became known as Crystal Palace and still is) and was finally destroyed by fire in 1936. The vacated land in Hyde Park was subsequently turned into public playing fields and tennis courts.

doned, tossed away. The only new information my study of it has afforded is that when it was used it must have bitten hard. There was considerable splashback. The wielder must have been saturated with gore."

"Is that why he took Wiggins clothes?"

"Certainly a man who must have been stained as much as the fellow holding this pocket knife was would draw attention from passers-by. There is…"

We were interrupted by the florid duty sergeant, announcing the arrival of three 'persons' to see 'Mr 'Olmes'. His disapproval of them was evident, but my friend's lips curved into a tiny smile at the sight of the disreputable trio.

Of the party I knew but one of them, and scarcely, for he had much grown and bulked out since I had seen him last seven or eight years before. "Is that Dikkon Small?" I asked incredulously. "Not so small now!"

The street-tough had not lost his cheeky grin, although he may not have washed since I saw him last as one of Wiggins' running-mates in Holmes' street-Arab gang long before Reichenbach.[40] He was dressed now as a dock-idler and bore upon his fists the signs of one who indulged in bare-knuckle fighting. "Dikkon Small it is, Doctor Watson!" the youth proclaimed, and then added to Holmes, "I found one."

Small gestured at a thin, shabby woman of the lowest class, a poorly-dressed doxy dolled with curled ringlets and too much rouge. She was accompanied by a sour-faced woman of middle years with similar but better-applied facial paints. I concluded that the girl was one of the many *demi-monde* who ply a trade amongst the lower parts of the city and her companion was the hostess in whose establishment she laboured.

"Mrs Perrett," Holmes identified the older female. "Small has indicated the nature and reason for my enquiry?"

"He h'as," the madam replied. "If it h'andn't been for young Wiggins going missing then h'ai'm sure we could not h'ave h'elped you."

Holmes ignored and abandoned Frome and guided his guests not to the interview rooms that were little more than cells but to the cosy little station canteen where he could provide mugs of oxtail soup and interrogate his witnesses with more delicacy.

"Dikkon says you was h'a-looking for some mariners what h'ad just come off a ship from the West h'Indies," Mrs Perrett mentioned, lean-

---

40 Holmes was lost over the falls at Reichenbach, Interlaken on Monday, 4th May 1891, a little over eleven years after Holmes and Watson had begun their partnership, and was considered dead until his return on Thursday, 5th April, 1894. The following month the recently bereaved widower Watson sold his Kensington medical practice and moved back to Baker Street.

ing in intimately. "H'in particcerlar, you wanted men h'oo 'ad boasted of h'unusual weather or h'events, anything h'out of the h'ordinary."

"Soosie 'ad a bloke like that," Small interrupted eagerly. "Last night."

Mrs Perrett glared at him. "H'as h'ai was saying, h'ai happened to h'ost a number of merchant seamen yesterday h'evening what h'ad travelled in from them parts, and one of them h'appened to mention such a thing to my dear ward Soosie. There is maybe a reward for h'information uncovered?"

"There may be," Holmes answered her. "That is in addition to my over-looking the matter of the sale of items of clothing inadvertently misplaced at your establishment to Messer Lumpwish of Totter's Yard, which could be misconstrued as theft and handling of stolen property. Now pray re-frain, Mrs Perrett, and let us hear from the girl herself." He turned to the doxy. "Soosie? You are come up from the country, I perceive, but have made a living in London for a year or more now. The right information would earn you a good reward, even after Mrs Perrett's share, and would go a long way towards the sum that you hope to save to settle down with your young man."

The girl's eyes flared wide, but Mrs Perrett evidently knew Holmes of old, for she calmed her 'ward' down and commanded her to reveal what she had been told.

The girl seemed chronically shy in our presence, in the Police House, and her tale came out slowly and falteringly. Stripped of hesitation and circumlocution, it was this: that last night around tennish, Soosie and her colleagues had entertained a party of seven or eight Dutchmen, merchant sailors new in port and just paid their wages. One of the fellows, taking a fancy to Soosie, had guided her to a side-room. He had been much in his cups and had not been able to immediately satisfy his desire, but had talked rapidly and in a difficult accent about his wide travels.

Chief amongst the seafarer's boasts had been that had survived a great hurricane off Puerto Rico two summers past, where he had witnessed another ship founder in the tempest and go down. Soosie had been en-thralled and chilled at his description of the struggling schooner as it was dashed upon the cliffs of a tropical isle.

But Soosie's caller had not ended his tale there. Having witnessed the tragedy during Hurricane San Roque some sixteen months ago, the same sailor had returned on his ship seeking to salvage the lost barque, not once but three times since.

"Diving down into the ruins, they did," Soosie confided, clutching her cup tight. "In one o' them bells, 'e said."

"Lost gold, they reckoned," Mrs Perett opined, unable to restrain herself any longer. "Though you should never believe w'hat a fellow tries to tell you!"

Holmes waved her to silence. His sharp questioning of the harbour doxy was not done. Three weeks after the hurricane and the disasters at sea it wrought, her visitor's ship had been recalled to the port of Orange in Dutch Sint Eustatius, one of the tiny Leeward Islands.[41] The cutter formed part of the rescue flotilla seeking several vessels that were missing after the tempest, dispatched to find the ship that it had witnessed being lost.

The Dutchman told Soosie of the terrible damage that San Roque had wrought in its tempestuous passage; of broken shorelines, of the tree-stripped landfalls, of floods caused by more than two inches of rain in an hour, of ruined coffee plantations and wrecked harbours, and of the turbulent void where sea had claimed what was once land. And he had described finding wreckage of that foundered ship, caught by the great waves of the heaving sea during the tempest and dashed upon rocks at the base of the white cliffs of Mona Island.[42]

"Mona!" I recognised. Sir Hugh evidently knew his subject.

It had not then been possible to reach the lost vessel. It lay wrecked in shallow turbulent waters ringed by jagged rocks, unassailable by land or sea, but its position had been marked. The sailor and his ship had returned to that location twice in subsequent months to try and salvage the beached wreck but in that time it had been consumed by the waves. It was only in autumn of last year, more than a twelvemonth since the hurricane, that a third visit had relocated the ruined cutter and used divers and special equipment to retrieve some of its cargo.

"What cargo?" I asked Sookie, as excited by her account as the girl had been.

"Gold!" she confided delightedly, confirming her madam's claim. "If it weren't bars *and bars* of bullion gold! They 'ad ter 'aul it out and take it back to h'Amsterdam, y'see? It was government gold, is what it was!"

Holmes took details of the sailor's appearance and that of his fellows, and commissioned Frome to locate the ship and secure its captain for interview. The inclement weather meant that a sailing vessel of any size could not yet have navigated out of Thames Bowl. He demanded runners to brave the climate and take urgent messages to Admiralty House and to Lloyds Shipping Insurers,[43] rousing after-hours clerks as necessary. "We

---

41 The island of Sint Eustatius or Statia covers 8.12 square miles. Its city and port are now usually named Oranjestad, capital of the Caribbean Netherlands.

42 Sint Eustatius lies 326 miles south and east of Isla Mona.

43 In 1686, Edward Lloyd began using his coffee house as a base to offer shipping insur-

must identify the ships, Watson – the one that found the bullion and the one that foundered. Such lost treasure, buried as it was under sea and mud, has surely some connection with the detritus in Wiggins' coat."

"And might the men from this vessel supply those lurkers whom we have spied today?" I wondered.

Holmes did not think so. "Regular seamen have a distinctive gait and would have left tell-tale marks in the imprints they made. Our pursuers were men of a different order. Some might have had shipboard experience but... no, not only sailors."

We thanked Small, made appropriate initial recompense to the women with promises of a handsome bonus if their information proved of special value, and settled down to wait for more information from the expert sources we had consulted.

I took advantage of the delay. At the back of the Police House was an old courtyard square. To one side was a coach house and stables, the other a line of ramshackle sheds. I bespoke the farrier and secured loan of a pleasant cob; on this bitter evening no cabs traversed the streets.

I took the borrowed police horse out along the Ring and left the park at Victoria Gate to trot along to Baker Street. I assured myself of Jenny's wellbeing in Mrs Hudson's care, quieted our landlady's fears for the missing Wiggins as best I could, and retrieved my Beaumont Adams[44] in case I should need it.

It occurred to me that nobody had asked Jenny where she thought

---

ance to his maritime customers. The business prospered as the Society of Lloyds at the Royal Exchange in Cornhill, City of London, and eventually managed to obtain from parliament the *Lloyds Act* 1871 that set out underwriting in its modern form. Lloyds is now an entire insurance market, a partially-mutualised marketplace where financial backers in syndicates pool together to spread risk. It is one of the most senior and influential financial institutions of Britain.

Lloyd's Shipping Register rose from its original core business of underwriting ships and their cargoes. Dating from 1760, the Register was (and is) a complete list of all significant seagoing vessels, including their construction port, technical details, estimated condition, and carrying capacity, to aid insurers in assessing risk. The Register's estimate of top ship quality from 1775/6 onwards has given us the phrase 'A1'.

44 The Beaumont Adams revolver was the standard British Army handgun from 1862 to 1880, favoured because of it was the first true double action firearm (cocked by either the hammer or trigger) and delivered a hefty 54 bore, .422 calibre bullet. It was replaced by the Enfield mark 1 as the army's weapon of choice the year that Dr Watson was pensioned out. By the 1890s the Beaumont Adams was rather out of date but Watson found it "trusty" and used it as his weapon of choice on several occasions. The firearm's speed of fire for close-quarters combat and significant stopping power made it an ideal adventurer's weapon.

her husband might have gone to ground. "It's hard to say," the gravid young woman responded sensibly and soberly. "He knows every street better than a cabbie and all the short-cuts and rat-runs, of course. But this weather is unlike anything I remember. All the narrow ways must be choked." She snorted something between a reminiscent laugh and a present sob. "Why last Sunday, when I wanted to go to chapel and it was so icy out and all that sleet, he wouldn't 'ear of me trudging through the snow in my condition. So what does 'e do but take to the cellar? And from there is a brick wall with a door in it to the next cellar along, and then another after, where they used to collect night soil in the old king's day – all scoured clean now, you understand, and dry and snow-free. At the end of the row there's a shallow tunnel, we 'ad to bend a bit like, but it was one of them forgotten storm drains what got cut off when the new sewers was laid, twenty, thirty year back. And then the cellar of the Crown and Ball, believe it or not! A nice thing to go to chapel through the basement of a public house, eh? But I speak God's truth, Dr Watson, when I tell you 'e got me the best part of the way to Sunday service underground, and us only 'aving to go out into the nasty weather but three short times."

I agreed that Wiggins was an ingenious fellow and exhorted Jenny not to let her spirits become low; Sherlock Holmes was seeking him. Still, as I rode back to Hyde Park in the frosty, gusty darkness and heard the clocks tolling seven, I could not help but wonder whether the next time I spoke to Jenny Wiggins she might be a widow.

I returned to find that Holmes had received several reports. I seized upon the medical examination of the Serpentine corpse first: The right lung showed basilar atelectasis due to the hemothorax caused by a stab wound. The lesion was four inches deep into the right pleural cavity, which when thawed had yielded around a twentieth of a fluid ounce of blood. Otherwise the external appearance of the sectioned surface evidenced no focal lesion; there was no indication of foreign material, infarction or neoplasm.[45]

In short, the man had been stabbed from behind as we had concluded,

---

45 It is perhaps unusual for Dr Watson's accounts to include detailed medical jargon. One might assume his original editor Dr Doyle chose to excise such material as unsuitable for lay readers, or that Watson himself revised his content in cases he selected for publication in his lifetime.

with a short blade that had punctured his lung and led to his drowning in his own fluids. It was certainly murder and probably competent murder.

Holmes had acquired charts of the Leeward Islands and the wider Caribbean Sea, showing the layout of the landmasses there. That chain of small isles is a hotch-potch of national holdings. To north and west, Britain holds Anguilla. Below that, France holds the northern half of Saint Martin and the Dutch the southern part. Next, Saint Barthélémy is French. Some twenty miles or so south from there, Saba and Sint Eustatius are Dutch. Only three or four miles southeast again, St Kitts and Nevis belong to Her Majesty. The whole area is rife with smuggling and intrigue, with political gamesmanship and naval manoeuvring between great nations.

Further north and west along the archipelago, after the British and American Virgin Islands, comes the territory of Spanish Puerto Rico and then the Dominican Republic. Mona is third-largest of the Puerto Rican islands there, some four miles by seven. Holmes' scribbled side-notes indicated that the place was now largely unpopulated except for men who collected its copious deposits of bat and gull guano for the phosphate trade, and that there were around two hundred caves there whose walls were decorated with native art designs and the carved names of early settlers; one had been hideout for the notorious Captain Kidd.[46]

Holmes had also gathered weather reports, including Met Office[47] and Admiralty records for 1893. "The year before last was a bad time for Atlantic winds," I recognised. "Ten hurricanes and two other tropical storms. San Roque was the third of them, formed on August 13th east of the Lesser Antilles, strengthening to a hurricane over the Leeward Islands. Three days later it reached Puerto Rico with 120 mile-an-hour winds. There were heavy rains over the chain, causing much damage and costing four lives."[48]

---

46 Scottish sailor Captain William Kidd (c.1655-1701), master of the *Adventure Galley*, was declared pirate by the Royal Navy. He hid out at Mona in 1699, one brief leg in a long fugitive career that ended when he was arrested on his return to Britain, tried and executed for piracy.

47 Britain's Meteorological Office, established in 1854 by the Board of Trade to provide weather forecasts for mariners.

48 By 22nd August 1893, San Roque was one of four active hurricanes in the Atlantic. Landfall at Patillas weakened the storm but it regained major hurricane status as it approached the Bahamas. It curved northward and made landfall in St. Margaret's Bay near Halifax, Nova Scotia as "the Second Great August Gale", a non-tropical category 1 storm that sank the vessels Dorcan and Etta Stewart and claimed twenty-five lives.
   Hurricane San Roque shares its name with a similar storm that was reported devastating Puerto Rico in 1508 by Juan Ponce de León, and another in 1788.

"It was at that time that the Dutch packet Hr. Ms.[49] *Jacob Remmessens* was lost with no survivors," Holmes confirmed, indicating a brief reply from the Admiralty. "It was spied in the Mona Passage between the Dominican Republic and Puerto Rico, foundering in heavy seas with a mast lost, and then reported wrecked on the southern coast of Mona Isle. There is more information in that envelope below Mycroft's message."

I was distracted by the telegram beside that report, delivered less than a quarter hour ago from Holmes' brother. That strange missive consisted entirely of seemingly-random letters:

KNNIK VNV URFRVD E CZFNC ZCEP HRYUL MSF YXZEK XP
KRBGN VVR RLCV EUPFK V VR KUXG FH UYHD JGLJQR RYB
QILC NIPWR VCK YNMFV NZZ CRKY OE YLNB P YRTF PWHL
ULR FYCN MPWJV ONE ILRF KWJP YRJ TZLD EJN N AJAV

Sherlock Holmes had provided the decryption and written the message in plain text below. Although there was no sign as to how he had unravelled the missive then, I asked about it later. It turned out to be what Holmes called, "A childish substitution cypher that Mycroft and I amused ourselves with as children. The method is simple and the text hardly secure, but it sufficed for the moment given the circumstances."

I took the trouble to master the method, which did not seem simple to me.

"One first removes all the spaces from the text," my friend explained. "They are extraneous, added quite randomly to deceive."

That left us with:

KNNIKVNVURFRVDECZFNCZCEPHRYULMSFYXZEKXPKRB
GNVVRRLCVEUPFKVVRKUXGFHUYHDJGLJQRRYBQILCNIP
WRVCKYNMFVNZZCRKYOEYLNBPYRTFPWHLULRFYCNMP
WJVONEILRFKWJPYRJTZLDEJNNADAV

From this stream of letters one then extracted every fourth character, replacing it with a space, to break the remaining list into blocks of three:

KNN KVN URF VDE ZFN ZCE HRY LMS YXZ KXP RBG VVR
LCV UPF VVR UXG HUY DJG JQR YBQ LCN PWR KYN FVN

---

49 Hr. Ms., Harer Majesteits (Her Majesty's) or Zr. Ms., Zijner Majesteits (His Majesty's) are the prefix of Dutch ship names as HMS is for British Royal navy vessels and USS for American military ones, although the modern international prefix for Dutch navy ships is HNLMS (His/Her Netherlands Majesty's Ship).

ZCR YOE LNB YRT PWH ULR YCN PWJ ONE LRF WJP RJT LDE
NNA AV

The rest was not a substitution of letters, where B stood for A etcetera, but rather *three* such substitutions. The first letter in each block was shifted through the alphabet by eight, so that A became H. The second letter was shifted by ten, so that A became J. The third shifted by fourteen, making A into N. The translation grid therefore looked thus:

0	A	B	C	D	E	F	G	H	I	J	K	L	M	N	O	P	Q	R	S	T	U	V	W	X	Y	Z
1	H	I	J	K	L	M	N	O	P	Q	R	S	T	U	V	W	X	Y	Z	A	B	C	D	E	F	G
2	J	K	L	M	N	O	P	Q	R	S	T	U	V	W	X	Y	Z	A	B	C	D	E	F	G	H	I
3	N	O	P	Q	R	S	T	U	V	W	X	Y	Z	A	B	C	D	E	F	G	H	I	J	K	L	M

Using that procedure, the blocks became:

DEA DMA NIS OUR SWA STR AIL EDF ROM DOC KST OME ETI
NGS OME NOT ALL WAT CHE RSD ETA INE DPA YMA STE RFR
EEO RIG INU NCE RTA INW HER EIS PAC KAG EUR GEN TM

Adding spacings in the appropriate places brought us to the message that Holmes had scrawled under the coded telegram text:

DEAD MAN IS OURS WAS TRAILED FROM DOCKS TO MEETING
SOME NOT ALL WATCHERS DETAINED PAYMASTER FREE
ORIGIN UNCERTAIN WHERE IS PACKAGE URGENT M

In this way we learned that Wiggins had likely been discovered because his contact was already identified and followed. Unknown adversaries had waited for the exchange and had then sought to intercept both men. Mycroft had captured some of the small-fry in the plot but they had not given up the organiser behind them or his hidden purpose.

Holmes intimated that the discarded fourth letters in the message were present only for padding, to confound translation, but when I was learning the cypher later I made an interesting discovery. The unregarded characters formed the string:

IVRCCPUFEKNREKKFHLRIIVCNZKYPFLFMVIKYZJJ

Using a substitution of eighteen letters, so that A became R, I uncovered the following additional memorandum:

0	A	B	C	D	E	F	G	H	I	J	K	L	M	N	O	P	Q	R	S	T	U	V	W	X	Y	Z
4	R	S	T	U	V	W	X	Y	Z	A	B	C	D	E	F	G	H	I	J	K	L	M	N	O	P	Q

REALLY DONT WANT TO QUARREL WITH YOU OVER THIS S

As I absorbed the telegram, Holmes was in deep study of some other document, but when I set Mycroft's message aside he absently passed me another dossier. This was information on the *Jacob Remmessens*, a three-masted tern schooner with a length of 117 feet. The vessel was reported sunk on August 16th, 1893, the day that the storm had raked the Antilles. Lloyds *Shipping Register* listed cause of loss of the Netherlands navy courier as shipwreck, indicating that it had foundered in the gale and been pressed by wild waves onto the cliffs of Mona.

"I see that the *Jacob Remmessens* was carrying a shipment of bullion," I said.

"It is the vessel to which the sailor alluded," Holmes assured me. "The Dutch navy schooner departed Orange, Sint Eustatius, with the second tide on Tuesday the 15th. It was ironically hoping to avoid the storm, evacuating the Dutch administrative port of its treasury and valuables ahead of expected damage to the island."

"But Hurricane San Roque shifted course unexpectedly," I saw from the charts we had been sent. "Sint Eustatius was skirted but the courier ship bearing valuable cargo and people to safety was caught up in the heart of the tempest. It was wrecked on the Mona cliffs, ground up on the shore-rocks where rescue was impossible. Within hours the *Jacob Remmessens* was submerged, lost with all hands and passengers, some twenty-five souls."

I shuddered at such loss of life in such dire circumstance. "That was why the wreck was so hard to locate, then. It sank and shifted in the torrent, its cargo falling to a sea bed that was guarded by jagged boat-snagging rocks."

"Indeed. Had not a passing merchantman observed it's sinking and marked its general position it may never have been found."

"The merchantman was that from which Soosie's guest originated."

"The *Fazant*, registered out of Rotterdam," Holmes supplied. "Once the paper trail was located, all became quite clear. *Fazant* is a brigantine plying the trade routes from the Guianas to the Gold Coast then up the Spanish and French Mains. She seldom comes to London, but the night before last she beat a difficult voyage along the Channel and arrived here, making port just before the Thames Estuary was iced shut. Captain de Haas is being brought here with all haste."

"Her purpose here was trade?"

"Everything seems to be in order, but I detect my brother's hand. *Fazant*'s owners were commissioned to deliver a shipment of fabrics and spices to London before completing their usual route. It is as if some valued agent was aboard the brig and required an excuse to disembark at the East Docks."

"The dead naval man? Mycroft wrote..."

"Possibly, but we cannot be more certain until de Haas makes an identification. Even then we may not be positive without Mycroft's confirmation. For now let us entertain the hypothesis that our victim was the man whom Wiggins was to encounter, and that he brought with him some artefact or item retrieved at last along with the bullion from the wreck of the *Jacob Remmessens*."

"Perhaps a sealed watertight packet, naturally bearing traces of the Caribbean mud in which it had been submerged."

"Just so. And, since it was still somewhat crusted when it entered Wiggins' pocket, an item that must not have been greatly inspected by its deliverer. It is possible that the courier also had his orders in that regard."

I was still at a loss as to how something retrieved from a sunken Dutch naval vessel half a world away could account for the absolute disappearance of our former Irregular.

"The answer lies in Mycroft's urgent secrecy, Watson. A ship of the line entrusted with a cargo of gold for Her Majesty Queen Wilhelmina or her government might well carry other items of great value and interest. A packet of government documents would be of no particular significance to salvaging sailors but of immense value to whichever state the materials referred, or to their rivals."

"The positioning of Sint Eustatius amongst so many competing territories makes it an ideal place for espionage or secret diplomacy," I understood.

"And all the more likely that some diplomatic pouch was included with the evacuated treasure."

"By the third attempt to recover the *Jacob Remmessens*' lost cargo someone may have been placed on the crew to retrieve such a package."

Our deliberations were interrupted by the arrival of a Dutch sea-captain, a huge fellow with a huger beard who strode into the Police House as if taking command of a poopdeck. "Where is Sherlock Holmes?" he demanded.

"Everything seems to be in order, but I detect my brother's hand."

The detective identified himself. De Haas shrugged off his constabulary escort as irrelevant and took a central position in the Inspector's Office, shedding snow across the floor. "Why have I been dragged from my ship?" the captain snarled.

Holmes eyes him coolly. "You were not dragged, but politely invited. You must have suspected a visit, for you were already dressed and prepared to leave your ship and travel through bad weather to an interview. We are not the first to make enquiries about your voyages and adventures."

"What are your enquiries to me?"

"They are police business," Inspector Frome cautioned the seaman. "We are investigating a murder."

De Haas' brows furrowed. "Murder? *Moord*?"

"You had better step over and see if you recognise the fellow," Holmes told him.

The dead man had by then been transferred to the mortuary at Scotland Yard but a good police sketch had been made and was available. Captain de Haas was shown the picture and evinced a hiss of recognition. "He is mine. I knew it. Visser is too good a mate to stay out past his leave and..." He caught himself, straightened up, and declared, "This man is one of my crew, second mate André Visser. He was a fine sailor. What became of him?"

Holmes learned that Visser had joined the *Fazant* in June of last year, coming with excellent references and proving himself a superior mariner. His papers showed him to have served aboard several Dutch Navy ships at the rank of Lieutenant before retiring to merchant work. He was well-liked and kept himself to himself. De Haas knew of no family, but the company that owned and operated *Fazant* would have a next-of-kin on record.

We had little time to exchange information before we were interrupted again, this time by a fussy-looking official and his agitated assistant bursting in without even removing their hats. "Stop this!" he demanded. "How dare you detain and interrogate a subject of Her Majesty Queen Wilhelmina in this manner?"

"What's this?" Frome retorted, his temper frayed by a long, difficult day. "Who the devil are you, sir, to barge in like this to a...?"

Holmes intervened. "This gentleman is a representative of the Dutch embassy, I fancy. He has just now been apprised of the interest in Captain de Haas and the doings of *Fazant* and has abandoned his excellent dinner of quail in aspic to hasten here and defend his countryman. I would be interested to know the source of his intelligence."

"The captain isn't under arrest," I assured the ruffled envoy. "He is help-ing us to fathom a difficult murder and a mysterious disappearance. This is Mr Sherlock Holmes and…"

"I know who this is. I know everything!" the official snapped. "Do not believe that you can ride rough-shod over the sovereignty of the Netherlands! You will not question this captain without legal counsel present and the support of his native embassy!"

"Will we not?" Frome snarled back. "This, sir, is England, and…"

"And in England as in every *civilised* country there are diplomatic pro-tocols!" another sharp voice broke in. At the doorway behind the Dutch official appeared another gentleman of advancing years. This specimen had thinning silver hair and a grey moustache and was still swathed in a thick fashionable Burberry long-coat.

The Dutchman swung around as if a wasp had stung him. "This is a matter of deep concern for Her Majesty's government!" he warned.

"And a deeper matter of concern for *Her* Majesty's government," the newcomer insisted. He deigned to turn aside to Frome and identify him-self. "Leslie, Foreign Office. I am here to *deal* with Mr Van der Linden's interference."

"Interference! Is the embassy to sit idle while our citizens are hauled away by *your* Empire's policemen to be interrogated in secret during the night? Do you imagine that the Duchy of the Netherlands will ignore such an insult?"

"Do you believe that diplomatic courtesies allow you to interfere in a security and legal investigation of significance to the British Crown and people?"

I felt as if I should intervene and perhaps avoid another Anglo-Dutch war. "Gentlemen, I feel perhaps there has been misunderstanding…"

Holmes has less tolerance for interruption. "There are questions to answer, sirs, on the matter of shipwrecked bullion lost during the San Roque hurricane," he cut in, trapping the diplomats with his stare. "The shipment from the colonial centre at Oranje Stad, en-route to the Dutch Bank in Paramaribo?[50] Lost aboard the Hr. Ms. *Jacob Remmessens* with all hands."

He gestured to the worried-looking sea captain. "There are matters to clear up regarding Captain de Haas' commissioning to salvage the cargo;

---

50 The capital city of Dutch Guiana, the nation now known as Suriname, on the north-eastern coast of South America.

who issued such orders three times since the tragedy of the schooner's loss, under what warranty, and to whom such cargo was returned." He pointed to the stricken-looking out-of-his-depth Frome. "There is an ongoing investigation of murder, seeking the killer of *Fazant*'s Second Mate who called himself André Visser. There is a missing young man whose life may be in peril. If either of you is prepared to answer any of those questions and assist me in untangling this affair then by all means remain. If you are here to obfuscate and obstruct this investigation then you must do so where you are not in my way!"

Heren Van der Linden's face suffused scarlet. "You may not tell an accredited official of the Embassy of the Netherlands that..."

Mr Leslie likewise cavilled at such speech. "How dare you sir, address..."

Holmes stabbed one long, bony finger at them. "You apprehend who I am, gentlemen? The name of Sherlock Holmes is certainly known in Whitehall, and I am sure my brother is very well known to you, Leslie, since it was he who disturbed your ease a half-hour ago and sent you scurrying here. I'd warrant my fame is not unheard of in Amsterdam either. You will recognise, then, that I am not a fellow whose attention men – or nations – with unscrupulous secrets may wish to attract. You are both perilously close to becoming such men. I advise you, therefore, to take your wranglings regarding Captain de Haas out of this office, and not to return unless you are willing to submit to my cross-examination. This, gentlemen, is your *only* warning!"

Such a caution from a man of Sherlock Holmes' capacity could not be easily dismissed. Frome, after a moment of shock at such procedural nightmares as rarely trouble a Hyde Park Police Inspector, roused himself and said to the diplomats, "Perhaps we might resolve questions of protocol away from the active investigation, sirs?"

"You will not question Captain de Haas without my presence and that of counsel," Van der Linden still insisted, if a little less shrilly than before.

"Then he may not be interviewed at all without a representative of the Foreign Office and a Queen's Counsel also present," Leslie replied.

Holmes quelled them both again with his gimlet gaze, then swung back to the unfortunate sea captain. "There is one enquiry that I will insist upon before you go, De Haas. Ignore these others, attend to me! Apart from Visser, has any other of your crew departed or been unaccounted for since you came to port? Or at all, in any port, since you retrieved the bullion? In particular, any other sailor who joined your compliment some time since you survived Hurricane San Roque and witnessed the destruction of the *Jacob Remmessens*?"

The master of the *Fazant* frowned in memory. "There are two who are no longer with us. Pieter Kleij was a deckhand who came to us a year since. He was lost in November in high seas at the Bay of Biscay. Hans Molenaar joined us as cook at *Pasen* - Easter last - in Lisbon. I dismissed him for drunkenness four weeks ago in Bilbao. No other is presently absent from my crew as far as I know."

Holmes turned to me as if vindicated, though I did not then follow his conclusion that Molenaar might also have been an agent, working against Visser in the matter of the *Jacob Remmessens* salvage. Dismissal for inebriation may have been a ruse to secure Molenaar's plausible departure from the ship to warn of the forthcoming diversion to London. If the unfortunate Kleij had also been more than he seemed, his employment had come to an abrupt end in the apparent accident that saw him lost overboard during an Atlantic tempest.

It was clear from the jealous bickering of the diplomats and the increasing agitation of the sea captain that no other enquiry would presently be successful. Holmes dismissed them all, calling on Frome to usher them off to an interview cell where they could continue their arguments and invoke their respective authorities without interrupting our case. The inspector was more deferential in removing the important personages but eventually left Holmes and I alone before the Enquiry Room fire to discuss what we had heard.

"The matter becomes ever more complicated," I complained as Holmes regained his temper.

He scowled and leaned over to rummage through Frome's desk drawers, dragging out stationary to scribble on. "Nothing so far has proved the hypothesis that Mycroft's desired package is recovered documents," my friend conceded. "With so little time and so great a distance there is no further we can go on that course, except to discover such documents if they may be found. However, the involvement of Dutch diplomatic force and its countering by British officialdom is suggestive that we may be on the right path. Meanwhile, whilst we are distracted by these fellows, Mycroft has been studying photographic copies of these charts."

And Mycroft Holmes was not above seeking to divert his brother. I joined Holmes in reviewing the pile of maps laid out across the inspector's desk.

"I had not expected so much detail and so many features," I admitted. "This park is very old and has changed much since it was seized from Westminster Abbey to make a hunting estate for Henry VIII. The whole of modern London has grown up around it."

"And being so close to the seat of power it has been well-documented," Holmes replied. "I had these older maps hauled down here from the British Library; they are hardly needed for policing Hyde Park today. The oldest of these plans represents the time that Queen Caroline ordained the creation of Kensington Gardens in 1728. Here is a layout of the works set in place for Her Majesty by landscape gardener Charles Bridgeman. He was ironically a key force in moving popular British taste from formal Anglo-Dutch parterres and straight avenues to that more naturalistic style that now characterises the great English estates and public parks. The Dutch were out of fashion, you see."

Holmes is uncommonly ignorant on certain subjects that do not interest him and yet can offer up profound and unexpected insights into such a variety of topics. I looked over the brittle yellow drawings that had diverted the then-open River Westbourne, damming it to join together ecclesiastical fish-ponds into what was there titled the River Serpentine.

Lying open beside Holmes was the tome that had occupied his attention when I arrived, a bound edition of the *Transactions of the London and Middlesex Archaeological Society*, vol. VI.[51] An engraving therein traced the river's course from its rise at Hampstead Heath all the way to Hyde Park and from thence to the Thames. Of particular interest was the now-hidden route of the Tyburn Brook of which the Ranger had spoken. The plan showed approximately where it also entered the park, flowing south, and had originally joined with the Westbourne there.

Holmes indicated a thick volume of parliamentary proceedings that he had likewise ordered up. '*Reports of Committees: 1860, Contents of the Fourteenth Volume*,' I read. A glance inside guided me to the lengthy '192: REPORT of the Select Committee on the SERPENTINE; together with the PROCEEDING of the COMMITTEE, MINUTES of EVIDENCE, APPENDIX, and INDEX.' The whole took up half the volume, a bulky 320 pages.[52]

---

51 The document from the venerable, still-extant and active London and Middlesex Archaeological Society is available for .pdf download at their website, http://www.lamas. org.uk/archives/23-transactions.html. The date of original publication was 1890, not 1882 as Wikipedia reports. The relevant map is on page 273, illustrating an article on the Westbourne from J.W. Waller (page 272ff).

52 This august and weighty volume is now available free in .pdf format from https:// books.google.com/books?id=1axbAAAAQAAJ

"What aspect of the Serpentine required the appointment of a Select Committee?" I wondered.

"Why, the great London debate of the middle of our century," Holmes replied. "The only matter on any Londoner's mind after the 'Great Stink' of '58 was that of sewage; it's disposal and the methods thereof."[53]

"I see that the committee interviewed Sir Joseph Bazalgette, the engineer who designed and laid down our modern sewer system."

"And the questions to him well illustrate how carefully Parliament considered the issues of public hygiene and the wellbeing of this park. Amongst the concerns of the enquiry was how the creation of Bazalgette's proposed deep sewers might affect the water supply and drainage of the Serpentine. The eventual chosen course rerouted the underground flow of the Westbourne River and Tyburn Brook as we have heard. The next chart before you shows what was done."

An unrolled map below the book showed plan and cross-sectional representations of a covered drain to run east along the top-side of Hyde Park from the 'pumping house' where the Italian Gardens were later placed to a point beside Albion Gate, then sou'south east under the Meadow and Sheep Trough before swinging out beneath the Ring to round the end of the Serpentine. Indeed, the trenches looked to pass right beneath the very Police House where we stood, or else very near. The waters of the Serpentine and what had once been the River Westbourne were reunited at the Dell and taken through a series of cuts and gulleys to vanish underground again in Knightsbridge. On that map the outfall finally found the Thames just up from Chelsea Hospital, but Holmes directed me to subsequent alterations that had blocked off the sewage from ordinarily venting

---

53 The insanitary condition of the River Thames was cause for serious concern throughout the 1850s. Scientist Michael Faraday complained to *The Times* in 1855 that, "Near the bridges the feculence rolled up in clouds so dense that they were visible at the surface, even in water of this kind. ... The smell was very bad, and common to the whole of the water; it was the same as that which now comes up from the gully-holes in the streets; the whole river was for the time a real sewer." Charles Dickens wrote, "I can certify that the offensive smells, even in that short whiff, have been of a most head-and-stomach-distending nature."

Hot weather in July and August of 1858 caused the industrial waste and untreated human effluence in the River Thames to form a chocking miasma that brought London to a halt. The business of Parliament was affected, with lime-soaked curtains hung ineffectively to mask the stench; there was discussion about removing government to Oxford or St Albans.

The eventual response was one of the world's major engineering projects, the installation of 1,100 miles of new street sewers connecting to 82 miles of main sewers beneath the streets of the capital, under the supervision of Sir Joseph Bazalgette. The work involved creating the Victoria and Albert Embankments and reshaped significant parts of London. The cost was £4.2m, close to $450m today. So effective and of such capacity were these works that Bazalgette's sewers still cope with the vastly greater requirements of the significantly larger present population of London.

into the Thames at that point; although that exit still existed to cope with floods, the main Ranelagh Sewer now voided considerably further downstream, via the Chelsea Embankment as far as Bexham.

"This is fascinating, perhaps, to an industrial historian," I judged, "but how does this...?" I paused as the answer Holmes might have made dropped into my head. "Wiggins is an expert at hidden places, secret paths. And he vanished somehow even though we suspect he may have been under close hostile observation. Jenny told me only today how he was able to guide her across London through subterranean routes." I looked at the maps with renewed interest. "You suspect that Wiggins has found his way into the lost watercourses underneath us."

Holmes shifted aside the plump mackerel police station cat that had settled on the next vital documents. The modern Ordinance Survey sheet was a useful 1:500 scale representation with elevations and boundaries. Specific Hyde Park management plans indicated manhole covers and inspection shafts for the sewer and overflows. "When Bazalgette's work was done and the Serpentine uncoupled from is original source, elements of the old tunnels appear to have been left unused and dry. Other channels guiding Tyburn Brook may have been similarly redundant. I can nowhere discover accounts of them being filled in."

The station tom, unimpressed with the great detective, stalked away to curl before the hearth fire.

"There was extensive work at the head of the Long Water when Prince Albert had his Italian Gardens installed," I saw. "Something called Agnes Well was lost, and the level of the land altered."[54]

Holmes indicated a contemporary chart that marked a one-foot drain

54 Little is recorded of St Agnes' Well and its location is only marked today by a small grate amongst the flagstones between the Pumping House and the Italian Gardens. The nearby St Agnes Villas probably derive their name from the site.

Sir Richard Philips' *Modern London* (1804-05), records that "In the north-west corner of Hyde Park, beneath a row of trees running parallel with the keeper's garden, are two springs, greatly resorted to: one is a mineral and is drunk [St Agnes' Well]; the other is used to bathe weak eyes with [Dripping Well, later called St Govor's Well]. At the former, in fine weather, sits a woman, with a table and chair and glasses for the accommodation of visitors. People of fashion often go in their carriages to the entrance of this enclosure, which is more than a hundred yards from the first spring, and send their servants for jugs of water, and sometimes send their children to drink at the spring. The brim of the further spring is frequently surrounded with persons chiefly of the lower order, bathing their eyes. The water is constantly clear, from the vast quantity the spring casts up, and its continually running off by an outlet from a small square reservoir."

Minutes of the Proceedings of the Metropolitan Board of Works, 1881, pg 560 notes that a report was read "dated July 25th, 1861, on the Letter of the First Commissioner on Her Majesty's Works & c., with reference to a deficiency in the supply of water to St Agnes Well, Kensington Gardens, consequent on the construction of the Ranelagh Storm Overflow works." This report was approved and forwarded.

Thanks are due to author, researcher, and scholar David Furlong for his correspondence on this topic.

cover just a few feet from the Pumping House. "Here is the only access to the once-holy St Agnes' Well now, Watson. It is one of several ancient wells and courses that have been covered, but most of them have some kind of inspection access point. Our forebears were not men to neglect the possibility of maintenance being required. Provision was made, even if those ducts are now overgrown and overlooked."

I looked at the plans uncertainly. "I doubt even Wiggins could fit through a one-foot hatch. And would he not have disturbed the snow atop it and so left signs of his hiding place?"

"Of course he would, had he gone to Agnes' Well. But there are other underground spaces beneath Hyde Park. Some of them have less public and larger access points."

"Your brother has been studying these same charts."

"And receiving reports of the investigation as the evidence is uncovered. Given Mycroft's remarkable acuity he could have already untangled this plot – if he ever bothered to stir himself from his armchair! But there is much to be said for first-hand observation, for tactile investigation, Watson! We are *here*, and mobile, and prepared to trudge through the storm. And so we must go – there!"

Holmes indicated a largely unfeatured wooded portion of the map north and a little west of our present location at the Police House. A hand-written notation in faded brown ink marked a point with the initials 'S.D.', signifying 'Storm Drain'.

I considered the location. "If Wiggins tried to leave the park at Marble Arch but found his way barred, he might turn left along the Ring, along Carriageway Drive. That would take him past a number of other gates, any of which could grant him access across Bayswater Road into the laby-rinth of domestic streets beyond; all the way to 221b."

"But if he found those paths blocked too, and especially if he was in-jured, then he might break south over the Meadow and find this hatch. Remember, the weather was poor, visibility was very restricted, and snow was covering prints nearly as soon as they were laid. If Wiggins knew of the storm drain then he might seek refuge there until he was missed and help could come."

"A day and a half ago!" I pointed out. "Could a man survive so long crouched in some damp hole, exposed to these conditions?"

Holmes did not reply. He shrugged on his Inverness cape suitable for cold-weather outdoor work and prepared to venture into the snow.

"Should we bring Frome and his men? Or send to your brother?" I ven-tured.

"Not yet, Watson. There is still more about the circumstances of yesterday that we have not yet unearthed. I am not confident about all the players in our drama. Van der Linden and Leslie both made very convenient appearances. The limping man – the sea-cook Molenaar? - and his fellows are still looking for someone or something and are watching carefully. Frome has been given orders via the Chief Constable, perhaps from the Commissioner of Police, but from whence did those orders originate? No, my friend, I would prefer us to venture out privately for now. You have your firearm?"

I checked the Beaumont Adams in my pocket. "Let's brave the storm."

We took lensed storm-lanterns[55] and ventured into the darkened park. Beyond the blue lamp that burned outside Police House and a pair of street lights there was nothing but pale reflections from snow. The moon was nearly full but no glimmer penetrated the overcast sky. A bitter wind blew off the Thames, picking up small eddies of whirling flakes from the new-fallen drifts.

Holmes kept the lantern covered except for the focussed beam that guided our steps. If sentinels still lurked in the abandoned park we did not wish to betray our movements to them. We trudged over the six-way junction and then departed from the path. Our boots vanished fourteen inches deep in untrammelled snow, making our passage difficult.

Even with foreknowledge of the storm drain hatch we had some difficulty in locating it. Beyond the newer ordered plane tree plantings was a rise with a thick stand of clustered elms, one of the islands of primal forest still retained from older wilder years.[56] A vertical iron hatch some four

55 The safest form of portable outdoor lighting in the latter part of the 19th century was the hand-held kerosene, storm, or hurricane lantern, a flat-wick lamp with a thick glass bulb and protective metal frame. Air flow was carefully controlled to make the flame brighter and to keep out wind and water. Where something more akin to a modern torch with a focussed beam was required, the glass mantle was largely replaced with sheet metal except for a shutterable lens (a dark lantern). This allowed light to be directed without entirely spoiling a wielder's night vision and allowed for stealth.

56 During the Commonwealth (1649-53 and 1659-60) when royal properties were seized, Hyde Park was sold off in various lots. The new owners generally stripped the land of assets, including most of its mature and valuable timber trees, predominantly oaks and elms. When the monarchy was restored in 1660 and Hyde Park recovered, it was described at the time as "a barren field". A long period of replanting followed, and though paintings dating from around 1800 show many fully-grown and beautiful treescapes, the paucity of trees was still drawing criticism on the Park Rangers in the early 19th century. Many of the prevalent plane trees in the park were planted in response.

Hyde Park's remaining distinctive and characterful old elm trees were lost to Dutch

feet tall was let into the side of the mound, sheltered from view by thick snow-covered brambles.

We might have taken longer to find it had there not been traces of recent human movement across the white slope. Several sets of tracks were still visible under the last snowfall.

"The most recent were less than two hours ago," Holmes judged. "The oldest I can discern would be... perhaps four hours back, when the glass fell again and the wind turned to the south? Look at how the snow has filled the imprints, Watson. The direction of drift tells everything."

The tracks had lost definition but Holmes carefully dusted away flakes to reveal a half-frozen tread with enough detail for him to read. "A size eight, square-toed all-purpose work-boot. The seaming and cobbling are distinctive of the wholesale manufactory of Mr John Branch of 87, Bethnal Green Road.[57] You see the relevance?"

I did not immediately follow Holmes' line of reasoning.

"The Diogenes Club supplies its staff with uniforms. Those footmen and functionaries whose work is entirely indoors in that sanctum of silence wear soft quiet shoes, naturally, but staff whose labours take them outside the premises are provided with boots from Mr Branch. This is the imprint of someone who wore footwear like that issued to the more active personnel of the Diogenes."

"Mycroft dispatched someone to find this storm drain before us."

"A pair of someones, probably, judging by the spread of half-erased tracks. They were the most recent visitors here before us, but not the only ones. Let me see if we might uncover some trace of our size ten and a half, hob-nailed, round toed with a right heel chip."

I was eager to approach the trap door but Holmes demanded method. He brushed away more snow, and although he failed to find treads of our covert watcher he unearthed another, more sinister trace.

The lantern beam shined on snow stained red. "Blood!" I cried.

Drifts had covered these marks very well. Holmes scraped away a good four or five inches before he found better splashes. "These drops

Elm Disease in the 1970s.

57 Mr John Branch and his factory were favourably described in *Toilers in London; or Inquiries concerning Female Labour in the Metropolis* (1889), Chapter XXIII, "Boot and Shoe Makers," as follows: "One of the best manufactories is that of Mr. John Branch, in the Bethnal Green Road. Mr. John Branch takes great interest in his female hands, and the arrangements made for their comfort contrast favourably with other factories. The girls are kept on all the year round; they work in a large, airy room, have full time allowed for meals, and tea provided on the premises." An advertisement with testimonials for the company appears in *Health: A Weekly Journal of Sanitary Science (Exhibition Supplement)* October 24th 1884, available in collected form as a free .pdf at https://books.google.com/books?id=oXoFAAAAQAAJ

were shed yesterday," Holmes opined. "More recent falls have obscured but preserved them. Now they may tell their tale."

I looked at the sprinkling of sanguine splashes that Holmes had scraped out, trying to see them as Holmes would.

"Here is where Mycroft fails," my friend assured me. "No minion could make competent observations nor draw accurate conclusions. Yet *we* see that the effusion of blood is periodic, not constant – a drip and a dribble, not a flowing stream. The bleeder was wounded in the arm – the right, if I am not mistaken, with a trail of blood trickling down his sleeve."

"Wiggins! The injury suggested by the marks on his coat…!"

"Most likely. Any footprints he might have made would be long gone, of course, even an hour or two after he passed this way, but blood tells." Holmes rose from where he squatted over the excavated snowbank. "Now to the hatch."

We approached the cut in the side of the hill and the metal door let into a shallow brick facing. The thick thorns that had overgrown it had been hacked aside very recently to open a clearer path to the hatch. The padlock on the clasp had been struck away.

Holmes restrained me from rushing forward. He retrieved a fluttering thread of cloth from one of the damaged brambles. It was a dull beige of some heavy weave and it too was dark with crusted blood.

"That is not from Wiggins jacket," I objected.

Holmes shook his head, looking satisfied. He carefully folded the scrap away and gestured for us to approach the door.

The ground around the old drain access was partly sheltered by the remaining bushes, so it retained traces of people's movement. "Two visits at least by three men in all," Holmes confirmed. "The hob-nailed boots were first. Not our limping man, but someone who shares his cobbler. It was he who trimmed back the foliage, I see. The pair in Diogenes Club footwear came later."

"And we came last – too late," I worried.

Holmes offered a non-committal shrug." There are no signs of anyone being dragged or carried out of here."

"There's more blood," I spotted. "There, on the ridge of the door. Has someone tried to wipe it off?"

"Ah, you apprehended that. Yes, the smear is where someone with a bloody cuff would brush it as the hatch was hauled open. But it was not Wiggins."

"But… Wiggins' shirt was the one that was stained to the cuff, and

I looked at the sprinkling of sanguine splashes that Holmes had scraped out...

since Visser was not wearing it when the injury was taken…"

"They may have exchanged clothes before this, but that is irrelevant. Observe this hatch. It hinges on the left. The mark is on the edge that opens. The only way to leave such a trace would be for a man to pull upon the door with his left hand. With the right he would instead leave a trace upon the outer frame."

"Visser was left handed," I recalled; and then further remembered, "The bloody shirt and coat were stained on the right sleeve!"

Holmes wagged a finger at me to indicate that I had taken the point. "Now we begin to understand why Wiggins and Visser may have exchanged clothes. There were two possibilities, but examining this entrance I am inclined to dismiss one of them. There is no evidence that Wiggins was forced here or dragged here."

"And the other possibility?"

"Suppose that Wiggins and Visser met as intended. We may now imagine that their encounter was observed. Visser passes his package to Wiggins and the two head off in different ways; or perhaps Visser trails behind Wiggins hoping to see him safe or to spot anyone who was following after. Whatever happened, Wiggins must have felt that his way back to St James's was blocked. He makes for another exit, Cumberland Gate by Hyde Park – also guarded!"

"He knew he was followed," I chimed in. "He made himself obvious at Speaker's Corner so he would be remembered when we came looking."

"He was not then injured. It would have been noticed when he drew attention to himself with his heckling. Thereafter he turns aside from Cumberland Lodge and perhaps tries for one of the other northern exits onto Bayswater Road, to no avail."

"But he did not call upon the ready assistance of local authorities," I objected. "The Police House, the Ranger's Lodge, the Gatehouse were all in easy reach." It was the problem that had puzzled us before.

Holmes set that point aside for now. "Wiggins, facing adversaries with obvious numerical advantage, but adept at avoiding pursuit and somewhat on his own territory, manages to avoid their attention for some time. But not forever. At some point he is discovered and comes to grips with an enemy. He is wounded by his hunter's knife."

"Here?" I asked, looking at the doorway into the storm drain.

"I fancy not. The signs are that whoever first broke this lock and prised open the cover was already bloodied. Wiggins may have escaped his attacker, or defeated him, or been rescued. It could have taken place anywhere across the snowstorm-obscured Meadows. I suspect that either then or after, Visser intervened to save Wiggins and fought off an assailant. The result, I believe, was that the enemy was overcome and probably killed – bloodily – by Visser. You recall the pocket-knife."

"No such body has been found."

"No such body has been found by us," Holmes corrected me. "There have been other searchers abroad in the Park since Wiggins vanished. If the dead assailant's allies found him they might easily spirit his body away. The weather would quickly bury any physical traces."

I wondered why we were hesitating to enter the storm drain when an injured Wiggins might be laid inside, but then I saw Holmes watching down the slope in the direction from which we had come. There was the faintest twinkle of a lantern before the darkness swallowed any sign.

"The police?" I wondered. "Mycroft's agents? Rangers? Or is it the fellows in the hob-nailed boots who followed us before?"

Even Sherlock Holmes could not tell. He went on with his hypothesis. "The bloody left cuff indicates the truth, Watson. Visser was drenched in blood. Not his own, not then, but some enemy's. His clothing was sufficiently stained that he could not pass without drawing significant attention. Wiggins was actually wounded but apart from some small markings on his right arm his clothing was still unmarred."

"You suggest that Visser helped the wounded Wiggins to shelter here," I caught up. "Wiggins knew of the place. Visser bore him to cover and gained entry, leaving the mark from his bloody sleeve."

"Very good. *Now* our story takes us into the drain, Watson. Be careful not to expose the light. Let those lantern-bearers below remain ignorant of our exact location. They will discover our trail eventually, but I would prefer it not be so soon."

Holmes eased open the heavy metal door, scraping aside a shallow mound of snow that had drifted up even in the brief time since the way had last been used. "Be careful now," he murmured. "This short section of tunnel has been redundant for more than thirty years, drained and dry since the Westbourne was diverted as the Ranelagh Sewer; but that was before recent heavy snows and ice disrupted the usual watercourses."

I prepared my service revolver and turned my lantern's lensed beam into the tunnel.

A vertical shaft lay before us, with a rusted iron ladder let into the brickwork. A fall of perhaps six yards ended at a dirty flagstone floor that was now shallowly covered with slush washed down from some surface inlet.

Holmes indicated a couple more traces of blood on the decayed ladder rungs and the mashed indentations of boots on the wet snow below. "We can now say where Wiggins' trousers acquired their rust stains," he remarked.

He climbed down the shaft. I closed the metal door behind me and followed him.

The old water channel was different from the modern sewers I had visited. Instead of a tunnel like a circular or oval pipe, the bottom third laid over a bed of Portland cement with water-sealed courses of glazed brickwork, we found ourselves in a barrel-roofed cut with an almost-flat floor that angled only slightly to a central gulley. Headroom was no more than six feet, requiring us to be careful when we moved away from the middle of the cut. The construction was old stone, much larger blocks than the regulation London stock brick, and the floor was of great shaped plates that gave it an almost mediaeval aspect.

We played our lights along the passageway. It ran northwards about fifty feet before terminating in a wall bricked with newer materials. Tree roots had broken through the ceiling at that end, causing a small landslide. A cascade of icicles like glass stalagmites betrayed where water had found access again to its former course.

The other way bent south and east. We had to trudge through the slush, following the imprints of previous searchers. I was struck how cold it was down here, like being in an ice-house. I feared that any wounded man who sheltered here would not long endure the temperature.

Beyond the curve of the passage the old channel terminated in another broken wall, but in front of that was a platform of builders' rubbish and storm detritus that left dry ground above the wash of slush that otherwise covered the tunnel's base. Evidently the rainwater that found its way here also found escape beneath that raft of rubble but did not top it. And there, on that shallow shelf, was evidence that Holmes could use.

"See here!" the detective cried, striding onto the uneven platform and indicating discarded wads of blood-drenched *Morning Standard* newspaper. It was evident that it had been used to stanch and clean up a cut.

Holmes dropped to examine the traces there. "This is where an injured man laid. A discarded cloth was placed there; it had been used to clean the blood. Perhaps a scarf? It has since been removed. The crumpled broadsheets were piled neatly there. They have since been disturbed, raked over by more recent visitors after the stains had dried – the bleed patterns are incontrovertible. Other bloodstains there… Visser doffed his bloody coat?

Then this is where the two men exchanged outfits."

"Why?" I puzzled.

"Visser helped Wiggins out of his pea-coat and shirt to tend to his wound," Holmes suggested. "It became evident that Wiggins was in no condition to go back into the tempest and face more assailants. It was agreed that Visser must try and make for help, probably to the Diogenes, possibly to Baker Street. But to pass unremarked he must have apparel that was not sprayed with an enemy's blood. Outer garments were swapped. Wiggins remained here; see the markings where a man in still-sticky blood-marked clothing made himself as comfortable a nest for himself as might be possible in this miserable hole. Note the discarded sea-matches[58] and some regular lucifers.[59] There was only one stick left in the box we found. This was all they had for light. Hmm... were the common lucifers left with Wiggins, or are these stumps discarded by one of the set of searchers who found their way here? I'd expect Mycroft's men to be better provided with quality matches."

"Then Visser climbed out and tried to make for help," I imagined. "At some point he encountered the enemy again and was not so victorious a second time. He took his fatal wound and they threw him into the lake."

"I think not, Watson. I rather fancy that, having taken a wound he knew to be fatal, Visser used his last strength to hurl himself under the ice. In that way he denied his opponents the opportunity to search him. They could not know whether the packet they sought went with him into the water."

I wondered how we might know that the enemy had not searched the body then dumped it.

"A search would have left unmistakable traces," Holmes insisted. "Visser was still bleeding. Shifting the corpse would have altered the stain patterns. Nor were his clothing seams disturbed, which any competent searcher would have investigated, even if the package they sought was simply in his pocket. No, be certain that Visser's last act was to deny his

---

58 Sea-matches or storm matches have a strikeable tip similar to a normal match but the combustible compound and oxidiser coats half of a longer waterproof-coated stick. Sea-matches burn even in strong winds and can spontaneously re-ignite after brief immersion in water. They are often included in modern emergency kits.

59 The lucifer match was patented in the 1830s by Samuel Jones, based on work for Scots inventor Sir Isaac Holden. Although soon replaced by Charles Suria's design that substituted unpredictable antimony sulphide with white phosphorous (the "Congreve", or the "loco foco" in the U.S.), then with paraffin (the "parlour match"), and finally by the red phosphorous "safety match", the term lucifer remained common well into the 20th century, referring to any crude cheap kind of match; c.f. "...while there's a lucifer to light my fag... [cigarette]" in the First World War Song *Pack Up Your Troubles*.

assailant an opportunity to discover whether he carried the object of their pursuit. They simply could not know if he took it with him under the frozen lake."

"Until the body was discovered and cut out of the ice."

Holmes frowned. "I wonder now if I should have taken the time to interview the person who first saw the body under Serpentine Bridge and alerted the police. It was a fortuitous discovery."

"You suspect that the enemy who fatally wounded him but lost him in the water might have conducted a search and then discovered his resting place?"

"There is no way to break through ice and haul a corpse out of the Long Water at Hyde Park without being noticed. Better to let the authorities do it and discover what he was carrying another way."

"By invading a police station?"

"You will recall that Wiggins was not confident enough to appeal to that station when he was being pursued. It may be that one or more of the officers there are not to be trusted."

"Frome?"

"Frome is under instruction. We do not know from whom those instructions actually precede. But it may not be him. It may not be any of them. All is speculation. We do not yet know – but we shall find out!"

"And Wiggins. What of him? He was here and is obviously gone now, but you say he was not taken?"

"There would be signs of struggle, or of an unconscious or dead body being lifted away. Besides, the recent searchers only found this place today, after it became clear that Visser did not carry the much-sought package from Sint Eustatius. As you noted, the chill down here would preclude any person from surviving here overnight."

"So where…?"

Holmes suddenly gestured for quiet. He tilted his head to listen. He sniffed deep.

I feared that whoever was behind us had located the drain entrance, but Holmes played his lamp over the uneven back wall that blocked the southern end of the old drainage sluice. "Do you hear running water?" he asked me. "Can you smell a faecal odour? We must be close to the juncture where the old passage joined into the new, improved waterway. It cannot be far past that sealed barrier."

Our lights revealed the shallow gap in the end wall that admitted the sound and smell of the Ranelagh Sewer. Courses of bricks at one side of the base had been broken down by time, the slow eroding flow of run-off water, and the intrusion of more elm-tree roots. Some of the broken blocks had been stuffed back into place to shut up the hole again.

There were more smears of blood near the rift in the wall.

"That gap," I asked, aghast at the possibility that came to me, "Is that sufficient for Wiggins to crawl through? Might he have climbed through there to better hide?" If so then he might still be there, frozen to death.

"If he went that way then someone took the trouble to place stones behind him. Look at how these bricks have been jammed in to cover the hole. This was certainly done very recently, in the last couple of days."

We set down our lamps and began to scrape out the debris that blocked the rent. The narrow opening in the bricks was no more than four courses high and perhaps three feet wide. The lower quarter was filled with ice-slush. A man might just about press through once the debris was again lifted clear.

Before the last of the rubble came loose we found the hole was also blocked by bundled cloth. We pulled out a sailor's coat of dull beige that was browned with clotted blood. Wrapped inside were a Fair Isle sweater, a cheap work-shirt, and a pair of burlap trousers, all equally marred by sanguine stains. "This overcoat matches the torn thread we found on the thorns outside," Holmes noted.

"Visser's clothes?" I asked incredulously.

"The sizes fit. The splash patterns suggest close arterial spray from the neck of a man of similar height at close quarters in front. This was a knife-fight, Watson, and Visser was a deadly opponent."

Yet not so deadly as the man who had pierced his chest cavity at the last, I reflected.

Holmes knelt down to shine his light past the opening where we had recovered the clothing. The passageway continued another twelve feet then ended in a weir that must once have fed water into the main channel beyond. A grill of sturdy iron bars six inches apart ran from floor to roof to block the route into the sewer main. There was no escape that way for any man.

A corpse lay face-down in the slush in the short connecting section. He wore nothing but his underwear. The rime of frost over his body was proof that he had been there for some time.

My heart sank again for poor Jenny Wiggins and her unborn, but even then Holmes was advising me, "It is not him."

I looked again. Wiggins had no beard and he lacked a shock of damp fair hair. This fellow was broader than our former Irregular and carried a crude and obscene tattoo on his left forearm.

I did not relish squeezing through that wet narrow gap to examine the corpse. Holmes, thinner but taller than I, evidently shared my caution. "Better to wait for the police to break the wall down, doctor," he advised me. "We shall draw what conclusions we can from what we see from here. There is much to be learned from the bloodstains on the frozen ice and from the disturbance patterns of the slush. I'll warrant I can reconstruct the scene from those alone, and from some other clues that are quite evident."

"If you can account for a second oddly-clad corpse then I should be glad to hear it, Holmes. The affair has become unpleasantly macabre."

"We posited that Visser left the injured Wiggins here and went to seek help. He left Wiggins a limited supply of matches. I have so far counted seventeen spent stalks. Wiggins improvised a small fire for a time by igniting a garment of clothing – the bloody scarf, for example. The burned remains of it are there by the weir. After Visser had gone, and with his impromptu camp-fire dying out, Wiggins looked about for some better hiding place."

"He found this gap. Or made it."

"He opened it up again, for certain. He crawled through and made himself as comfortable as he might on that mound of rubble there. You see the imprint? He was alone in the dark for some time."

I shuddered at the idea. Cold, wet, injured, and hunted, huddled in the absolute darkness of this forgotten sewer? It was not a situation I would relish.

"Remember, however, that he and Visser had left a trail. It would still then have been readable to an expert, or perhaps just a lucky hunter. In any case, one of those who searched for him found the drain hatch, discovered the broken padlock – not yet covered by the snow, I warrant – and followed down here. *His* were the common lucifers we discovered. He came to the end of the tunnel, where we are now, and saw the hole as we see it."

"It had not then been blocked up."

"I suspect Wiggins discovery of it came after Visser departed and our young friend felt somewhat recovered. When the searcher came, Wiggins was hidden on the other side of this wall, crouching in the darkness. He would see only a flickering match flame approaching but it would be enough to alert him."

I saw that the dead man's boots had been pulled off, doubtless so that his trousers might be stripped, and they lay discarded in the overflow. There were of the hob-nailed type that other unidentified hunters had worn.

"The fellow spotted the gap and shimmied through," Holmes went on. "Wiggins saw his only chance. As the stranger pushed his head through the gap, Wiggins struck with that brick there. You see the marks of skin, hair, and blood on it? I do not say that he meant to kill, but Wiggins was near-blind and half-dead with blood-loss and cold. The brick split this man's skull. You can read the wound."

"Wiggins dragged the body through the gap," I guessed, following Holmes' reconstruction. "He stripped the corpse's clothes to replace Visser's blood-ruined outfit so that he might pass outside without remark, perhaps even be mistaken by his pursuers for one of their own. Provided with the last of his assailant's lucifers to light his work, he sealed the hole behind him to hide the body and obscure his actions."

Holmes nodded approvingly.

Encouraged, I went on. "When it became evident that Visser was not returning with aid, and as night drew in and Wiggins had revived some more, or else become desperate, the lad decided to decamp under cover of darkness."

Holmes rose from the gap and stretched. He allowed his lantern to trace the line of the wall and the detritus that was stacked there. "Wiggins was always a bright fellow, Watson. He knew that given time either Mycroft or we would come looking for him. And he was confident that we would leave *no stone unturned.*"

Holmes spoke that last sentence as if it had special significance. I followed his gaze to the pile of rubble washed up in one corner of the rough platform where the youngster had first lain. All the broken rock and discarded mortar was covered in a greenish sheen of mould, except for one small flat limestone flake that was darker and uncrusted.

That stone had been shifted recently, turned over. It was nowhere near the stones that had plugged the wall-breach, of quite a different type.

Holmes retrieved the object. It was no larger than the palm of his hand. It would have been ideal for skimming across the Serpentine. On the obverse side, which had previously been its smooth upper side, crude scraping had etched letters and symbols on the rock:

"Wiggins left this?" I wondered.

"Of course, Watson." Holmes twisted the stone so that the pictograms stood in a vertical column. "The top two sigils are the address."

Looked at from that perspective, the first gravings were clearly letters of the alphabet. "S H... Sherlock Holmes! And the rest?"

"Of greater interest, conveying the message that young Wiggins wished to send in such a way as to be unintelligible if discovered by an enemy."

A dot inside a circle, a dot inside a square, three horizontal lines forming a grid with three verticals, and whatever the last complicated marking was did not mean anything to me.

"Nor would it," Holmes assured me, "or to any other who had not made a study of the marks left by tramps and itinerants to warn and advise one another of the neighbourhoods through which they pass. You will find these marks, and a dozen like them, chalked and scratched on walls and pavings throughout the city. Variants of them are found in any area of Britain you might choose. Similar but different systems are prevalent in Europe and North America."[60]

"You understand such symbols, and Wiggins knew you would. You can read them."

"Indeed. These kinds of sigils are left in warning, or to indicate where food or shelter may be found, or to convey the best means by which charity might be obtained from a particular house." Holmes traced the circle with the dot inside. "This warns of police presence, or that the householder may summon a constable. The next is a sign of danger or threat of violence; the dweller may give a beggar a drubbing or turn loose a dog. The next-to-last also refers to the police, and in particular to a police station or prison."

"And the final symbol? I thought it might be the numeral 10 until the axis of the images was shifted."

"That is the most interesting of all, for that is not a tramp sign, or at least none I have ever seen. If I am correct then that is the most telling part of the script."

"But what does it all mean in the context of Wiggins' message?"

60 American hobo signs from the 1890s to the present day have been well documented but there are fewer surveys of their British and European counterparts. A relatively early source is *The Tramp: his Meaning and Being* (1931) by Frank Grey, newspaper proprietor and MP for Oxford, who was at the forefront of social reform for care of vagrants and who in the 1920s went undercover as a vagrant to expose the harsh conditions which tramps faced. Samples of British vagrant signs can be found online at http://www.workhouses.org.uk/vagrants/signs.shtml, and extracts from Grey's book at http://www.workhouses.org.uk/Gray/

"Why, it tells us what he intended when he crept from this place. It warns us to beware either a policeman or someone dressed as such. It points us to where he is likely to be. It tells us where the packet might be now – depending upon the weather."

"The weather?" Had Wiggins hurled the documents into the Serpentine or Ranelagh Sewer or down St Agnes Well to prevent their capture by some enemy of the Crown? Were the secrets everyone sought now lost in the sewer outfalls to the icy Thames?

We were interrupted by sounds echoing down from the top of the access shaft. There was a shriek of rusted gate hinges as the drain door was pulled open.

"We are discovered, Holmes!" I did not like the tactical position we found ourselves in, at the dead end of a short curved tunnel.

Holmes evidently shared my view. He gestured for me to hurry and strode boldly back to the access ladder. "Constables?" he called. "Frome? Is that you?"

A light shone down the entrance shaft. "Mr Holmes?" a voice descended to us. "It is the police. Are you all right down there, sir?"

"I'm coming up," Holmes announced. He gestured for me to hang back at the bottom of the ladder until he had reached the summit.

"Is Dr Watson there with you?" the fellow shining the lantern wanted to know.

"Hold on," my friend answered, hastening up the rungs to the surface. "I shall be with you shortly."

I waited until Holmes climbed off the ladder and had scrambled through the small hatch before I came up after him. The man with the storm-lamp had to withdraw the light to allow Holmes egress and I had my own lamp blacked out, fastened to my belt.

Holmes made a terse, small 'stay back' gesture to warn me. He stretched upright outside the low threshold of the storm drain. "Did you find the missing packet, sir?" one of the bobbies enquired.

"I have three questions for you first," Holmes told the trio of constables clustered outside. "What sum of money must a man carry in his pocket to be immune to the charge of vagrancy? What is the significance of three shrill short blasts on your pea whistle? And what is the name of the Hyde Park Police House cat?"[61]

---

61 The correct answers would be:
The 1824 and 1838 *Vagrancy Acts* make no mention of any sum that is required to be carried, but were in fact a broad and bluntly-used pieces of legislation aimed at, "Every person wandering abroad, or placing himself or herself in a public place, street or highway, court or passage to beg or gather alms, or causing or procuring or encouraging any

"What?" the nearest constable asked, baffled by the string of questions.

"Come now," Holmes scorned as I took up position in cover inside the drain hatch. "Any bobby knows these things! What are your service numbers? It is there on your epaulette."

All three men peered instinctively at their shoulders. Holmes hit the nearest in the face with his heavy lantern, then turned and caught the second in some scientific *baritsu* toss. As the third fake constable raised a pistol I fired at close range and caught the fellow centre-chest.

Response shots returned at us from the dark brambles beyond. Holmes dropped down and ducked back through the storm drain gate.

Of the three men in constable's uniforms and police overcoats, two were insensible in the snow and the third twitched his last. Bullets from unseen enemies further away ricocheted off the brickwork of the inspection hatch.

We took sheltered positions behind the brick buttresses that supported the door. "How many?" I asked Holmes.

He drew his own revolver, a smart new Webley Bull-Dog,[62] and indicated three directions. "We are bracketed. These fellows know their business. The supposed policemen were meant to find out what we had discovered, if we had the package. The others are here to ensure that we do not leave alive."

"Now we know why Wiggins avoided the Police House," I guessed. "If those fellows impersonated bobbies when they came for him, he had no way of knowing if they were the real thing or not."

"That may be how he was wounded," Holmes suggested. "If a supposed constable called to him, approached him, he would see no reason to shy away."

"Impersonating a police officer is a serious crime."

"Murder is a capital offence. And despite these sham officers, I still suspect an informant inside the Hyde Park station. Someone sent word that we had slipped out; too late to trail us but in time to search for us. We

---

child or children so to do, [who] shall be deemed an idle and disorderly person."

Three short blasts on a constable's pea-whistle signified warning of a riot and required immediate response from other policemen.

History has not recorded the name of each particular police station cat but the breed was ubiquitous until well into the middle of the 20th century and, as the internet attests, is far from extinct today.

62 The Webley "British Bull-Dog" was a firearm designed to fit into a coat pocket. With only a 2½ inch barrel but firing five .44 Short Rimfire, .442 Webley, or .450 Adams cartridges, it was small but powerful. General Custer carried a pair at Little Big Horn. A Belgian-made copy was used to assassinate President Garfield.

"I have three questions for you first," Holmes told the trio of constables...

already know that Visser's secret meeting with Wiggins was revealed, but that is Mycroft's part of the problem. He can be relied upon to fathom that much."

A couple of shots rattled nearby, reminding us that we were under siege.

"More adversaries have arrived," Holmes noted. "Four, possibly five newcomers, and with rifles. Our enemies are concentrating their forces."

"And we are somewhat trapped here," I recognised.

Holmes shook his head. He actually looked satisfied. "On the contrary, Watson. *We* are trapping *them* here."

Before I could ask for clarification, we were called from the darkness. "Mister Sherlock Holmes. Doctor Watson. Do you hear me?"

"Quite plainly," Holmes called back.

"There is no reason for you to die. Give me the documents."

"What documents?"

"Do not imagine me a fool. Give me the documents or the footman dies."

Holmes snorted. "Do not imagine me a fool either, sir. You do not have him."

There was a pause and then the voice continued. "You know where he is, then?"

"If I do, then that information will not be shared with you." Holmes fired three more blind shots off, wasting ammunition.

His barrage provoked response. More missiles struck chips from the brickwork near us and *spanged* off the hatch's metal door. It took a moment for the gunplay to calm again.

"You are quite cornered," the unseen speaker warned. I fancied his voice had a foreign cadence but I could not place it. "I have men enough to overcome you. If I am forced to storm your position I guarantee that you will not survive it."

"Your thugs must be extremely loyal, then," I shouted back. "I promise you, the first half-dozen or so will certainly die. I wonder which will volunteer for that?"

Holmes glanced upward, tense. He abruptly flung open the door and hurled himself outside, landing full-length on his back in the tramped-hard snow. He raised his Bull-Dog two-handed and fired above the lintel of the hatch, where two men had crept round and approached from the crest of the hill in which our entrance was embedded.

The men, hampered by the thick ice-rimed brambles through which they had to press, were not quite in position. They tried to jump aside but were caught by tangles of thorns. Both men grunted, cried out, and fell limp.

The speaker had been distracting us while we were flanked. Holmes was smarter than that. I laid down covering fire as he scrambled back inside the head of the ladder-shaft.

"Your defiance changes nothing," our tormentor called. "If you do not give up the papers then we shall take them from your corpse."

Neither Holmes nor I felt the need to mention that we had not got the missing packet. Our only clue was the scratched stone that Wiggins has left for us.

"Perhaps you will satisfy my curiosity," Holmes called into the darkness. "Was it you who played the part of the cook Molenaar on the cutter *Fazant*? Were you there when the cargo of the *Jacob Remmessens* was salvaged?"

"I am not here to answer your questions, Mr Holmes. I am here for the property which is rightfully mine."

"You mean the property of your government?"

"I did not say that."

"You did not have to. It was you, then, who eliminated the agent Kleij in an Atlantic storm? You failed to identify Visser at that time, but did you finally discover him too as he tried to slip away from *Fazant* at the docks? Time enough to bring in your local allies, anyhow. You caught up with him at last near the Italian Gardens? Did he even see you before you stabbed him from behind?"

"You are too clever for your own good," our enemy responded. "Be clever enough to surrender that package now."

"I am too clever for *your* good, Heren Molenaar. Or is that 'Herr'?"

Our adversary paused just a second too long before replying.

"German, then," Holmes called out. "The quality of your operatives has declined somewhat since the dismissal of Otto von Bismarck. Chancellor Caprevi lacked his delicate touch and hardly tempered Kaiser Wilhelm II's unwise expansionist ambitions. Your present fellow, Hohenlohe, seems to have scarcely been able to find his desk."[63]

---

63 Otto Eduard Leopold, Prince of Bismarck, Duke of Lauenburg (1815-1898), known as "the Iron Chancellor", was the first Chancellor of the German Empire. From the 1860s he dominated European politics with a ruthless political genius, often in opposition to conflicting British interests, but maintained an uneasy and unprecedented peace across the Continent by diplomacy and manipulation. After the death of Kaiser Wilhelm I and the brief reign of Friedrich III, he clashed with Kaiser Wilhelm II who was eager to see Germany aggressively expand and claim its "place in the sun". Bismarck was finally dismissed from office in 1890 at the age of 75.

His replacement was Georg Leo Graf von Caprivi de Caprera de Montecuccoli (1831-1899), who reflected the young Kaiser's Neuer Kurs (Newer Course) martial and expansionist enthusiasms and who dismantled many of Bismarck's careful partnerships.

"I do not say I am German." Our opponent sounded angry now.

"You say it with every syllable you utter. To a trained ear the inflexion is obvious. The missing documents, then, are sensitive diplomatic correspondence between the German Empire and the Dutch. There has been much plotting to disrupt British colonies in the West Indies of late, to divert our nation's attention from other corners of our empire. And the Netherlands still sometimes smarts from territory they lost many years ago."[64]

I began to see why Mycroft had such a close interest in the papers. Private letters about coalitions against our overseas assets would be invaluable intelligence, and possibly tools to use against the correspondent governments. I also perceived why representatives of those governments might badly want to retrieve the missing documents – at whatever cost!

Molenaar, or whoever he really was, lost his patience. "You are wasting my time, Mr Holmes. I have given you a plain choice. Yield up the package and live. Withhold it and perish."

Holmes' reply was another shot into the night. A volley of enemy fire replied.

I checked my watch. It was closing on midnight. The weather was worsening again, with new flakes falling. With our remaining storm-lantern shuttered, the night was almost pitch black. Only the beam from Holmes' dropped lamp a couple of yards away sliced the darkness, reflecting off the snow to offer any definition to the scene. If visibility deteriorated more we would be hard-pressed to see attackers closing from all sides.

"We cannot hold out until morning," I judged.

"Nor need we," my friend replied. He let off another couple of deterrent shots, then reloaded.

"I see no means of escape, Holmes. Leaving the drain would be suicide. The only other exit is closed off by bars and leads to an icy fast-flowing sewer."

His plans to force Britain into closer alliance with Germany failed (how history repeats itself!) and ultimately brought the nations to greater odds.

The Kaiser dismissed Caprevi in 1894 and replaced him with Chlodwig Carl Viktor, Prince of Hohenlohe-Schillingsfürst, Prince of Ratibor and Corvey (1819-1901), then 75 years old and at the end of a long career of statesmanship, who continued in post until 1900.

In 1897, the year before his death, Bismarck warned that "...the crash will come twenty years after my departure if things go on like this," and that "One day the great European War will come out of some damned foolish thing in the Balkans."

64 The Dutch Empire lost New Netherlands, their significant holding in South America, to Britain in the Second Anglo-Dutch War 1664, and regained Ceylon that the British had captured in the Fourth Anglo-Dutch War 1780-84 only by yielding Indian holdings in compensation. When Ceylon was lost a second time it was retained by Britain, as was post-Napoleonic South Africa and Java.

"We need not escape, Watson. You forget where we are. The atypical weather has misled you. This is not some rural wilderness or hostile shore. We are in a royal park in the heart of London, less than a mile from Buckingham Palace. A short walk through the grounds takes us to the Albert Hall, to the Royal Geographical Society..."

"To Knightsbridge Barracks!" I realised. At the park's perimeter stood the base of the Household Cavalry Mounted Regiment, the Queen's own bodyguard. Sabre squadrons of the Life Guards and the Blue and Royals, a headquarters squadron, a cavalry training wing, all posted on ready watch.[65] "And gunfire travels."

"Enemies of our nation have brought armed conflict to Her Majesty's back garden, Watson. Whatever corruption or incompetence has prevailed so far, do you imagine that the Household Cavalry will sit idly now?"

I was seized with unholy glee at what would inevitably follow. "The finest riders in the British army will somewhat even the odds against us!"

Holmes let off more rounds. I realised now that his gunplay was by way of a signal, allowing the Household Division to orient on our position. These were ceremonial guards who also went to war; they were first in parade because they were first into battle. Fellows who excelled in dressage and precision riding had to be excellent horsemen - and Hyde Park was their riding ground.

"How long do you think, before a response?" I wondered.

"Not long, I deem. Mycroft will have been apprised of our vanishing from the Police House and has doubtless taken measures. Ah, listen! Is that the sound of hoofbeats on snow?"

In the growing swirl of blizzard the Cavalry had come upon our besiegers unawares. Now a brassy horn broke the stillness of the night. Troopers rode in from all sides, the red tunics and white plumes of the Life Guards and the blue tunics and red plumes of the Blue and Royals, implacable guardsmen bearing rifles and sabres and – heaven help the enemy – even a few lances. I remembered again that, for all their ceremonials, these were elements of the two senior regiments of the British Army, and they are also front-line combat units.

The Cavalry crashed down on the invaders with ruthless precision, as if there was no snowstorm, no icy terrain, no impediment to perfect mili-

---

65 The Household Cavalry of the 19th century was drawn exclusively from the British aristocracy and gentry and was considered the most prestigious place for military service. It holds order of precedence in any list and always parades at the extreme right of the line except when preceded by Royal Horse Artillery guns in a procession. It remains an elite force today (and is sometimes criticised for elitism). Princes William and Harry have both held commissions in the Blues and Royals.

tary discipline. *"Honi soit qui mal y pense!"*[66] I growled.

There were sparks of gunfire and a blaze of hand-lamps. Shocked thugs broke from cover but could not escape mounted soldiers. I swelled with patriotic pride.

Only a short while later, less than two minutes after the Cavalry had arrived, the battle was over.

There was some necessary sorting out. Holmes and I had to identify ourselves and explain things to the senior officer. Holmes tersely outlined enough of the circumstances to indicate our credibility and to account for nine unidentified men laying dead in a royal park in a snowstorm.

In the middle of the follow-up we were joined by more men with lanterns; Inspector Frome and a contingent from the Police House had found us at last, with help from some sullen sleep-deprived Rangers. Following the procession came Heren Van Der Linden and the ministry man Leslie and their retinues, struggling and bickering through the drifts.

I indicated the shaft to the abandoned drain, explained how to find the dead man beyond the wall, and left Frome and the Household Cavalry to argue jurisdictions. Our deceased attackers carried no identification in their pockets, only ammunition and knives similar to the one that ended Visser.

When the Cavalry's kills were laid in a row on the hillside, Van Der Linden shivered with more than cold, but he quickly disavowed any knowledge of the corpses or their identities. "All I can say for sure is that they are not my countrymen," the envoy from the Dutch Embassy insisted with clairvoyant certainty.

Holmes waited only long enough to be certain that the situation at the storm drain would be handled. He had no interest now in supervising the site or playing any part in the lengthy reconstruction of events. The Rangers and some constables were sending for scaffolding and sledge hammers to break down the barrier that barred them from the fellow who had come for Wiggins, but this was routine to the detective who had first located the corpse.

"You will understand that we have had a difficult night," he told Inspector Frome. "We shall return now to the warmth of the Police House, avail ourselves of something hot from your canteen kitchen, and await your return when your duties here are done."

66 Anglo-Norman for "Evil be to he who evil thinks," the motto of the Household Cavalry.

"A thorough search of the tunnel will be made," the policeman promised. "The Chief Constable is sending a specialist team of experts."

"There may be property down there..." Van Der Linden interjected. "Private, protected property of Her Majesty's Government of the Netherlands..."

Holmes did not wait to hear that tangled conversation. I turned my lamp down the hill and we backtracked along the tramped-down path that the stream of visitors had helpfully made for us. A uniformed constable trailed after us for security. It was not clear whether the Cavalry's charge had caught all the gunmen that had beset us. Some of the horsemen still hunted across their park. There was no proof that Molenaar was amongst the dead.

Holmes and I walked in single file because that was easier along this narrow trail. My friend turned to the bobby and said confidentially, "You may tell Mycroft that I do not have the package – yet. He need not waste time in the storm drain either; it is not there."

The man following us betrayed no surprise at having been identified as Mycroft Holmes' operative but he admitted nothing. He listened carefully and intelligently as Holmes outlined the principal points of the reconstruction of Wiggins movements: the initial contact with Visser, the intervention of Molenaar's minions disguised as British policemen guarding the exits of the park, Wiggins injury, his rescue by Visser, their sheltering in the storm drain, the exchange of clothes, Visser's subsequent attempt to find trusted help, his fatal last encounter with Molenaar, his final defiance of the enemy by pitching himself under the ice of the Long Water.

"And where is the footman Wiggins now, sir?" the supposed constable asked.

"He left his hiding place last night," Holmes replied. "He has been gone for twenty-four hours. You may assure your master that I will locate him and the Mona package." Holmes pointed eastward, towards Hyde Park Screen and St James. "Your way lies there. We shall be at the Police House if required."

So bluntly dismissed, Mycroft's spy had to turn aside and forge a path towards Serpentine Road and Nannies Lawn, and so to the Diogenes.

I knew Holmes' methods. "Where are we really going?" I asked once our escort had departed.

Holmes patted the pocket were Wiggins' inscription lay. "Why, to the Police House, Watson. You read the message."

"Police, danger, jail," I recalled.

The blue lamp loomed out of the gloom. We found the front door and bundled through it, out of the miserable night. The duty sergeant greeted us with questions about what was happening on the Meadow. Other than him, the station was almost stripped of personnel again.

We found the canteen and located the tureen of oxtail broth left on a low light to keep hot. Holmes insisted we pour ourselves mugs of it and prepared a third. "For Wiggins," he explained, pocketing a breadroll.

He waited for me to catch up. "Last night, Wiggins had to abandon the storm drain," I reasoned. "He had been discovered once, and in any case could not have survived for long in that freezing hole. Now that he had passable clothes from his assailant, had at least some chance of slipping unremarked past his hunters, he made his way up the ladder and out. But where then? Any policeman might be a fake. Or perhaps he suspected that some real officers were in his enemy's pay? The gates were probably still watched. Molenaar or Molenaar's German paymasters seem to have had plenty of men. He durst not seek help from strangers he could not trust. He could not call to the Rangers, the police…"

Holmes took up the spare mug and started off to the back of the station. A low doorway led from the house proper into the open square at the rear.

I was still thinking. "He needed a hiding place where he could stay warm and hidden until found by friends – by us. He had an idea where to go. He left a message to guide us after him."

The stables were lit but empty. The police horses, including the cob I had borrowed earlier, were presently all in use where the authorities swarmed the storm drain.

"In cold weather, there is no place warmer than the hay loft above a stable," I recognised. "There is soft bedding, heat from the animals below, access to fresh water… and in a police stable one is unlikely to encounter a large gang of armed assassins. Indeed, in a small station like this one, where every officer is known, any impostor would be immediately challenged."

We passed into the cobble-floored interior of the stable block. I caught familiar odours of horse sweat and fresh straw, of damp wood panels and leather tack. A kerosene lantern hung from a crossbeam and two old braziers heated the space.

"You are correct, Watson," Holmes approved. "And the more searchers who go forth to the hunt, the less men here to discover what is concealed. Mister Wiggins! You may come forth now!"

There was immediate movement in the loft above us. Shreds of straw drifted down as someone emerged from a cocoon of hay. "It's very good to see you, Mister 'Olmes, Doctor Watson," our missing Irregular called down. "Is that soup I smell?"

"And well deserved it is, Wiggins. Be careful on that ladder. Your arm will require some attention."

The young man was pale and weakened. He favoured his injury as he managed the steep treads from the hay loft to join us. I made a cursory check on the bandage he had improvised and decided I could not better it without a medical bag.

Wiggins fell upon the broth, torn between warming his hands on the cup and gulping down his first sustenance in thirty-six hours. "If I'd known it was going to be like this I'd have 'ad a bigger breakfast yesterday," he confided. "Visser got through to you?"

We had to break the news about the sailor's murder.

"Pity," Wiggins mourned. "That fellow saved my life. Some bloke got up like a copper cut me, and he'd have 'ad me for good on his next strike, but that Visser 'ad worked out that the game was up and we'd been rumbled. He jumped in with just that tiny pocket-knife and gutted the fellow like a fish with it. Gristly work, gory, but no doubt that man saved my life! And then we 'ad to leg it sharpish, because that weren't the only cove out after us. Visser 'elped me away and I took us to cover. Visser's done for, you say? Pity. 'E deserved better than a dagger in the ribs." The youngster was glum for a moment, then added, "Well I got one of 'em for it."

"We found him. And we are glad to find you at last. Jenny was worried."

"Jen? Oh, Lordy! Is she…?"

"Safe with Mrs Hudson," I promised Wiggins. "Worried, of course, but she knows your faith in Sherlock Holmes so she keeps hope too. Now we can take you to her."

We were all taken by surprise at the unmistakable noise of a pistol cocking. "You will go nowhere," Molenaar told us. "Do not turn around. Make no move. I am a professional and will not hesitate to kill you."

"A professional indeed," Holmes agreed. "There are few people who can trail me without my knowledge, even in blinding snow."

"I take the compliment," said the foreign agent. "You have caused me a good deal of trouble too, Mr Holmes. Almost as much as the boy there."

"We take the compliment too. But what do you expect to happen now? Gunshots here will doubtless alert the police in the adjacent building. Many armed soldiers are nearby. You have run out of minions to die while you escape. Might it not be better to simply disappear, Herr Molenaar?"

"There are other ways of dying than of a bullet. Ask Visser. But for now, I am satisfied to have the package your Mister Wiggins had from him."

The Irregular snorted. "I don't 'ave that, mate! Search me if you want."

"Then you know where it is. You will speak."

"You want to bet, matey?"

"He does not have it," Holmes intervened. "He sent it on. Look in my pocket." He made the smallest gesture to indicate the right hip of his Inverness cape.

He caught my eye and flicked his gaze to the storm lantern hanging close by.

"You will not move," Molenaar repeated, "except to carefully withdraw the packet and drop it on the floor."

Holmes lifted a thickly-packed brown envelope from his capacious pocket. I had no idea how it might have found its way there. He turned to face the foreign agent.

"Holmes, you can't!" I told him.

"Watson, we must give it to him," my old friend and ally told me. Message received.

Holmes tossed the envelope underarm. It arced close to Molenaar but fell short at his feet. As Molenaar's eyes naturally followed the object of his mission, I grasped the lamp and shattered it down on the cobbles, atop the packet.

The mantle splintered to shards, spilling blazing kerosene over the straw and the stuffed envelope.

Molenaar screamed in rage and squeezed off a shot at me. I was already diving for cover behind one of the wooden stalls. Holmes and Wiggins hurled themselves aside the other way.

The foreign agent reached into the spreading fire, heedless of the burns he took, and pulled the package clear. He wrapped his jacket around the smouldering bundle, dousing the flames that scorched one side.

By then I had drawn my Beaumont Adams and was ready to return fire. Holmes produced his Bull-Dog. Molenaar saw that he was outnumbered and outgunned and leapt for the door. Our shots were too late to stop him. He fled with the package.

"But...!" gasped Wiggins. The lad clutched his shoulder where his plunge had opened his wound.

I had no time to lose. I chased after Molenaar, into the night and the storm. The fellow had committed murder on British soil, had taken secrets required by our government, had brought battle to the beating heart of our nation; he would not escape.

Molenaar saw my pursuit and fired at me. Still running, he could not sight accurately and I was making certain to dodge. He pelted away along Policeman's Path and I followed him. Holmes was racing behind me but I did not turn to know it then.

The night seemed to gather up all its frozen malice and hurl it as us as we ran. The wind bit our faces, lifting up drifts of snow to pelt us as we chased. The ground underfoot was icy and treacherous, layer upon frozen layer seeking to turn an ankle or break a leg. Visibility was poor even where the intermittent gas mantles burned to mark the otherwise anonymous white-shrouded road. My old wound slowed me slightly, but my quarry's limp evened the chase.

Molenaar fired again, not in hopes of hitting me but to delay my pursuit. I snapped off a shot back at him to break his confidence. He was not knifing an unarmed man now.

Policeman's Path threads down under heavy trees to Magazine Gate. Beyond that is the long straight road over Serpentine Bridge. Molenaar could not afford to use a route that gave me a clear sight-line. Instead he scrambled down the treacherous slope to the embankment path that runs beside the Long Water. Unlit, unswept, it was harder going but better for a man who sought to lose his enemies and escape with his prize.

Holmes caught up with me at last as we reached the bottom of the hill where the bank-path goes under the first arch of the bridge. "Watson, *hold!*" he called. "Look where you are!"

The graceful lines of the Serpentine Bridge ran away from us to our left, illuminated by ornate iron sconces holding modern gas lights. Below it, new snow had obscured the dividing line between shore and iced lake. Molenaar's scramble had taken him off his intended track, out onto the slippery surface of the frozen Long Water.

"This is where we found Visser," I recognised. "Where they cut him from the ice."

"Yes," Holmes agreed. "Where the broken ice is still very thin."

Molenaar was only a blur on the white shroud, half-lost out across the lake, but we were near enough to hear the fatal crack of a thin sheet breaking, to see the fleeing agent vanish through the fractured surface.

"The papers…!" I cried.

"He doesn't have them," Holmes replied dispassionately. "Come, Watson, you *saw* me raid Frome's stationary drawer. It occurred to me that a facsimile package might be useful later. Remember that Molenaar has never seen the real thing."

We heard splashing and struggling in the water. There was no call for help.

"That man is dying," I said to Holmes. "He cannot last long in freezing water."

"We cannot risk the ice to retrieve him. We cannot see them in the dark, but there are surely danger markers posted where the sheet was broken earlier. I will not risk my dear friend on a futile attempt to save a murderer."

A short while later the thrashing ceased and there was another corpse to lift from the ice come the morning.

It was almost dawn before we were able to finally quit the park and head for home. Frome looked haggard from more than a long day and night of manhunting. I never heard or fathomed from whom he or his Chief Constable were taking orders, though I gather that not all factions of the British civil service and of Her Majesty's government were behind Mycroft's treatment of the affair.

The British and Dutch diplomats arrived at an uncomfortable détente when they believed the papers had sunk with Molenaar, and departed with what dignity they could muster. Wiggins sent off a message of thanks to Dikkon, Soosie, and Mrs Perrett for their timely information, with promise of official rewards to follow. Holmes dispatched a brief message to Mycroft that was nothing more than more strings of letters and numbers but evidently made sense to the siblings.

And so to Baker Street. Jenny was dozing on a couch but woke soon enough as we returned with Wiggins. Mrs Hudson, indomitable in crisis, was close at hand with miraculous fortifying tea and subsequent buttered toast. Wiggins hugged his pregnant wife and assured her that the wound on his arm was trivial, soon mended. Their reunion was touching, worth every chill and ache we had suffered in those long bleak hours behind us.

Let Mycroft Holmes chase the greater good. I am content with the small good, like bringing two young people together again for the promise of a family future. It is that care that makes our civilisation worth preserving, and confound those who forget it.

I kicked off my wet cold boots and found my slippers warming by the fire. Only one question remained. "The actual package, Holmes… the one that Visser obtained from the wreck of the Dutch courier ship. Visser gave it to Wiggins, and then Wiggins hid it. Is it somewhere in Hyde Park still, waiting to be retrieved?"

Holmes chuckled and sat in his familiar chair. He gestured to Wiggins to answer me.

"I wouldn't trust to leaving something like that just lying around, Doctor Watson," the Irregular assured me. "Not with that many searchers, an' the snow leaving signs and the like. And I didn't know 'oo as to rely on, with maybe even coppers on the wrong side. All the gates was watched. So I did the only thing I could to get the package out of the park."

Holmes passed me the flat stone where Wiggins had scraped his message. "The last symbol, Watson. The one that isn't a letter or a tramp mark. It is simply a drawing."

I examined it again. It was a square except for a curved top surmounted by a dot, and inside it was a horizontal slit and a square below it. To my tired imagination it almost looked like… "A pillar post box?"

"There's one in Hyde Park," Wiggins revealed, "just down the road from the Police House. Emptied seven times a day. So I put the envelope in there."[67]

I laughed. Holmes laid his hand upon the pile of mail that sat on the salver by his side. "And here, I believe, it is, addressed to '*Mr Sherlock Holmes, 221B Baker Street, Marylebone, N.W., London.*' Well done, Wiggins! Never doubt the redoubtable institutions of our nation, Watson. The machinations of foreign agents have been thwarted by Her Majesty's Royal Mail service! Molenaar had already lost and he never suspected it."

"I am forbidden to open that, sir," Wiggins told Holmes anxiously.

"It doubtless contains secrets with drastic diplomatic consequences," Holmes reflected. "Men were willing to kill for it, to risk war for it. The future of the West Indies may hinge upon its contents." He tossed the packet unopened back upon his pile. "Mycroft may send for it when he wishes. It is of no interest to me and of no relevance to my calling."

He reached instead for a slice of toast and applied a generous daub of butter.

---

67 Remarkably, Victorian London enjoyed seven collections from each post box every day for five same-day deliveries except Sundays; for details refer to Mogg's *New Picture of London and Visitor's Guide to it Sights* (1844) or Dickens' *Dictionary of London* (1879) by Charles Dickens Jr. Unstamped letters were delivered on payment of the postal charge of 2d by the recipient (twice the cost of a stamped letter).

SHERLOCK HOLMES OF LONDON

GEOGRAPHICAL REFLECTIONS FROM I.A. WATSON

Despite the success of some modernised versions of Sherlock Holmes set in our current age, a key component of the Canon stories' appeal for contemporary readers is the historical setting. Holmes and Watson operate in another era of different social and technological standards. Their world is one of class-consciousness, of empire, or gender assumptions and limitations, of manners and prejudices. It is a world devoid of phones, televisions, the internet and the motor car, innocent even of the damages of two World Wars.

In some ways the trappings of Victoriana are as much a character as the brilliant eccentric detective and his admiring good-hearted companion. They at least form a distinctive backdrop that offers rich possibilities for memorable adventure.

"Hell is a city much like London," Percy Shelley famously opined. The larger part of Sir Arthur Conan Doyle's Holmes stories recount Holmes' investigations in the capital. The city was inextricably associated with the Victorian era, at a time when London arguably reached its zenith as the largest, richest, and most powerful metropolis on Earth and yet was still a place of immense poverty and crushing social injustice. The juxtaposition of orderly society and shocking outrage, of polite decency and venal exploitation, is at the heart of the Holmes mystery.

For all the ubiquity of London in Holmes' Canon, it is rarely described in any great detail. Doyle assumed his readers would know what they needed to without a travelogue (or footnotes) in the same way as they would know about the postal system, or tipping cabbies, or lawsuits for breach of promise over broken engagements; it was all common knowledge. Modern Holmes writers whose audience is not immersed in a bygone era require more context to enjoy the setting.

Even in Holmes' time, London was old. It was a place of history piled on history, of streets built atop streets built atop streets the Romans had trod. It was filled with traditions, with jealously-guarded ancient rights, with learned societies and belligerent commercial guilds, with thriving trade wharves and ancient public spaces. There were churches where fifty generations of Londoners had gone for baptism, marriage, and burial. Road names preserved the events of many years.

Yet Holmes' London was also forward-thinking, growing every year, thriving in the last great flowering of an empire "on which the sun never set."[1] New buildings replaced the old. Reformers demanded better housing, better labour conditions, universal schooling. Merchant-adventurers raised factories and markets and railway stations. Britain was striding forward and London was in the vanguard; what the capital did today would be mirrored in the provinces tomorrow and across the world after.

Holmes and Watson sit very comfortably in that contradictory, familiar, yet changing London. In their Baker Street flat they receive those with problems and offer comfort and justice. But then Holmes goes out in disguise and trawls through any tier of society in pursuit of the truth. He and Watson probe the dangerous and dark corners of the city and shine a modern light on ugly old crimes. London suits our heroes well.

Because Doyle shied from much addressing contemporary events in his narratives (for reasons of taste and perhaps because that would have "dated" stories that were meant to be set in "the present"), we never see Holmes and Watson plunge much into the history and geography of London. There is no Canon reference of the Krakatoa tragedy that was on every lip in 1883 or the massive 1887 celebrations for Queen Victoria's Golden Jubilee, no mention of the Fourth Anglo-Ashanti War (1894), the Second Matabele War (1897), the Boxer Rebellion (1889-1901) and the Second Boer War (1889-1902).[2][3] Nothing is said of the hard winter of

---

1 So called because there was no time of any 24-hour period when some part of the British Empire was not in daylight. By 1913, the British Empire ruled 412 million people, 23% of the world population, and by 1920 it covered 13,700,000 sq mi (35,500,000 km^2), 24% of the Earth's total land area, and was the largest empire in history.

2 Also the Anglo-Zanzibar War of 27th August 1896, 9.02-9.40am, the shortest war in recorded history.

3 The notable exception is "His Last Bow. The War Service of Sherlock Holmes", later titled "His Last Bow: An Epilogue of Sherlock Holmes", first published in September 1917 in Strand Magazine and, then collected in *His Last Bow: Some Reminiscences of Sherlock Holmes* (October 1917). This atypical story written in the third person is set on the eve of the First World War and the antagonist is a German agent. Chronologically it is by far Holmes and Watson's latest Canon appearance, and concludes with Holmes' final recorded words, as pointed a political statement as ever appears in the literature:

"Good old Watson! You are the one fixed point in a changing age. There's an east wind coming all the same, such a wind as never blew on England yet. It will be cold and bitter, Watson, and a good many of us may wither before its blast. But it's God's own wind none the less, and a cleaner, better, stronger land will lie in the sunshine when the storm has cleared."

1894/5, though it had a massive real-world effect.

Watson might be seen as deliberately obfuscating the location of Holmes' exploits. He seldom mentions recognisable addresses; even 221 was not an actual house number on Baker Street until the 1930s. Perhaps the same deference with which other identities are kept private is extended to places too.

However...

There is within the broad range of detective fiction a strand of investigative adventure in which a mystery unfolds through geographical exploration. The hunt for the missing man is a common one in literature and it is often expressed in terms of a physical search. Holmes is occasionally called upon to find someone, but it is seldom that he is required to expend physical as well as cognitive effort to discover his quarry.

There seemed to me to be a gap, then, for a Holmes story which included a number of previously unused, uncombined elements: a splash of history in the form of a particular weather event and a significant global catastrophe; an unusually detailed physical landscape that offers some unique story elements; a still-seldom-used emotional stake by threatening a known and liked supporting character; a political element allowing another outing for the eccentric Mycroft Holmes; and even a proper gun-battle with the logical consequences of opening fire within a mile of Buckingham Palace.

For that reason the most significant guest star of the preceding story is actually Hyde Park. It plays a meaty role: antagonist, backdrop, suspect and executioner all in one. This remarkable ancient space so close to the centre of power, with such significance in the lives of citizens of London, offers a lot of material. Admit the forgotten rivers of London as well and an editor might forgive a double-sized story turning up.

221B Baker Street, Marylebone, N.W., London is Holmes' address. We know he and Watson fit perfectly into Baker Street. It was interesting to pan out and show him of Marylebone, adjacent to the royal parks of Hyde Park and Kensington Gardens, with the Tyburn Brook running under his feet, and of London, operating on that urban home soil where he has such deep knowledge and such deep resource.

Part of Holmes' appeal is time and place. This story places emphasis on the place.

Ian Watson
March 2018
Out of the cold

Sherlock Holmes

in

"The Ghost of Otis Maunder"

By
David Friend

ince several of the most stimulating cases investigated by my friend Mr Sherlock Holmes first became a matter of public record, my own name has become better known than any provincial medical practitioner may reasonably deserve. Although, with some justification, it is Holmes who has remained the keen focus of attention, I have had occasion myself to be greeted enthusiastically by followers of his exploits. These instances, of course, do not present themselves when such good people see my face but when they recognize my name. Although not troublesome in itself, this does become a bother when they are also patients and insist on asking questions of my famous friend instead of allowing me to administer to them.

The instance of which I shall record occurred one cold November day in 1896. Sherlock Holmes was back in the country after a five week, cross-continental case involving his former nemesis Brigadier Horrigan and the Nostradamus legacy and I had not yet welcomed him home. I was, instead, at my practice undertaking my duties. The fog was swirling languidly without and pressed against the windows as though it wanted to come in and join me. I wanted dearly to return to the hearth and read *An Outcast of the Islands*, but considering the number of patients waiting in the hallway, it seemed I would be occupied for some time.

"I had not the devilish notion just where she was stepping out each night."

"Raise your arm, please, Mr Bickerstaff," I asked politely. The old man was too distracted by his own words to detect my weariness.

He lifted his left arm mechanically, but did not cease his chatter. "Just why, I asked myself, was the blessed Effie visiting the house next door?"

"Er... your *other* arm, Mr Bickerstaff. The arm you are so concerned about."

My patient managed to obey the instruction, but continued nonetheless. "And as I read on—with still no answer of my own and worrying for poor Mr Grant Munro—your clever friend Mr Holmes had sorted it as well as always." He shook his head with awe, his white curls shaking with the motion.

"Perhaps you can bend your elbow for me," I requested.

"It was Effie's first husband in the house, you see." He began to lift up the wrong arm again, but I stopped him. "She had been married once before to a black-American lawyer named John Hebron."

"Mr Bickerstaff, I urge you to concentrate." There was pleading in my voice now.

"They had a daughter together named Lucy, you see, and it's believed he had died of Yellow Fever."

I returned behind the desk and sat down heavily with a sigh. "Mr Bickerstaff, you are aware I was with Holmes at the time? And I understood the situation comprehensively enough to write it all down?" I looked at him squarely. "Which is the only way *you* know about it."

Mr Bickerstaff stared at me for a long moment. I truly believed he was now grasping the point. "It was the daughter's face Mr Munro had seen in the window!"

Even war does not prepare a man for such things.

"Am I right in saying, Mr Bickerstaff," I said, trying to remain unflustered, "that you have no real ailment to speak of? That the only reason you have visited my practice today is to discuss the remembrances of my friend Mr Holmes?"

My patient suddenly looked quite awkward and I decided I had heard enough.

I marched out of the room and found over two dozen men and women waiting without. I had never seen the place so occupied. I turned to face them all with a grim and, I thought, forthright countenance.

"Can everyone here who does *not* wish to consult me for genuine medical purposes but instead to discuss Sherlock Holmes please leave?"

For a moment, nobody moved, and I felt a flicker of relief. Perhaps I had misjudged the situation and this was to be a regular day at the practice after all. Then, in one fluid movement, my supposed patients suddenly arose from their seats and began heading for the doors. There were so many, and so close, that their bodies ploughed determinedly into mine and I felt myself being pushed back and rendered off-balance.

The doors shut behind them and I was left in an empty waiting room. I sighed deeply, trying to rid myself of the annoyances of the day. Then my consulting room door opened and I realised one of them still remained.

"You see, Effie had hidden the girl because she thought—"

"Mr Bickerstaff!" I yelled.

Without giving him another moment to respond, or to explain any more of the retched case, I took the little man by the shoulder and frog-marched him to the door. Slamming it closed after him was the most satisfying thing I had done all day.

I was heading back to collect my coat when I bumped into Mrs Agnew. She was a short, elderly woman with a permanently knotted brow.

"Mrs Agnew," I said lamentably, "it's been an absolute fifteen puzzle here this morning. If I screw my eyes shut and think hard, I can almost remember when this was a normal practice and my patients wanted nothing more than medical advice. Nowadays, all they do is press me for news about Holmes. *Has he had any baffling cases recently? Can I speak about them? When will there be another account?*"

I would never describe Mrs Agnew as a sympathetic person, even if she did spend her days around the sick and infirm, and she was typically indifferent now. "Can these people not simply visit Mr Holmes himself?"

"I thought so too," I agreed. "He told his landlady to keep them away. I heard one man kept pestering him to find his missing cat and began knocking on the door at all hours of the day and night."

The old lady could not have looked more cross if she had been harassed herself. "What did Mr Holmes do?"

I smiled with dark humour. "He poked his head out of the window and catapulted the fellow with a stone."

Mrs Agnew seemed to think this was a sensible idea, so I elected to leave before she suggested I try it myself. With no other patient waiting to consult me, a free afternoon clearly beckoned. I felt weary, as though I had already worked a whole day. Despite my friend indirectly causing such interruptions to my professional duties, I decided to return to him at Baker Street.

With a slow and leisurely gait, I set off in that direction. I began passing Georgian houses and hansom cabs patiently waiting for customers. The mentioning of a previous case by Mr Bickerstaff brought to my mind many others. I wondered about my friend's former clients: Mr Jabez Wilson, the red-headed pawnbroker, and the strange circumstances involving the *Encyclopædia Britannica*; Miss Mary Sutherland and her suitor, and Mr. Victor Hatherley and his thumb. I realised, poignantly, that neither Holmes nor I had ever encountered such clients again. He helped them at the time and they, satisfied, returned to their lives, melting back into the millions that made up our metropolis. How they lived or what they then did was as much of a mystery as the ones they had presented to Holmes in the first place.

Such nostalgia, however, would be entirely alien to my friend. Rarely had he made known his memories. The ones he had conveyed were inevitably bound up in another adventure. Clients to him, I fancied, were merely vessels bringing to him a perplexing problem. In his own small way, he cared for them, in that he was happy to end their distress, and certainly endeavoured to save their lives, but foremost of all was the case itself. It was a way in which he could marshal his motor signals. The moment the case was solved, the client was of no further use to him and he looked with impatience to the next.

As I perambulated down Baker Street, I believed only companionable silences and the occasional quiet conversation were to follow. However, when I reached the door, it jutted open suddenly and I found my friend standing framed on the threshold. He was wearing his top hat and frock coat and clutching his cane. He did not even cast me a glance as he stepped purposefully forward.

"Quickly, Watson!" he cried.

He gestured urgently to a dog-cart across the street and it lumbered over to us. Holmes jumped smoothly aboard.

"What is all this?" I asked, bewildered, as I dropped down beside him.

Still, Holmes didn't look at me. He was studying his pocket-watch with beetled brows. "I have had a cable from Inspector Bradstreet," he said. He looked about him, searching for shorter routes to whatever destination he was so keen to reach. "Nothing interests me less than the news of an arrested murderer, Watson. By definition, all mystery has withered to nought. However, this matter is unprecedented. I dare say you remember Miss Violet Hunter and how her position as a governess in Winchester brought her some considerable concern."

"Yes!" I exclaimed. My mind swivelled back ten years. "Her employer, Mr Rucastle, forced her to impersonate his daughter, Alice, as he had locked—"

"Watson, I share full knowledge of the case in question. I did, after all, solve it myself."

I realised, with a wince, that I had repeated Mr Bickerstaff's mistake from earlier that afternoon. "But what of it?" I said, desperate to understand. "What is going on?"

Holmes's face tightened, his head hung low. "I am afraid," said Holmes, "that Miss Hunter has been arrested for murder."

"What in the—?"

"Horace!" he barked at the cabbie; who swerved to a hasty halt outside the police station.

Holmes leapt out. He headed for the station, his strides long and loping. With a firm push, the doors swept open and he entered the foyer. I finally reached him and can bear witness to the fierce look in his cold-grey eyes.

A wiry young man was moving swiftly past in a curious half-run, his arms hung still and his feet like those of a duck paddling through water.

"Constable Cook!"

The man stopped and turned. "Mr Holmes!"

My friend stepped closer and I noticed he was keeping a tight grip on his cane. "I must see Inspector Bradstreet at once," he said seriously. "It is a matter of great importance."

The constable led us through to a small, cramped room on the west side of the building. Inspector Bradstreet was hunkered over a desk, his not inconsiderable bulge pressed hard against the wood as though it were trying to push it away. I had not seen him since the business of Sir Thaddeus Fowler and the Onondaga treasure, though I knew he had so-licited Holmes's help on several subsequent occasions. He lifted his large, bearded head and looked at us in surprise.

"Inspector," said Holmes, as Cook took his place beside the door. "I would appreciate it if you could furnish us with the facts." He didn't take a seat, nor did he take off his hat.

Inspector Bradstreet's brows were raised so high they were almost ob-scured by his hairline. I observed in him a faint air of triumph, as though he were pleased to have solved a case without the help of London's famous consulting detective. Holmes, however, had not come here to give his con-gratulations, however much Bradstreet would have liked to have heard it.

"Mr Holmes, I am sure you can understand that this case is now closed."

There was a rickety chair opposite and, without a glance, Holmes seat-ed himself on its edge. "It is about to be open again," he said quietly. "Why have you arrested Miss Violet Hunter?"

His stare was absolute and seemed to displease the Yard man.

"The same reason we arrest anyone," was the terse reply. "Because she's guilty."

Holmes leant back. "You belong in the music hall!" he said bitterly.

"Holmes!" I admonished.

Constable Cook, I noticed, had taken out his notebook and had begun scribbling furiously.

"Don't write any of this, Cook," said Bradstreet impatiently. He turned back to Holmes with an awkward look. "The constable here is recording some of my cases," he explained. "Much as Dr Watson has with yours." He sounded guilty and looked suddenly embarrassed. I wondered if Holmes would feature at all in the chronicles of the cases they had shared.

My friend looked as though he was about to emit a derisive laugh and I spoke quickly to stop him. "We would like to see Miss Hunter," I said, my voice firm.

The Inspector looked irritated. "You will be wasting everyone's time," he warned. "As I said, the case is closed. But, by all means, cause yourselves embarrassment. It would make an amusing addition to my memoirs."

Constable Cook led us on another journey across the police station, during which I caught glimpses of other associates from cases past, all crooked over desks, including Inspector Patterson, Inspector Gregory and Constable Pollock. We finished up in the cells, and Cook revealed to us Miss Violet Hunter.

She had been sitting on a bench and had risen at the tinkle of keys. Her appearance was much the same as it had been ten years earlier, when Holmes had rescued her from the sadistic Mr Jephro Rucastle. Her face was pale and lightly freckled, her hair still curled and auburn, while the only difference I could see was the look of frozen horror in her eyes which I suspected she had held for some time.

"Mr Holmes!"

She stepped widely towards us, relief spread across her face.

Holmes moved to the bench and sat down as though he himself was now a prisoner. "Miss Hunter," he said earnestly, "if we are to help you, you must tell us all."

Miss Hunter was still registering the surprise of our arrival. She lifted a hand and rubbed her temple, clearly trying to focus. "It is such a shock to see you," she said quietly. She quickly marshalled and slowly began pacing the cell. Within moments, she was telling her tale.

"My life has recently become one of change," she said. "I became betrothed last summer to a young man named Mr Marcus Housley, an Alderman in Penshurst. I have become a schoolteacher since I last saw you and have also been a headmistress. A few weeks ago, I received a letter. The headmaster of a public school, a Mr Otis Maunder, was retiring and had recommended me as his successor. Well, I could scarcely believe it." She shook her head, still apparently bemused. "Not only was it strange to receive such a letter without warning, but I had never met this gentleman. However, I knew better than to disregard such an offer and accepted it gladly. I went there and started work. The name of my predecessor, however, kept returning to me, and queerly, I began to feel as though I had heard it before.

"I spent the first Friday unpacking my belongings in my office. In one of the drawers of this desk, I found lots of old photographs, mainly of the school through the years. There was only one portrait. A framed photograph covered in dust. In it was a man I supposed was Mr Maunder. It must have been from long ago as he looked to be in his late thirties, with thinning dark hair combed briskly to the left and a cool, absent stare as though he wasn't aware he was standing for his likeness at all. I thought again of his name and it seemed to tug at something at the back of my mind.

"Then I remembered. My late father, Pheaphilus, had mentioned him quite frequently at one time. They and two others had set up the Sevenoaks Secretarial College for Gentlewomen. If I remembered rightly, it came to light that Mr Maunder had embezzled funds. However, instead of informing the police, my father and his friends were lenient and agreed that Mr Maunder should simply leave the firm. I remember Father being disappointed, but apart from that, it is all I recall about the affair.

"I finished sorting and my new secretary, Mrs Burton, appeared. She is quite a gentle lady, with a grey bun and an open, pleasant face. I wanted to ask about Mr Maunder. It still troubled me why he would recommend me for such a position. Perhaps, I considered, he was grateful to my father for not telling the police of what he had done.

"Mrs Burton told me how he had left the school quite quickly, leaving only a hasty recommendation for his successor, and had died soon after from heart failure. I asked what she knew of the college and, at the very mention of it, the old lady's face turned sour. She said she didn't know the particulars; just that he had been forced to leave and had always been bitter and furious because of it. Whenever the girls at the school expressed an interest in proceeding to the college, Mr Maunder virtually forbade it. He said the people there had done him a great disservice and he would never forgive them. He would, apparently, tremble with the rage it brought him."

"That night, I continued with work far into the evening. It had turned quite cold and I tested the fire. Then, as I often did while a governess elsewhere, I took a walk around the grounds. The moon was out and though dimmed by clouds, I could clearly make out the lake. I moved towards it, breathing in that brand of evening air which is so fresh and chilled that you can taste it. All I could hear was silence. With the school behind me, I could only see woods and country ahead. I looked towards the lake, a couple of yards distant, and saw how it stretched far and deep into darkness. And that was when I noticed something.

"A curious shape seemed to have formed and was slinking slowly across

"That night it had turned quite cold and I tested the fire.

the water. It was a good way out from the edge, not at all near the shallow part, and at first I had to strain my eyes. It was a man, I could tell, but his footfalls were firm upon the water. How in the world was he doing it? My heart began to race. As he moved closer, I recognized his face. It was the young Mr Maunder, just as he had been in the photograph. My throat was suddenly dry and I couldn't even muster the energy to scream.

"'Avenge me!' wailed this impossible spectre. 'Avenge me!'

"Breathless, I spun around and dashed back in the direction of the school. I was breathing heavily, even hoarsely, as I stamped across the grounds, and my feet were hurting like never before. I found my way inside and didn't stop until I had reached my office and shut the door. For a reason I didn't even register, I turned the key in the lock and stood as far away from it as possible. There, in the darkness of the office—a room which didn't look at all familiar anymore—I cowered. Shivering with fright, I turned away, my eyes falling to the desk and the photograph of Mr Maunder. Quite witless, I took it from its frame, tore it in two and threw it into the fire.

"I needn't add that I barely slept that night. Even on the morrow, the memory of whatever it was I had seen haunted me still. I felt compelled to tell someone and so I told Mrs Burton. The old lady humoured me, of course, telling me it was the excitement and nerves of starting in a new position. But I knew what I had seen.

"I think myself practical, Mr Holmes, and it was in such manner that I set about researching Mr Otis Maunder. I searched in various books and documents and asked others too. I learned how he had become headmaster in the late '60s and that he had set up the college with my father and two men named Edwin Luckett and Nathaniel Farley. Both men lived in the nearby village of Riverhead. I heard again that Mr Maunder had never forgiven any of them and that while they had become rich and successful, he had become progressively miserable until he recently resigned.

"In looking for papers which could help me in my quest, I happened upon a letter. I am not of a mind to pry into other people's correspondences, Mr Holmes, but I read the first line almost accidentally and I confess its bluntness gripped me. I remember it vividly:

"I sense there are spirits here in this house. Nobody may believe me, but it is what I know to be true. In the dark of night, when the world is otherwise silent, I can hear noises. I wander and hope to find them. Alas, I have not yet, but I shall one day and I dread it. I even consider leaving here and escaping once and for all. But something makes me stay. A sort of indescribable hold."

"Naturally, I was staggered. The handwriting was rough, as though the person writing it was scared."

"Was there an address?" asked Holmes. He had remained sitting, his head tilted back against the bars, his eyes closed.

"No. It appeared to be unfinished."

"Proceed."

"Well, it frightened me even more. I felt like he had led me to this letter, to prove to me that what I had seen was real. I was desperate to speak to those who had known him. It so occurred to me that I should speak with his former associates—presumably, the people his ghost wanted me to avenge. I took a trap to Riverhead and saw Mr Luckett and Mr Farley wandering the village. I wondered what I could say. Part of me wanted to tell them what I had seen, but I was worried they would consider me mad. I was prevaricating still when a policeman passed.

"'You want to speak to those men?' he asked curiously.

"'I mustn't,' I said. 'What I have to say would only scare them.'

"And so I returned to the school. I decided that I must now forget what I had seen. I was still trying to do this, some days later, when the police arrived. They began questioning me immediately. In Riverhead, they said, two middle-aged men had been stabbed to death in their houses. Their corpses had been covered in violets."

I jerked back a step in surprise. "Violets?" I repeated. I looked at Holmes, but he did not seem remotely surprised.

"They had been picked from the surrounding gardens," Miss Hunter explained. "As such, no violets could now be found in any garden at that end of the village. They believed I was responsible; that a clue had been deliberately left as a twisted joke. The killer was a violet hunter, and I am a Violet Hunter.

"The police discovered that I had been asking about both men, had traced them to Riverend and had watched them. One of their own constables was a witness! They also spoke to Mrs Burton, who told them how convinced I was that I had seen the ghost of Otis Maunder. They believe me insane, Mr Holmes, and want me to hang!"

As she finished, Miss Hunter and I turned to Holmes expectantly. He remained still. If he had been anyone else, I would have assumed he had fallen asleep. But then, his eyes blazed open and he sprang to his feet.

He moved to the door of the cell, about to leave, then whirled suddenly around like a sequined cobra.

"Miss Hunter," he said quietly. "I cannot promise you anything."

It occurred to me, as we left the cells and the eerie silence of those within them, just how little we knew about Miss Violet Hunter and whether, as a medical man, I could vouch for her mental stability. Perhaps, I considered, her experience at the Copper Beeches had affected her more than we had realised.

I met Holmes in the corridor, his long loping legs having conveyed him there faster, and gave voice to my concerns.

He pondered a moment. "It is true that some cases may take their toll on those with a weaker constitution than others," he accepted. "Your old friend Mr Percy Phelps, for example, was a man in deep distress."

"Yes," I said, nodding at the memory. "He doesn't work for the government anymore, apparently. The pressure didn't sit well with him."

Holmes sniffed. "As I recall, it wasn't his personal qualities which afforded him the position in the first place."

"Do you suppose that case could have affected Miss Hunter's mental health? Ten and a half years later?"

Holmes paused again, his brow furrowed. Then his eyes seemed to spark and, turning on his heel, he headed off down the corridor.

Ten minutes later and two streets away, Holmes and I entered a dimly-lit office. It was lined with bookshelves with small, curtained windows and a narrow desk in the corner. A short man was seated behind it. Dr Marcellus Chappell had a wide, domed forehead and a bushy Van Dyke beard, rather like Carl Zeller. The hair on the back of his head was brushed up untidily as though he wanted to remind people that he had at least some of it left.

"My name is Sherlock Holmes and this is my friend and col-"

"Ah," said Dr Chappell in surprise and let out a hand for my friend to shake. "It is good to meet you, Mr Holmes." He stared at my friend and hadn't, it seemed, even seen me.

I coughed lightly. "And I'm Dr Wat—"

"I have enjoyed reading your observations, Mr Holmes," the alienist interrupted.

Holmes smiled thinly and I could tell he was greatly pleased.

"I shall be writing another soon," I promised.

Dr Chappell turned to me for the first time with a frozen expression. "Excuse me, but I was referring to Mr Holmes's monograph on enigmatic writing." He looked at Holmes. "Who is this?" he asked bluntly.

Holmes made no effort to disguise his amusement. "This is my friend Dr Watson," he said. "He has written up some of my exploits for an undiscerning public."

Dr Chappell nodded cautiously. "I am unfamiliar with such work," he said.

Holmes looked even more delighted. I expected him to substitute my friendship for that of this other doctor at any moment.

"What can you tell us about Miss Violet Hunter?" I asked the alienist testily.

Dr Chappell's eyes widened at the remembrance of our curious client.

"I concluded that Miss Hunter is mad," he said candidly. "She has convinced herself that she had seen Mr Maunder's ghost. She may even believe that it was possessing her. As I see it, Miss Hunter was suffering from guilt."

"Guilt?" I echoed. "Why must she feel guilty?"

Dr Chappell continued as though I had not said a word. "We have spoken extensively about her experiences," he said, looking at Holmes. "I understand her father and Mr Maunder, among others, had founded a college together, but Mr Maunder had been forced to resign. It would seem he was willing to forgive her father and, as a symbol of this, he recommended Miss Hunter to succeed him as head-teacher. She felt she could return this favour by punishing those who had wronged him."

"But that would be..." Any word I considered seemed somehow inadequate. "Don't you think?" I added, omitting the word entirely.

Dr Chappell, nevertheless, seemed to understand. "Miss Hunter is clearly unwell," he reminded us. "This was hardly the action of a sound mind."

I could see the doctor's reasoning, but somehow did not want to accept it. I seized upon the question of the violets.

Dr Chappell tilted his head ponderously as though he was only now considering the matter. "I would suggest Miss Hunter's subconscious mind had selected the violets and left them on the bodies as a clue to her identity," he said. "It is not an unusual occurrence for the culprit to desire capture and therefore punishment for his crimes, particularly if there is a large degree of guilt involved, which there may be in this case as Miss Hunter perhaps feels she has benefited from her predecessor's death."

"And the ghost?" I asked.

"A vivid dream," said Dr Chappell dismissively. "They can often be confused with reality. If I recall, Miss Hunter believes she encountered the ghost at night time, which would make perfect sense."

"It would indeed," Holmes agreed. I had almost forgotten he was there. "Thank you for your time, Dr Chappell."

"Not at all. I look forward to more of your monographs, Mr Holmes."

Holmes's mouth curved into a smile.

We moved towards to the door, but then I paused. "Perhaps," I added hopefully, "you may like to read one of my accounts of Mr Holmes's cases."

Dr Chappell's eyes dimmed at the words. "I only read academic journals," he said blankly and returned to his work.

A short hour later, Holmes and I were taking a train from Charing Cross to Sevenoaks. Holmes was silent for much of the journey and stared blankly at the floor, as though there were not any sumptuously golden fields lying flat beyond the window. After a while, I too was seized by thoughts of that mysterious phantom striding across the lake. On reflection, that month, so suspiciously near to All Hallow's Eve, was a decidedly unnerving one, and would also see us contemplating the wrath of a Peruvian vampire.

The rest of the afternoon was spent visiting the school over which Miss Hunter had presided and speaking with those who had known her. Mrs Burton, her secretary, attested that Miss Hunter had confided in her about the alleged ghost. The old lady seemed quite shocked at the subsequent events, but was certain that her headmistress was unwell.

Holmes also managed to discover that another teacher, Mr Lucian Devitt, was the only teacher who found Miss Hunter's presence at the school disagreeable. This was due to the fact that he had expected to inherit Mr Maunder's position himself. We met him briefly in one of the many labyrinthine corridors and he certainly seemed unconcerned about the circumstances in which his headmistress had now found herself. He was an astonishingly long-limbed man with jagged sideburns and flamboyant curls, though his stare alone made him worthy of note. It was cold and intense, his damnably blue eyes seemingly fixed so hard that nothing would pry them away. Thankfully, he became distracted when he recognized one of the boys—the school's most infamous practical joker, apparently—and began telling him off.

It became clear that we were to spend more than just a day in Sevenoaks and Holmes suggested I find us accommodation for the night. I went to the village and settled upon The Ploughman's Inn. It was a quiet and comfortable place and Holmes was to join me there that evening for a steak and ale pie. I waited for him at the bar and mulled over the ghost who walked on water.

In our time together, there had been moments when I'd had cause to question the rational outlook of my friend, not least during the Erasmus Brew case of 1889. Both as a doctor and a soldier, I had borne witness to occurrences which could not be explained by anyone but the churchman. I pictured what Miss Hunter had seen that night upon the water and I tried to adopt my friend's certainty.

A little after six O'clock, Holmes joined me. I noticed a gleam in his eyes which could only tell of success.

"I have had a most invigorating session at the school library," he said.

"Good to hear," I said between mouthfuls.

"Miss Hunter's father, Pheaphilus Hunter, was indeed in business with Otis Maunder, Nathaniel Farley and Edwin Luckett," he said. "They were rather entrepreneurial men, having noticed the growing demand for female clerks and the need to equip them with the skills of shorthand and typing. Luckett had a friend, G. E. Clark, who had founded a secretarial college in Southgate Road in 1880, and wanted to do the same here. So it was that the four men founded the Sevenoaks Secretarial College for Gentlewomen. They hoped it would emulate the success of Skerry's College, which provides young men with civil service training and has colleges all around the country. However, it soon became apparent that Maunder was embezzling funds and, just as Miss Hunter said, the other three men did not inform the police. This, by the way, is Maunder."

He had taken out a photograph and I examined it with interest. Mr Otis Maunder had been stout and of medium height, with only a few forgotten hairs left on his head, and a downturned mouth which made him appear somewhat brusque.

Holmes was about to speak again when he noticed something through the window of the pub. "Ah!" he said. "Come, Watson." He leapt from his chair and threaded quickly through the inn's other customers. "This," he told me in a low voice as we made our way outside, "will be Ambrose, an odd-job man from Sturridge. I had the landlord summon him here to clean the windows quite urgently."

"Why would windows need to be cleaned urgently?" I asked.

"Because we won't be here for long, Watson, and this man is the son of Otis Maunder."

We turned a corner and approached a figure pressing a rag against one of the windows. He looked nothing like his father. Whereas the older Maunder had been paunchy, Ambrose was tall and lithe, his face thin with sucked-in cheeks and a pencil moustache sat astride his mouth.

"Good evening," said my friend merrily. "We would like to speak with you about a young lady named Miss Violet Hunter."

The young man turned and eyed Holmes suspiciously. "I'm not talking about her," he said quietly. He seemed to grip the cloth harder and turned back to the glass. "I'm busy."

"If you insist," said Holmes, "Watson here will wash those windows for you."

I looked at my friend in surprise. "I will?"

"Most certainly," said Holmes, as though he himself was offering to help.

Ambrose paused reluctantly, but nodded to a bucket on the ground. I picked it up and stared into it with distaste. It was half filled with dirty water, with pieces of old moss and floating dead beetles. I shook my head resignedly, squeezed the cloth out and applied it firmly to the window.

"How do you feel about your father's—ah—*ghost* being seen?" Holmes asked the young man.

"It's not true," he said stonily. "It's a fairy tale. Margaret Oliphant nonsense."

"Have you considered asking Miss Hunter about it? I don't think you have visited her yet, have you?"

The young man's lips pulled back into a bitter grimace. "And I won't either," he said. "My father has been dead five months and now this mad woman is trying to start rumours. I won't have his memory upset like that."

Holmes nodded, as though none of this was unexpected. "Your father once embezzled funds from a company he ran with his friends."

I paused in my endeavours, shoulders sagging with disappointment. Holmes was capable of tenderness and tact, but exhibited it with astonishing inconsistency.

"I won't have his memory upset by you either," Ambrose said harshly.

"We already know it to be true," Holmes pointed out. "I grieve to tell you that speaking ill of the dead is a necessity in my profession."

Ambrose seemed to consider for a moment. "He needed the money." He said it quickly, as though he had been bursting to support his father for a long time and was now finally able to. "But he always thought the other three should have given him a second chance. And I did too."

Holmes nodded, unsurprised. "One other matter, Mr Maunder, to

I squeezed out the cloth and applied it firmly to the window.

which I hope you will submit your attention." He fished a piece of paper from the inside pocket of his coat and presented it to the young man, who looked at it indifferently. "Is this your father's handwriting?" he asked.

Ambrose shifted, unsure. "It's been a long time," he said, "but I think so."

"Thank you," said Holmes. I glanced back at him and noticed his smile was less fleeting than usual. He was clearly pleased about something.

We returned indoors and found our table again.

"I didn't like to mention his mother's alcoholism," he volunteered before I could even ask. I looked at him incredulously. "The letter I showed Ambrose," he explained. "It is the one Miss Hunter found. It seemed to describe how his father thought there were spirits roaming the house at night, how he could hear them, how they frightened him and how he was considering moving away just to be rid of them. Rather, of course, the letter wasn't about ghosts at all."

"What is it you mean?"

"His wife was addicted to drink," he said. "She swore to her husband that she was addicted no more, yet she hid these bottles of spirits in the house. He became suspicious and was determined to find them. She would drink them at night, coming downstairs and taking them from their secret hiding places, where they would tinkle and unknowingly disturb him upstairs. In his despair, Maunder even considered leaving her. The letter was written to his son, explaining the situation, and the handwriting was shaky as Maunder was upset. "

I was about to congratulate Holmes when I noticed his face twisting into a perplexed frown. "There's something else," I detected.

He nodded. "I cannot say here," he said, his eyes flitting fretfully about the snug.

We took the stairs to the first landing, each of our rooms in opposite directions. Holmes stood over the banister, his hands gripping it tightly as he spoke. "Otis Maunder," he said, "never forgave his former associates. He was resentful of his lost opportunity. The other three went on to become wealthy and Maunder did not. He was furious. Ambrose admits that he is too. No doubt the old man poisoned his mind. I believe that, before he died, Otis Maunder thought of a plan in which he could exact his revenge.

"Pheaphilus Hunter, of course, had since died and so it was necessary to punish his daughter instead. He discovered Miss Hunter was now a teacher and headmistress and was, as it happened, searching for a new position. Maunder retired and recommended Miss Hunter as his successor. He fully intended to carry out the rest of his plan, but died of heart failure before he was able. I fancy that Ambrose knew of what his father was up to and decided to continue himself."

I stared at my friend keenly. "What was the plan?"

Holmes let go of the banisters and threw his hands up in the air as though admitting defeat. "It is a hypothesis which cannot work," he said. "I believed that it was Ambrose who Miss Hunter had seen that night. Just how he managed to walk on water, I do not yet know. But I was sure it had to be him." He smiled grimly. "But Ambrose looks nothing like his father. Even if he had stuffed a cushion up his shirt, he would still not have looked convincing. From the moment we learned this ghost was supposed to be Otis Maunder as a young man, I wondered why. Surely a ghost would look like a man at whatever age he died, not as he was in his prime? Alas, Ambrose could not, I fancy, look like the photograph of his father which Miss Hunter had seen. His father carried too much weight. In other words, we still do not know what happened."

The following morning, we took a dogcart to the school, but Holmes elected not to trouble any of its staff again. Neither of us spoke for some time. I followed my friend through the grounds and noticed with concern how sombre he seemed. He moved briskly, the ground dipping slightly into a curve, and reached the lake.

"How, Watson? How?" he murmured as I joined him.

I was about to reply when he suddenly charged into the water, splashing like a mad seal until he finally halted, over two yards away. The water came up to his knees.

"There would have to be a platform of some sort," he speculated.

Again, I was about to answer him, when he jumped up and, in another splash, disappeared beneath the surface. There he remained for what felt like minutes, until I began feeling rather worried. I stared hard into the water but could not see through the murkiness. Something, I felt, was wrong. I stepped forward and was about to totter into the stillness myself when there was a sudden burst a mere foot away.

I smiled with relief as I watched Holmes, curled into a ball near the very edge of the lake, unfurl into a stand. Every inch of him appeared soaked. He clambered out, dripping onto the ground.

"Find anything?" I asked.

Holmes shook his head and water sprayed off his hair. "Nothing. Just blackness, mud and moss."

He looked about him, his face tight with concentration. He was searching for something. I looked about me but could see nothing unusual. His eyes then widened and one side of his mouth twisted shyly into a smile.

"Halloa!" he cried and sprang forwards into a run. He stopped some yards away, then bent down and picked something up and held it aloft like a schoolboy who had just won a prize.

"A dead fish," I said, upon seeing what it was. Holmes examined it minutely. "How do you suppose it got so far from the lake?" I asked. "I know they can leap out of a stream but they couldn't get this far."

Holmes remained mute and I knew I would get no answers—at least, not yet.

"Come Watson," he said finally. "We shall discover nothing more here."

He turned and, with surprising dignity, walked off, his clothes still dripping water wherever he went.

We returned to the Ploughman's Inn and he took the opportunity to change into dry clothes. I thought it likely that we would be staying for a few days and asked the landlord if the rooms were to remain available. It was typical of my friend, however, to suggest something completely contrary to my expectations. When he returned, I noticed a keen look of determination on his face.

"We must return to London," he announced.

And so it was that we met with Miss Hunter again. This time, we shared her cell with Inspector Bradstreet, who took prime position on the bench, and Constable Cook, who seemed again to be making a series of copious notes.

"How do you spell aquiline?" he asked me.

"I don't," I lied.

Holmes brushed a piece of fluff from his sleeve with a weak-fisted wave. He was set to begin. "It occurred to me, Miss Hunter," he said, "that we only ever had your confirmation that the man in the picture was indeed Otis Maunder."

Miss Violet Hunter looked shocked. "Mr Holmes! Are you accusing me of lying?"

Holmes's expression almost mirrors hers. "Not in the least," he said. "I simply mean that you would not know what a young Otis Maunder looked like. The photographs in the drawer did not include any other. I am suggesting it was not the late Mr Maunder in that picture at all."

Miss Hunter, Inspector Bradstreet and Constable Cook all shared the same frown.

"Who could it have been?" she asked.

"His son Ambrose," said Holmes. "I was always convinced it was he, though I could not reason just how he had managed it. But then it became clear. Instead of using a photograph of his father, of whom he looked nothing alike, he used a photograph of himself. He put it in an old frame, covered it with dust and planted it in the drawer. He wanted you to believe it was his father and you did not question the implication for a moment."

Holmes gestured to me, clearly unwilling to continue his explanation himself.

"Ambrose," I said, remembering what Holmes had told me on the way back to the capital, "had his father's key to the school and every night he would steal into the office and check to see if the photograph had been moved. When he found it was missing, he knew it was time to put the rest of his plan into action. As an odd-job man, he does a little work in the grounds every now and then. He had seen you walking around the lake and learned that it was your custom to do so every night. Holmes and I have visited the lake. Now, if we remember, the end you saw is rather narrow at only two yards across, and the ground beside it is only an inch or two higher. There is also quite a curvature in the ground's formation, meaning that it can retain water when it rains and make a puddle."

"I believe," Holmes went on, "that soon before you ventured out for your walk, Miss Hunter, Ambrose came to the lake and filled a bucket with its water. He then poured it thickly across the ground and kept doing so until he had created a very large puddle, as Watson just indicated. It stretched out wide until it reached the edges of the lake itself. From a distance, the join between lake and puddle could not be discerned. To all purposes, the lake had been extended a little. Ambrose then positioned himself in the middle and waited.

"Soon after, you arrived, Miss Hunter. In the dim moonlight, with the barest hint showing from behind the clouds, you did not have the surest notion of where, precisely, you were standing. Neither did you realise that the lake was apparently nearer than usual. All you knew was that a figure was out on the lake and moving towards you. His feet, in fact, were touching the ground underfoot but, from all outward appearances, he was walking on water. To your startled eyes, Otis Maunder had returned as a ghost!

"Over the following few days, you learned of his life and death and that his former associates Edwin Luckett and Nathaniel Farley lived in nearby Riverend. You even visited the place and saw them from afar, which not even Ambrose could have anticipated. He worked in many gardens and had been in Riverend for a couple of weeks already. He collected together a bunch of violets. He then visited both of the men's houses and killed them, leaving the flowers on their corpses. He hoped the police would understand the message and they did. The killer was apparently announcing himself as a violet hunter and you are indeed a Violet Hunter."

Inspector Bradstreet's face had paled. He looked from Holmes to our client and back again. Constable Cook, meanwhile, struggled to keep speed with Holmes.

"They believed you were quite literally mad, leaving a cryptic clue as you avenged Otis Maunder. And with the questions and the spying and this talk of a ghost, it is no wonder they had you see an alienist."

Miss Hunter looked awed. "But we can understand your conviction," I added, at pains to soothe her. "I'm sure even Mr Holmes himself would have been deceived."

"I wouldn't quite say that, Watson," said Holmes harshly.

"But Mr Holmes," said Miss Hunter, "how do you know this?"

Holmes lifted a hand like a magician producing a pigeon. "You ripped the photograph in two and threw it into the fire. Considering your temper at the time, you were too distracted to tell if it had properly burned. I checked, and I was fortunate, for one piece had fallen behind the lumber." He took it from his pocket and revealed it to us. It was the upper half of the photograph and was clearly Ambrose, not his father.

Inspector Bradstreet looked sceptical. "What about the lake?"

"Upon inspection of the ground nearest to the lake, I found a small, dead fish. Ambrose had clearly scooped it in his bucket before pouring the water onto the ground. He was too rushed to notice it. I had visited Ambrose and had also seen pieces of moss in the bucket which I believe had also come from the lake. I tried to have Watson retrieve it, but he started washing windows instead."

Miss Hunter remained worried. "But how will the police stop believing it is me?"

"Rest assured," said Holmes, "I would wager that even the inspector here will secure a confession from Ambrose Maunder. Leaving you, Miss Hunter, free to marry Mr Marcus Housley and continue your career as a headmistress."

Miss Hunter's frown cleared as he said this. "Mr Holmes," she said, "I cannot adequately thank you!"

Holmes opened the cell door and she sauntered happily out of it.

Cook followed us, frowning at his notes. "I don't think I've copied this down properly," he told me. "What's the fish got to do with anything?"

Inspector Bradstreet remained sitting on the bench, frowning at the wall and thinking over all he had heard. Holmes quietly closed the door of the cell, locking the oblivious inspector inside. My friend looked at me with a mischievous smile and a finger raised in silence and I said nothing as we moved away.

"*Now* the case is closed, inspector!" called Holmes and I could hear the man's guttural cry of indignation as we left.

THE END

DAVID FRIEND - lives in North Wales, UK, where he divides his time between watching old detective films and thinking about old detective films. He's been scribbling out stories since he was seven years old and hopes, some day, to write something half-decent. Most of what he pens is set in a 1930s world of non-stop adventure with debonair sleuths, kick-ass damsels, criminal masterminds and narrow escapes and he wishes he could live there. At the moment, he's working on something in the vein of the British pulps, like Sexton Blake, Bulldog Drummond and The Saint, and the iconic 1960s television series *The Avengers*. He thinks of it as P.G. Wodehouse crossed with Edgar Allen Poe, only not as good.

Sherlock Holmes

in

"The Case of the Singular Tragedy"

By
Raymond Louis James Lovato

it has been my singular honor to have accompanied my companion, Sherlock Holmes, on many a great adventure into exploring the depth of human depravity and the undiscovered decency in people's souls. We have unraveled mysteries in the most ornate and palatial estates of England, been involved in international intrigue and solved the mystery of a troublesome inheritance. My friend and companion had solved them all with his uncanny powers of detection and observation, all with the detachment of a man solving a puzzle at his table on a rainy afternoon. But there was one case that my friend was deeply and emotionally involved in, more so than I have ever seen. All during the case, there was a fierce determination on my companion's face, and I knew that this was unlike any other case that Holmes had ever undertaken. The detective was not going to stop until he solved this seemingly insoluble crime. This time, it was personal.

A brisk chill swept through London on this October morning as I entered the sitting room to find the usual tableau, my friend seated in his wing-back chair with a newspaper in front of him, scones, honey, and butter with a hot pot of tea delivered by Mrs. Hudson resting on the table.

"Good morning, Watson," said Holmes, hidden behind the impenetrable screen made by the Daily Courier.

"Good morning to you also."

"Interesting story on page five concerning the apparent loss of four army carrier pigeons from the camp in south London." The paper rustled slightly.

"Could this be a portent of war," I smiled, "or could it just be some poor chaps in search of a meal."

"This could be something worth looking into," said the voice behind the paper.

Our friendly banter was abruptly interrupted by the banging on the front door.

"It must be very important judging by the hour and the obvious need to attract our attention," said Holmes, allowing the paper to fold down in half so that he could peer over it.

Since I had not yet taken a seat and was closest to the stairs, it was natural that I answered the urgent summons. Upon opening the front door, I found one of the ragged and unwashed Baker Street Irregulars.

"I must talk to Master Holmes. It's very 'portant." Before I could protest, the little scamp bolted past me and up the stairs.

By the time I had retraced my steps, the little urchin was standing in front of Holmes, talking hurriedly in a low voice. All I could make out was "two men—murder—Thames—friends." Holmes bolted out of his chair, reached down to scoop up a few pence from the table and handed it to the boy.

Then my companion hurried to his wardrobe, shouting from his room, "Doctor, please grab your hat and coat and follow me downstairs as I hail a cab. We must hurry to the River Thames."

Once on the street and having secured a Hansom carriage, Holmes commanded the driver to proceed to Elaine's Buttress and that there would be a handsome payment upon arrival if he would race there at top speed. As the cab took off with a sudden jerk, I was thrown back against the seat. My curiosity about our destination and the haste at which we must arrive could not be contained.

The detective looked out of the window, consumed in deep thought. "Holmes," I finally said, "would you care to inform me as to where we are going and why such haste?"

The detective turned his head slightly, but stared at the floor, not looking at me. "Watson, if what I was told is true, there was a murder most foul last night on the banks of the River Thames and the victims may be Pete the Greek and Dead Fish Barney, two old friends and informants who choose to survive by their wits on the cruel streets." He didn't offer any other words.

The quickest way to the Thames was St. Paul's Road to Mile End Road past Tower Hamlets Cemetery. It took approximately twenty minutes as the boulevards were sparsely occupied at this early hour. When we reached the River Thames, my companion exited quickly. We both pulled our collars up as the crisp autumn morning became damper. I paid our driver generously as Holmes had instructed and bade him to wait here for us. My friend was already walking briskly toward the embankment overlooking the River Thames, a filthy, polluted, garbage disposal for both human and animal waste. Its muddy banks were heavily strewn with wet rocks, rubble and wooden debris from the evening's tide. At the cobblestones' edge, Holmes descended a moss-encrusted, wooden ladder to the sandy soil below, heavily carpeted in rocks, then advanced with haste down the sloping incline. Following him, I cautiously made the climb downward and set foot on the rocky ground. Carefully, I moved to the embankment, treading an unexpectedly well-worn path, only to see Holmes speaking with Inspector Lestrade. I heard my friend say, "Good morning, Inspector. How is it that you are assigned here?"

"Do you think I want to be here on this smelly, muddy, pile of rocks, Holmes?" said Lestrade. "There is a flu going around the division, so they expect me to cover everything. This is a case for Billson. The waterfront's his. He had another bum die along here a night ago. The chap took quite a beating."

Holmes turned away quickly, saying nothing more to Lestrade.

As I arrived, I added, "Good morning, Inspector. It is lucky for you that you have avoided catching this flu. It's a minor inconvenience as it lasts for only a few days at most. I had a touch of it last week. Just a minor cough, really, nothing serious."

I turned and saw my companion squatting over a body that was leaning against a wooden brace at the top of the steep incline about six feet from a rusty steel barrel filled with ashes half-burned driftwood, and small, charred planks of crates that served as a campfire. Holmes picked up a long stick from the ground, bent over the barrel, and poked at the wood and ashes.

After he finished, he walked around to observe the two filthy blankets spread on the ground, along with some branches and sticks strewn haphazardly and a small, old tarp that covered a neatly stacked pile of wooden planks. There were several pots, tin plates and a half-filled bottle of ale set beside it.

"Are these, indeed, your friends?" said I.

"Yes, Watson, they are. Two men that I have known and worked with down here for several years. Men who shared their confidential information with me. A pair whose character was beyond reproach, men of their word and resolute souls. It was only by the hand of fate that they had such a hard lot."

"This is Dead Fish Barney," said Holmes. He paused and looked around. "It appears that none of their possessions had been stolen. That rules out robbery by a derelict. Since there are no signs of movement by him and one set of boot prints directly in front of him. Barney was murdered right where he sat. You can see that the right side of Barney's skull has been crushed in. That would suggest that his attacker was a left-handed person."

Holmes moved over to the other body that was to our right, which lay face down on a patch of weeds. "This, regrettably, is Pete the Greek. Notice the rather sizable hole in the sole of his left shoe, Watson. Observe that down this slope there is a body-size indentation in the mud close to the river bank. Something happened down there. Also, leading up from that spot, there are deep drag marks in the soil and disturbed rocks to where his body is laying now. But the heavy boot prints of whoever placed him here have no traces of a hole on its left boot. And, certainly, Pete did not drag himself up to here. Inspector, who found the bodies?"

"Young Hennigan here," Lestrade jerked his thumb at the lanky patrolman standing beside him. "He spotted them on his morning patrol."

"Young Hennigan, come here." The detective pointed to the tall Bobbie clad in his single-breasted Melton wool uniform with his Metropolitan custodial cork helmet. The policeman's face showed his immediate displeasure at my friend's order. The constable didn't move.

"Here." Holmes' voice was unmistakably commanding.

The Bobbie turned to Lestrade and asked, "Am I taking orders from this man, Inspector?"

"Get down there now, Hennigan," said Lestrade, as he ran his finger across his short moustache. The constable moved several steps down the embankment, stopping short of the mud.

"Where did you find the body?" Holmes asked looking up.

"Over there," the Bobbie pointed towards the Thames.

The detective took a step forward. "Over there? Floating in the Thames? Sitting on the other side of the river? Over by the Tower of London? Show me exactly where and be quick about it."

Hennigan stepped cautiously past Holmes through the slippery mud, always looking down at his boots. "Right here," he said, pointing down to the wide, polluted indentation.

"And how was the body positioned?"

"He was on the ground."

Holmes took several forceful strides forward, stopping only one meter from the copper's face. The Bobbie quickly lurched backward.

"You will answer all of my questions precisely and accurately. Do you understand? Did you find the body on his side? Face up or face down?" The detective's voice wavered between anger and disgust.

It seemed to me that the constable wanted desperately to look back at Lestrade, but obviously thought better of turning away from the detective's icy stare. "He was face down, sir, arms spread out to his sides."

"Did you drag that man's body up the bank from that indentation?"

"Yes, I did."

"And why would you do that?"

"Because there's grass up there. Less mud," Hennigan said meekly.

Holmes turned to Lestrade, with displeasure etched on his face. "How many times have I asked you not to disturb or remove anything at the scene of a crime?" Lestrade also looked down at his muddy shoes and didn't respond.

To the left of Dead Fish Barney were two sets of boot prints that led down to the Thames. But there was only a second, single trail that returned back up the sloppy embankment. I could see Holmes, his thin, bony fingers resting on his sharp chin, as he began to reconstruct the crime by following the distinct sets of boot steps in the mud down to the river bank. The detective scoured every inch of the muddy trail, moving cautiously, so as not to further disturb the area around the scene of the murders.

He retraced the foot prints going down the embankment towards the river. "The tangled mess of foot prints tells me that the two of them struggled briefly, then Pete broke away and started running towards the Thames."

"His pursuer chased him to about here," Holmes strode back up the bank to where one set of the shoe prints ended, "and his attacker slid to a halt there. Pete's foot prints stop about five-meters in front of the killer where my old friend was shot twice in the back. That is elementary, as I observed two holes in his wool jacket where he now lies up there with you. The force of the bullets pushed his body forward and it eventually slid to a halt and lay face down in this cavity. He died right here.

"The other footprints leading from Pete's final resting place are all, obviously, from our overzealous Yarder because there would be no need for the killer to drag Pete up the incline and deposit the body next to Barney, as the foul deed had already been done."

I was still examining poor Barney's mangled skull with the Inspector standing beside me, when I looked up and said, "Good Lord, Holmes, how do you know that?"

"It's elementary, my dear Watson," Holmes called up from his position down the slope. "The set of shoe prints leading up to this indentation in the mud could only be made by Pete, as they show a distinguishable hole on the left foot print. Since there are no other foot prints around this small crater, Pete had to have been shot in the back while running towards the Thames. The second set of different boot prints are to his left and stop several yards back there behind where Pete came to rest. I believe our killer was right-handed as he chased Pete slightly from the left. Pete then hit the ground hard and slid forward in the damp river bank, stopping right here as shown by the disturbance of soil and rocks leading to this muddy, hollow space."

"Holmes, do be careful," I called out. "You are sloshing around that swampy, filthy ground that is filled with muckworms. Those buggers live in manure and feces."

"Watson, you know that I will always go wherever the case shall lead me. I'm glad we arrived here before the morning tide, or making any sense of this murder scene would have been virtually impossible."

"Holmes slowly made his way back up to where I was with Lestrade. As he did, he stopped several meters from the barrel, bent down and picked up a small handful of wet black powder next to two small muddy shards, dirty rags and several pieces of driftwood. He lifted his hand to his nose and drew in a short, deep breath. Looking over to where I was kneeling over Pete's body, he called out, "Dr. Watson, before I traverse this muddy slope to join you, please tell me, in your learned opinion, would you hazard a guess as to what type of weapon was used on Pete? Would you say it was fired from a revolver, and not from a very old flintlock pistol?"

The question seemed odd; but, then again, I was very use to odd questions from the detective. "Yes, Holmes, from the size of the entry wound, I would hazard a guess that it was from a revolver."

My friend let the black grains fall from his hand, stood up, and continued to survey the entire scene laid out before him. Hennigan had beaten a hasty retreat to Lestrade's side. Holmes eventually made his way back to Pete's body at the top of the mud-spattered slope. Pulling out his magnifying glass, he examined the two bullet wounds in his friend's back.

The detective then moved over to Barney's blood-soaked body and inspected the gaping, caved in head wound. "These wounds were made by several repeated blows to the skull? A ghastly way to die." He looked around at the impressions made by the attacker.

"Barney was the first to meet his death," said Holmes, "as he was the first person the attackers would have encountered when they appeared. He put up no struggle and was murdered where he sat. His murderer either snuck up on him or he was familiar with him and not afraid of the person. Watson, notice the boot prints around Barney's body. This set of footprints leads to right here, then stop in front of Barney to inflict this carnage. There were definitely two assailants to accomplish this. These footprints reveal that Barney's killer are worn deeper on the inside of each boot than they are the outer side of the boot prints which lead towards the river to our left. This man has a distinguishable gait, perhaps because of an accident. And yet, there were three men involved" said Holmes.

"Three," said I. "How in deuces do you know that?"

"On the way down I noticed another set of boot prints to the far left of where all of us descended the ladder and made our way down here. The last man stood off to the side up there so as to clearly observe his cohorts as they carried out their lethal mission. Those footprints lead to a spot where he stood and then, after it was over, departed. He was obviously the leader of this vicious raid, as he didn't have to sully his boots."

Holmes stood silent; surveying the Thames with its many ships anchored in the middle of the river and then perused the buildings in the immediate area. "Since there are no buildings or warehouses behind us, only an open field, let's visit the ones directly across the river to inquire if they noticed anything or had heard the two shots."

We bade Lestrade, who was rapidly filling his small note pad with my friend's observations, goodbye. The young Bobbie stepped back several paces as we passed him by.

Once we were seated in our Hansom's hard seats, my friend stared straight ahead. A moment later, he was his familiar animated self. "They were my friends who were murdered back there," he said," two unwavering men that I have known and worked with. Noble in their own way. How do you measure what a man's worth, Watson? Is it how did he live? How did he die? Or is it what did he contribute to civilization? I feel that, regardless of their station, it is truly if they had a great heart. They will be missed."

I turned to my companion. "I am most sorry for what befell your two friends."

"Thank you, Watson, but hold your sorrow for the depraved villains who did this to them when their time comes."

We took our cab across the bridge and headed for a two-story building set back a little ways from the cobblestone path which ended abruptly into a muddy mess that could only be referred to as a road in a most generous way. It led to a row of warehouses and beyond that was a two-story, faded white wooden building marked by a brass sign as *Her Majesty's Royal Naval Port Of London Office Of The Harbor Master.* I again paid the cabbie a handsome sum and instructed him to wait for us, which he was more than willing to do. The wrought iron gate to the Harbor Master's building was open, so I followed my companion up the very short brick path to the steps, through the door, and into the building.

I knew that the Harbor Master of the Royal Navy was in charge of the naval shipyard and dry docks for refitting naval vessels which were situated almost directly across from the scene of the crime. Looking to the west, you could see the Tower of London jutting out around the curving shoreline. Inside the first floor of the wooden building was a sort of waiting room with a bench against the wall, an old desk with papers strewn upon it, a stamp and ink pad beside them. Seeing no one there, Holmes, in one of his impatient moods, bounded up the stairs to the second floor.

That room appeared smaller because of its clutter. On one side was a bench turned towards the wall and several wooden life rings stacked next to it on the floor. The wall that faced us had a small table and chair next to a window that looked out to the River Thames. The wall to our right held a long, thin table with a Mid-shipman's sword mounted on two pegs and navel banners leaning against it. Next to the door in the far corner, there protruded a sign that read: Captain Tobias Payne, Harbor Master. Since the door was ajar, Holmes walked right in. Seated behind an overly large desk for such a small room, dressed in his blue frock coat with gold buttons and his rank worn on his sleeve, was the Harbor Master. Standing next to him was a Master's First Mate, a burly fellow wearing his naval hat.

"Who the hell are you?" Captain Payne demanded.

"Sherlock Holmes, Consulting Detective, Scotland Yard. I was wondering if you could indulge me and answer if anyone on your night watch reported any activity directly across the Thames last night."

"I'm too busy with important things to do than to talk to a fancy copper about naval business."

"I assure you that I am not a constable; merely an associate of Scotland Yard. I am seeking your help with a matter that occurred across the river last evening." While he spoke, Holmes had twisted his head slightly to one side. I had seen him do this before and I knew he was reading every paper, every bill of lading, on the Captain's desk top.

"No bloke with a parish pick ax is going to barge into my office and demand that I talk to him."

The detective ignored Payne's remark about his strong, hawk-like nose and continued. "Sir, two dispossessed men were murdered last evening on the opposite shore almost directly across the river. I am merely inquiring if anything was heard or reported over here? Gun fire, perhaps? After all, I assume you have nightly patrols to discourage smugglers and river pirates on the Thames."

"Are you insinuating that I have pirates and smugglers operating here in the Port of London?" Captain Payne shouted." How dare you make those accusations? That is an insult to me and the Royal Navy."

The Harbor Master turned angrily to his First Mate. "Jenkins, remove this man at once. I am proud of my impeccable record and I'll not have my reputation besmirched by these wild accusations of crimes on my watch."

Quite suddenly, a second naval Mate appeared at the door behind us. He was slightly larger than Jenkins.

"Marston, help Jenkins escort these men to the gate and make sure that they never come back," the Captain said.

"No need," said Holmes, "we can find our way out without any assistance."

On the lengthy ride home, the detective only commented on the uncooperative stance of the Harbor Master and of Holmes' lingering, extreme displeasure about the near destruction of the scene of the crime by the young Bobby. Otherwise, he was silent, looking out of the Hansom window at the cloudy sky. I felt that the dreary weather perfectly matched his mood.

Upon arriving back home at Baker Street, Holmes immediately retired to his small corner where he sat in front of his oval vanity mirror, the small dresser top cluttered with tins of makeup, cloths and various brushes, along with several strange appliances. My friend first placed a painful looking contraption inside his lower lip giving the outward appearance of crooked and broken teeth. Afterword, he began applying a thin layer of putty transforming his strong nose into a sloped, broad nose that tipped up ever so slightly. Then he put on makeup that gave his cheeks a sallow, yellowish tint.

"May I inquire who is going out on the town tonight?" said I.

"An old salt that hasn't been seen in many months, but can freely navigate the seedier drinking establishments of the East End."

"Holmes, that is not the healthiest of places to walk around. Those slums are notorious for violence, crime and vicious criminals. It is considered Hell on earth."

"If it helps to solve this conundrum, then I shall go to Hell and back," said Holmes.

"Then I am accompanying you, carrying my service revolver."

"You can come if you wish, Watson, but only if you stay clear of me. Old

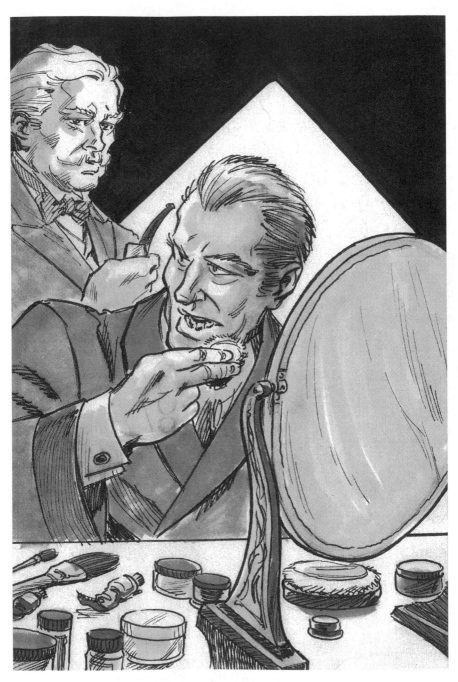

"If it helps to solve this conundrum, then I shall go to Hell and back."

Alfred Beanes works alone," he said, smearing on a brown substance to make his upper teeth appear discolored and rotted.

The carriage moved slowly through the muddy paths of London's East End as the cobblestone streets had ended a ways back. The late afternoon sun began to slide westward, casting long shadows over the already coal-fueled, blackened sky. There was a perpetual fog blanketing the small alleys and the overcrowded, rickety houses resting on no foundations. From everywhere, your nose was assaulted by the stench of raw sewage, the smell of human waste and the dung of cows and chickens being raised in small backyards. There was more than ample reason that this was called Dirty Old London.

Upon arriving at a dilapidated building, marked by a small sign that read THE PIG'S WHISTLE, my companion instructed the driver to stop further down the road and remain there. "Watson, you will please stay with the carriage as protection, as you would undoubtedly stand out once inside this tavern."

Holmes, with his true face unrecognizable, then affected a slight limp and proceeded inside the narrow tavern door. I sat quietly inside the carriage as it moved down the muddy lane. But, as I viewed the denizens skulking through the muck, I became more concerned for my friend's safety. It was unimaginable to me that my companion would constantly partake in such dangerous sorties as this all the time. Flinging open the door, I stepped out of the carriage, reminded the driver to wait for us, and walked carefully through the mire back to the drinking hole.

As unobtrusively as possible, I positioned myself by the small window outside and peered in. The place was dimly lit inside by the flicker of flame obscured by filthy glass globes on lanterns hung on wooden pillars. From my position, I saw small, mismatched tables, wooden benches and stools. Straw was strewn all over the floor. Even through the window I could smell stale urine. I observed Holmes as he stopped, scanned the room, and then proceeded to a spot at the bar next to the biggest, burliest lout covered with tattoos in the place. It wasn't so much as a proper bar; it was just a large plank held up at both ends by barrels.

I put my face as close to the glass as I could, attempting to hear or try to read lips, as my companion had been instructing me in that art. After getting his ale, the detective turned to speak to the brute beside him.

Unfortunately, that shielded his face from my sight. But it was very apparent that he was slowly aggravating the fellow. It was then that I noticed the two ruffians, both in extremely worn blue sweaters and red wool-knit caps at the far end of the bar start to circle behind Holmes. I could wait no more. I moved quietly into the tavern, slid around the door, and sat myself in the shadows in the nearest corner.

Suddenly, the thug at the bar took a swing at the detective, who adroitly ducked under the punch and countered with a solid blow to the man's stomach. Holmes then grabbed the back of the lout's neck and slammed his face solidly into the plank. The two ratbags behind my companion rushed forward, one brandishing a knife. Holmes met the first attacker with a sharp kick to the knee, a devastating move that he had mastered from savate, sending the man collapsing to the dirty, straw floorboards. As the second foe lurched forward with his blade, Holmes weaved to the left, letting his opponent's looping swing meet empty air.

My companion countered with a powerful chop to the attacker's throat, who immediately began to choke; grabbing his wind pipe as if that would afford him more air. Still, in his almost disabled state, the ruffian drew his arm back to attempt to plunge his blade at my friend. The detective threw a straight right hand into the attacker's jaw, sending him to the foul floor.

As the first hooligan regained his feet, I stood and fired my revolver into the air. Everyone in the bar became as statues, except the two goons who pushed themselves from the putrid straw, and scampered past me to the front door. One of them stopped to stare at me. I lowered my arm towards the lout to remind him that I had a revolver and he straight away disappeared into the night.

Holmes helped the brute next to him off of the bar, a thin stream of blood trickled down the man's face. "'Ere, let me 'elp ya," my companion said, "and don't mind 'im," he cocked his thumb over his shoulder, "'e's my friend. He's a dizzy age. Really old. Been followin' me 'round for a week. But 'e's 'andy to have 'round with that pistol."

As the thug wiped blood from his nose, Holmes continued, "Let's 'ave a shant of bivvy together." The barkeep quickly brought over two pints of beer. They began drinking together like old friends. "What's yur name?" the detective asked.

"Duncan. What's yours?"

"Alfred Beanes."

"Wait, yur Freddie Beanes? Blimey, I just got whipped by Freddie Beanes. Pleased to meet ya, Mister Beanes. It's a real pleasure. I done heard that you was gone."

"Yes, 'bout five months up in Glouster. Worked ev'ry day. Made me some real quid." Holmes proceeded to buy Duncan another pint and they talked about local dock rumors. His new friend boasted that there's a lot of nighttime activity going on at one of the warehouses.

"Strange to be slogging away at night. You gotta be a bricky bloke to take that pay. Gotta be fearless to work the river at night."

Holmes eventually brought the conversation around to his friends, Pete the Greek and Dead Fish Barney, asking Duncan if he knew of them.

"Yes, I kno's who they are. Funny you should ask 'bout 'em. A few nights ago, two nasty lookin' blokes dressed all in black come in 'ere. They stood real straight, like coppers. Real scary dockers. Both had pistols tucked in their belts. Then, they start banging pint glasses off the floor and shouting they want to find Pete an' Barney. Since Pete an' Barney wasn't 'ere, nobody says nothing."

"Hmm," said Holmes, "Do you know where they might be now? Pete an' Barney."

"Well's, they usually comes in 'ere an drink wit' Wheezy Rourke. Wheezy's a strange bloke, him wit' his giggle mug. Never stops smiling, that one. They sit in the back corner all night whenever they got money." Both Duncan and Holmes laughed loudly.

"I know ol' Wheezy from way back," Holmes said. "I'd like to 'ook up with 'im again. Ya know where 'e hangs out?"

"Rourke? Usually at that harlot's house around the corner, The Crowing Cock, when he's not 'ere."

Finally, Duncan had too many pints and his head, once more, slammed down on the wooden plank. Holmes tossed a few pence on the bar. "Please take good care o-my friend 'ere. Let 'em sleep it off on a bench back there. An' sorry 'bout the row. 'Ope this covers it." The barkeep smiled a toothless grin, and scooped up the money.

We left the tavern together and got in the carriage. "That certainly ended well," I said.

Holmes turned abruptly towards me. "Don't ever again step in when I am working. I don't tell you how to minister to your patients, do I?" He then shouted our destination to the driver and settled back in his seat. Silently, he began to remove all of his makeup and drop it in a case on the floor.

It was a short ride around the corner through the muddy East End streets. Our carriage pulled up in front of a large, old brick building with two lanterns out front. Their glow was a pale scarlet due to the glass being lightly tinged with red paint. Underneath them was a hand-painted sign that read The Crowing Cock. The letters were in a ghastly, faded crimson, with an absolutely garish painted red door beneath it to match. My companion instructed the driver to again wait for us and we proceeded up the steps, which was crowded with men coming and going with bowed heads.

Once inside the door, I could barely see as the air was heavy with smoke. I noticed that my friend was warmly greeted by the madam, a robust, mature woman with flaming red hair, who wore a bright ruby-sleeved corset with stays and ribbons crossed over her ample bosom. I was not about to ask my friend how he knew this matron for him to receive such a warm welcome. The velvet-draped parlor was filled with all types of men, accompanied by all shapes and sizes of fallen women, who walked around in black or pink lingerie, thigh-length black stockings, and the type of dressing gowns and robes de chambers only seen in the boudoir. Almost every one of them was smoking some sort of hand-rolled cigarette. In front of me passed two plump women walking around with their bodices unlaced, all wearing too much face powder.

The madam left us, only to return a minute later with a slim, relatively attractive girl with wavy, brushed back hair caught up in curls, as was the style of the time. She was almost clothed in washed-out bloomers and a peacock blue corset. Holmes nodded, took her hand and escorted her over to a garishly upholstered settee where I joined them. Apparently, the young woman was Wheezy Rourke's favorite girl. With a little financial encouragement, she related to us the last time that she saw Wheezy. At the time, he was rather intoxicated, and he had confided in her saying that Rourke's friends, Barney and Pete, had a big secret. But they weren't telling anyone until they could sell the story to one of the daily papers like the *Telegraph* or *Express* for big money. Plus, Wheezy related that Barney and Pete were very interested in an Oliver Mullberry.

"And do you know who this Oliver Mullberry might be?" said Holmes.

"Rourke only says he was a skilamalink by the river."

"Skilamalink?" I repeated.

"A shady character," Holmes explained. "And one last question, do you know where I might find Wheezy Rourke?"

"Na, he disappeared right after 'e told me his story. Ain't come round in a few days. Don't know where 'e is."

"How very odd. Thank you, Miss," said the detective, reaching into his jacket pocket and handing the girl another three farthings.

"This is the usual rate. For another tupence I'll entertain you both. You want to go upstairs now?" she asked.

"No, thank you. You've given me everything I needed right here."

Before we left, Holmes sought out the madam, and spoke a few words to her. As he lifted up her hand up and kissed the back of it, he slipped a quid to her, and then bade her good night. I thought I saw her blush, as if that was possible in a place like this. Once outside on the stoop, we observed that there was no one else around. No bustle of men coming and going.

We then spotted Lestrade across the street surrounded by a flurry of activity by a dozen of Scotland Yarders. Their activities were concentrated on an old, slightly out of kilter, one-story building, notable only by a rather small hand-painted sign that read "Daisy's Parlor." I could not help but notice one tall, exceptionally thin man being chased by constables. The man was desperately trying to cover his total lack of clothing with a too small mauve woman's robe with a fur collar. An overweight man in his long johns was being ushered into one of the two police wagons. Into the other wagon, the coppers were dragging several fallen women, in various stages of undress, who were kicking and screaming. The noise raised by this police raid was deafening. To my surprise, at the top of the steps across the street, a woman, totally naked except for high-laced black boots, was being hauled away, lashing out at both constables who tightly held her arms.

Lestrade turned and caught a glimpse of Holmes and myself leaving The Crowing Cock.

"And what brings the noted Sherlock Holmes down to a brothel in London's East End?" he said, a wry smile crossing his lips. "Reduced to visiting bordellos late at night, are we? The strain and stress of your consulting detectiving cause you to seek an evening out?"

"Inspector, I might ask you the same question. We are all here in the name of pursuing the truth. Am I not correct?"

"What, pursuing your profession or the world's oldest profession?" the Inspector grinned.

"A fine jest, indeed, Lestrade, but are you certain that you are here as a staunch upholder of the law? Even you must surely know that prostitution is perfectly legal. So, it is either that you and your constables are here to make threats in order to gain certain favors later or simply wished to see bare, naked ladies."

"This here is official police business and none of your business," said Lestrade. "It was reported that there were too many cases of syphilis coming from this harlot house and not all these wagtails were clean. We got enough diseases running around London."

"Lestrade, I am positive that one of your hard-working sergeants reported that opinion and he encouraged you to make this raid, correct? The only reason you are here tonight, Inspector, is because that bordello is late in their monthly protection payment to that particular Sergeant. It's bad form having some mutton shunter, as they call them down here, unlawfully extorting money from these legal establishments. Perhaps, that might be the crime you should be investigating."

"As I said, this is none of your business."

"You know that I make it my business to know as much about everything as I need to know. May I suggest that you keep a close eye on that stocky, bearded sergeant standing at the bottom of the stoop, as he might bear some investigating himself. Please let me know the results of your inquiry. We will both benefit from that in the long run."

Lestrade was speechless. "What...I...Holmes, how dare you make that accusation?"

"I make it with the utmost certitude. Good night, Inspector. Come, Watson, our work here is done."

As we settled into our carriage, I immediately asked, "How in blazes did you know to make that accusation against Scotland Yard without full proof?" The detective let that infrequent, sly grin appear for only a second.

"Folks in the East End have been talking about some burly constable keeping close tabs on all of the disorderly houses down here to see which ones that he could intimidate," my friend said. "You remember Red Rosie, the madam we met in The Crowing Cock. She is, indeed, one of my most useful informants. Most helpful in that case several months ago in giving me information that put me onto the true culprit. The case that you wrote about as The Case of the Silver Secret, a most appalling appellation by the way. After obtaining the information that I sought, she made me aware of this situation, telling me of a sergeant with a full red beard who was behind these extortions. Tonight, I spotted a red-bearded sergeant on the steps of Daisy's Parlor, and from there it was elementary, Watson. I noticed that as all of the fallen women passed by the sergeant, they stared directly at him. Some spat at only him, not the other Yarders. I felt it was my duty to put a word in Lestrade's ear."

"Holmes," my mouth suddenly became dry, "I am reticent to bring this up, but you are well aware that I am no stranger to the fairer sex and that I have shared my bed with many a women before; but I would beseech you, as my friend, to keep the knowledge of this little excursion a secret from my Mary? She might not approve of my visiting such places with you, even in the pursuit of murderers."

"Doctor, as far as I'm concerned, as a physician, you are very familiar with the human anatomy of both sexes. And, I, as a professional on official business, shall keep my lips sealed."

I thought in the dim light that I saw that same wry smile appear for a split second. The hour was late and it began to rain again; so my friend decided that we should start up again tomorrow morning. He was obviously deep in thought as the drops continued to come down slowly, as if the dark London sky was weeping.

Finally, Holmes broke his silence saying, "I'm not sure what to make of tonight. Pete and Barney would only take employment as dustmen, rat catchers or nightmen cleaning the cesspools of human waste behind shabby houses. I've known them for too many years. They knew many of the secrets of the East End, but very few that would be of any interest to a newspaper."

"Well, it's a side of London that I never visited before. These conditions, those people, the way of life down here. I wish that there was something that I could do for them."

"They want to make their own way, Watson. They know no other way of life than this. They all learn the art of survival at an early age or they will have a very short existence. Having a slice of bread is to them the equivalent of our tea, jelly, and crumpets in the morning."

After a long ride, we arrived at 221 B, Baker Street, only to find a two-wheeled Hansom cab waiting in front of the apartment. The rain was now coming down harder and the wind began to swell. The waiting cab door swung open and the large, unmistakable form of Mycroft Holmes slowly moved down the carriage step, noticeably tilting the buggy to the right. Obviously, Mycroft forgot his rain napper at his office as he stood unprotected in the heavy shower. Since the detective also had no umbrella, the two men faced each other in the pouring English rain.

"Aren't you going to invite me inside, Sherlock?" said Mycroft.

"No, unfortunately not, as I have no time for social visits; although your visits, brother, are hardly ever social."

"Well, if we are going to stand out here in this God awful weather, then I shall be brief."

"I doubt you know the meaning of the word 'brief', Mycroft."

"You will treat this as an important matter, little brother. You may want to destroy your professional reputation as a consulting detective, but I will not let you destroy my reputation in her Majesty's Service."

"Mycroft, you have finally acknowledged that being a consulting detective is a profession. How very open-minded of you."

"I didn't come here to play word games with you, Sherlock."

"And I have no time for playing games either, dear brother."

"Sherlock, I have spent the entire afternoon in my office being admonished and reprimanded by Vice Admiral Whitenhall himself. A man in my position should not have to receive a tongue lashing from some pompous, over-decorated sailor who could not find a ship in all of London's harbors if his life depended on it. And all because the great Sherlock Holmes decided to barge in unannounced at the office of the Royal Navy's Harbor Master of the River Thames. Her Majesties' Royal Navy will not tolerate interruptions and unfounded accusations directed at the Harbor Master as you have done by verbally assaulting the Captain responsible for overseeing the dry dock for the entire Royal Navy."

A roar of thunder echoed above from the black sky as if to accentuate the clash below. Exasperation was very clearly etched on Mycroft's face as the rain poured off his hat like tiny waterfalls. "Sherlock, this is not a suggestion. It is a warning. Choose someone else to harass. There is surely almost nothing in the world that I cannot save you from, except the Royal Admiralty. And, most certainly, not from yourself."

My friend stepped forward, now standing closer to his older brother. The chill in the air could not match the cold stare of the detective. "I will pursue this through the Royal Navy, through the monarchy and through you if I must to get to the truth."

The detective turned his back, quickly ascended the steps, thrust his key into the lock and disappeared into the house. I watched as Mycroft hoisted his ample frame back into the carriage.

We both rose early the next morning and were already ensconced in the sitting room when Mrs. Hudson brought up the morning's repast. Holmes seemed particularly occupied as he perused the morning newspapers. After a quick breakfast, we hailed a Hansom and were off to Scotland Yard to meet with Inspector Lestrade. Our driver knew of a short cut, as the road was clogged with morning traffic. He turned the carriage down a narrow street off of the boulevard to avoid the slow crush of carriages.

Just as we approached a side alley, a hay cart was suddenly shoved in front of our cab, totally blocking our progress and causing the driver to quickly rein in his horse.

Out of the alley bounded two ruffians, wearing worn pea coats and black wool stocking caps. They wore dark kerchiefs wrapped on their faces, covering both their noses and mouths. One carried a kosh, but it was an unusually large sock filled with sand, while the other brandished a truncheon and proceeded forward to attack our carriage. I waited until the hooligan who had veered off to my side of the cab was almost upon me. With as much force as I could muster, I swung open the carriage door and caught my attacker full in the face, knocking him down to the cobblestones.

Glancing over to the other side of the carriage, I saw Holmes had immediately jumped out and taken two strides forward to greet his opponent. Just as the man was upon him, the detective leaned back, putting his weight on his left foot and lashed out with his right leg. His foot caught the hooligan square in the stomach, stopping the burly thug and sending him reeling backwards. I now turned my full attention to my situation. I stepped out of the carriage holding my teak cane which I brought along, as I knew that I would be involved in much walking today with my companion. The ruffian in front of me had just righted himself and began to swing his blackjack over his head with his right hand. This gave me the opening that I needed. I swung my cane hard to the left side of his head, delivering a glancing blow to his skull. He staggered back and slumped to the ground.

On the other side of the carriage, Holmes took advantage of the space now created between himself and his attacker. Stepping forward, the detective reached out and grabbed the driver's buggy whip from the coach. When the thug once again advanced, waving the billy club back and forth in front of him in his left hand. Holmes lashed out. I could hear the whip snap as it sliced the ruffian on his right cheek, immediately drawing blood. The goon let out a sharp scream, dropped his truncheon and placed both hands on his face. He then beat a hasty retreat to the alley. As I looked down, the lout that I had floored picked himself up and followed his companion down the dark alleyway.

"That was more excitement than I anticipated on a carriage ride," said I.

"Well played, Watson. Whoever they were, they surely had been following us. When the street congestion held us up, they obviously raced ahead of us when were able to finally turn down this narrow lane and set up

I swung my cane hard to the left side of his head, delivering a glancing blow.

this ambush. But more importantly, why were we the target of this attack? Perhaps they were the two men we heard about from the tavern who were seeking information about Pete and Barney. They wore the same type of clothing. Most curious. Now, Watson, if you would be so kind as to help the driver and me push that hay wagon out of our way, we can proceed to our destination."

Arriving at Scotland Yard, we made our way back to Lestrade's office to find the Inspector peering up over disheveled stacks of paperwork. His usual look of aggravation upon seeing Holmes dropped over his face like a veil. "Good morning, Lestrade," said my companion.

"It was a good morning until you arrived," said Lestrade. "And what have you come to bother me with today?"

"Why, Inspector, you know that I only come to you when the most pertinent information is required and I am confident that you can be of great service. What does the Yard officially know about a Mister Mullberry and any business that he might have along the Thames?"

"Horace Mullberry? We were watching him awhile back. Seems he started out as dock worker and, eventually, became a dock boss for a year. Then one day, he showed up with a barrel of money and brought one of the warehouses."

"I see. Which warehouse might that be, Inspector?"

"The rather new one on the north side of the river, just east of the Tower of London."

"Unofficially, what does Scotland Yard know about him?" said Holmes.

The detective's question was met with a frown, but Lestrade continued, "We were suspicious of where all his money came from, so, we had two Bobbies watch him for a while at first. But it seems he is only importing oriental cooking ware, household goods, cut-rate vases, and small, cheap statues from China. Nothing suspicious. We questioned a few of his workers, you know, the usual way, and they confessed to seeing no untaxed liqueur or any smuggled China-men of any kind." There was a slight smile on Lestrade's face. "There hasn't been any increase of criminal activity in the East End. Well, no more than usual. So we left him alone."

"Inspector, would you happen to know where I might find Horace Mullberry this time of day?"

"As I recall, he always had lunch at that posh private club, the, ah, what's its name. Oh, yeah, the St. Thomas Club," he paused, "Holmes, you wouldn't be thinking about causing any trouble now, would you?"

"Inspector, you know me better than that. Thank you, Lestrade, you've been more than helpful, as always. Good day."

I saw the hint of astonishment on the Inspector's face. It wasn't often that he was complimented by the detective.

About twenty minutes later we were at the St. Thomas Club, a stately building with pillars carved into its facade. Fancy carriages were parked in front. We ascended the steps, entered a small but stylish anteroom, and approached an ornate podium. An elderly man, wearing an impeccable long-tailed tuxedo, inquired how he could be of service.

"Where is Mr. Horace Mulberry seated?" Holmes said.

The host motioned to a rather corpulent man sitting towards the middle of the room.

"We are here to see him. He is expecting us."

"I'm terribly sorry, sir. Mr. Mullberry didn't say that he was expecting guests. And seeing as you are not members, I'm going to have to ask you to leave."

"Really?" the detective said, raising one of his animated eyebrows. "Doctor Watson, would you be so kind as to show this fellow your business card."

I immediately retrieved one of my cards from the case inside my jacket pocket and handed it over, not sure how complying with my friend's request was going to aid us in getting into the dining room.

"As you can see, my good fellow," Holmes said, "this man is a doctor and is working with the City of London's Department of Proper Health Services. There have been several complaints about the size of the rats in your kitchen. Now, unless you want him to inspect said kitchen and shut you down post haste, I would suggest that you look the other way while I see Mr. Mullberry."

"Yes, quite," I quickly added." It has been reported that the rats are the size of small terriers. Very unsanitary. Very bad for business in such a fine establishment. I'd hate to shut you down in the middle of such a crowded lunch. It might cause some consternation with your members."

In the meantime, Holmes had been using my distraction to observe his quarry. Then my companion slipped away, leaving me to further occupy and intimidate the good fellow as the detective marched over to the table. Mullberry was an obese man, poorly dressed in an ill-fitting frock coat. The detective walked up to him most deliberately so that everyone dining would notice. I could hear his conversation quite clearly.

"Allow me to introduce myself. I am Sherlock Holmes and I would like a few words with you about your business on the Thames."

"I don't care who you are. I don't know you. You leave me alone right now."

"I don't think so, Mullberry. You will talk to me or else I will very loudly point out what a fraud you are posing as a gentleman member of this club.

"Why, sir, you assault me," Mullberry sputtered.

Holmes leaned in closer. "That's 'insult you' and I will do more than that right now. Your coat is the coat of a poseur, very thread-bare and frayed at the edges and your ascot is improperly tied. Your double-breasted vest is missing one stud. A true gentleman wears one ring, whereas your four rings betray how ostentatious you are. You have been eating with your elbows on the table during your entire meal. A gentleman covers his mouth with a napkin to remove any fish bones he finds, not pick his teeth with his fingers."

Mullberry was totally perplexed. "We can keep this between ourselves, can't we?"

The detective leaned in even closer. "Certainly. Now, about your recently purchased warehouse, where did you obtain the funds to buy it?"

"I won the money fair and square gambling."

"Sir, do you play me for a fool? You could never win that amount of money and walk out of a gaming house alive."

"Oh, I forgot, I got a real big inheritance from me old auntie. Then I went to several gaming houses and won just a little at each and every one." His face was turning red.

"So, you are either the luckiest man in England or someone gave it to you then."

Mullberry looked extremely uncomfortable.

"I will state that it was given to you. And who might that have been?"

"I don't know, sir, honestly. It was all done by some mean-looking thugs. It was always done at night."

"Do you recall if your benefactor was left-handed or right-handed?"

"What does have to do with anything?" Mullberry was looking around to see if any of the patrons seated near him were taking notice of this interrogation.

"It matters to me. That's all you need to know."

"I... I don't remember."

"I suggest you do remember," Holmes' voice became louder.

"I, um, I think that he handed me the money in an envelope in his left hand. I'm pretty sure of that. Yes, left hand. Or maybe right hand."

"What were they wearing?"

"Wearing? I don't know. A pea coat or something. You know, like a dock worker. The two of them approached me in an alley outside a tavern in the upper East End. I was drinking a lot, you know. I really don't remember much, except that they liked to stand in the shadows. It was such a good and sound offer. I was going to get my own warehouse where I could unload and store cargo. I was going to be the boss. I had to do it." The poor man was now fidgeting noticeably in his chair.

"Exactly what do you import and store in your warehouse, Mr. Mullberry?" said Holmes.

"It's a lot of Chinese stuff, bowls, plates, cups, vases, small tables, and things. That's all. People like that China stuff. I'm an honest business man," he pleaded, beads of sweat rolling down his face and onto his collar.

"Lastly, do you know two men called Dead Fish Barney and Pete the Greek?"

"No, sir, I truly don't."

"Then, there is no further need for this conversation. I bid you good day," said my companion, as three waiters appeared behind him.

Holmes and I returned to Baker Street, slowly climbing its seventeen steps to the second floor. An hour later, as we sat smoking a bowl, Mrs. Hudson knocked on the door to announce that Inspector Lestrade was here wishing to speak with us. My companion thanked her and said that it was all right to let him enter.

The Inspector wasted no time, waving his bowler emphatically in his hand. "Holmes, what in Hades are you doing? I've an official complaint about you from the St. Thomas Club. You remember, the one you asked me about this very morning and said that you weren't going to cause any trouble in. You have to stop bothering very important business men in their private club, or I'll have you arrested for being a public nuisance, trespassing, disturbing the peace, and— I'll think of some more things later. If this is connected with that case down by the Thames, just stop all these silly questions about a murder case that will never be solved."

The veins bulged in my friend's neck. "So, you want to simply write this off because those murdered men weren't merchants who your coppers take apples from? Or affluent politicians, or well connected business men? Those murdered souls were honorable men. Those men have names. And I will do what you apparently can't. Good day, Inspector."

Holmes turned away from Lestrade, walked over to the small table by the window and picked up his pipe. The Inspector mumbled something under his breath and left. The air reeked of anger and resolve.

Later that evening, I walked into the setting room as Holmes was putting on his heavy coat and familiar hat. "Are we going somewhere?" I inquired.

"Yes, Watson, I must go back to the scene of the crime. I'm sure there's something I missed. All I have so far is a bunch of meaningless names, no motive and no trail to follow. I am no closer to solving my friend's murders than I was when we started."

"Can I be of any assistance?" I said.

"Watson, I would be most grateful for another pair of eyes."

We secured a carriage and headed off for the Thames. Holmes revealed to me that he wanted to survey the scene during the night, when the crime occurred. The Hansom stopped after arriving at the river and parked under the balustrade. Before going down the steep bank, we both lit the lanterns that we brought along. The lights cast an eerie glow in the fog and mist.

"Holmes, are you sure that going down there in the dead of night is such a good idea?"

A simple 'yes' was his answer. I knew that disagreeing with him would be pointless. We cautiously slid down the embankment, careful not to slip or fall.

The first thing the detective noticed was that all of the lights on both sides of the Thames in this location were not lit. They were all blacked out, something he would never have noticed during the day. Holmes suddenly brought his finger to his mouth. "Shhh," he hissed. "Watson, quickly turn your lantern down as low as you can and put it behind your back."

My friend cupped his hand to his ear and leaned forward. You could faintly hear what sounded like the regular rhythm of oars out on the river. But there were no boat lights to be seen. The sound gradually faded. He then turned his lantern up and I followed suit. When he arrived at the river's edge, he crouched down to closely examine the soft, muddy ground. With his gloved hand he began to pick through the flotsam and jetsam strewn by the last tide. A piece of rope, bottles and excrement tangled up in weeds and paper. To his left he spied a small, jagged plank broken off of a larger crate. He carefully brought it up to his lantern to better see the markings burnt into its side.

"This water-logged piece of wood must have been washing in and out with the tide. It wasn't here when I surveyed the scene that morning. Look at this, Watson, the markings burnt onto this plank. Too bad it is only a small broken piece off of the entire crate. I can make out, 'OUTH' and

'RICA'." I could see that the detective was retreating into his memory rooms to decipher what this might mean and if it had any bearing on the case.

"Well, the last word could be 'America,'" said I. "And the first word 'South'."

"Perhaps, Watson, perhaps."

Holmes continued to look around. There, to the far left of the mostly washed away impression of where Pete's body had fallen, his light reflected off a mud-caked button half-hidden by the ever-present algae, laying just at the edge of the tide's grasp. He picked it up and ran his thumb over it to clean off the moist soil. It appeared to be a gold-gilded button with some sort of worn, scuffed crown and another scratched imprint. He put it in his pocket and continued to carefully scour the scene for a half hour and then slowly climbed back up the steep embankment by lantern light.

"Watson, I know this a special favor to ask at this time of night, but could I drop you off at the London Council Hall of Records so that you can make an inquiry for me?"

"Holmes, you know that the Council Hall building will be closed at this time of night. No one will be there."

"Dear Watson, I am very confident that, with your influence and contacts, that you know someone who can return there, meet you, and do you the courtesy of finding this information, even at this late hour."

For the first time in days, I could see the old fire in his eyes. "Holmes, I will gladly undertake this mission for you." I could now detect a slight grin wind across his narrow lips.

Upon my successful return to Baker Street with the information that my companion had requested, I hung up my hat and coat and then relayed the information to Holmes. He was very appreciative for the information and for my efforts. He then bade me good night, turned, and walked across the sitting room. He picked up his Stradivarius and cradled it under his chin. I said, 'good night,' but I knew my companion didn't hear me. Retreating to my room, I prepared myself for sleep. It was about ten when I got into bed. I could hear the music from his violin wafting in from the sitting room. Holmes was inevitably standing next to window, playing for the falling rain. My second best friend, my bull pup, quickly retreated to his favorite spot under my bed. At most times, Holmes' music calmed him. Gradually, I dozed off, only to be awoken by the forceful, angry tones of Wagner, his favorite composer. Getting back to sleep was slightly more difficult.

I next opened my eyes when I had to answer nature's call. Staring at the small mantle clock; it showed three-forty two, the veritable middle of the night. The music was more muted, almost like a funeral dirge. At first, I couldn't identify the tune; then it came to me. It was one of Holmes' own compositions that he hardly ever played. The solemn melody helped me to quickly fall back into Morpheus' embrace.

Approximately seven in the morning I awoke. Pushing back the heavy blanket, I sat up at the edge of the bed, my feet searching for my slippers on the floor. As I lathered up to shave at the hand bowl, it occurred to me that I no longer heard the violin strains from across the hall. I hurriedly shaved and dressed. A creaky floor board just prior to the doorway announced my arrival.

In the sitting room, dimly lit by a sun that was struggling to rise, I spied on the table the untouched dinner and, I assumed, a cold pot of tea that Mrs. Hudson had left for him. It rested on the acid-stained, deal-topped table next to two thick tomes. One was *Dunbar's Complete Book of Etiquette.* Diagonally on top of that was *Colonel Monstery's Self-defense for Gentlemen.* I suddenly recalled how my friend once summed them up for me. He said that a gentleman must know how to fence, box, shoot, ride, and swim. But above all, should always carry himself gracefully.

It was then that I wondered if my friend had partaken of his seven percent solution. I spied his Moroccan leather case still on his desk in the corner. He always said that his habit was necessary at times to coalesce the torrent of thoughts that swept through his mind like a raging river and then arrange the little bits into whole theories. Holmes was pacing with his pipe clenched firmly between his teeth, most certainly unaware that its bowl was exhausted of its strong, black tobacco. Deep in concentration, his eyes were distant and blank. I could see it was one of Holmes' intense moments. My friend's moods were a river with ebbs and tides.

"Watson, good morning. Could you quickly go down to the street and hail one of my Irregulars. I see one across the way, huddled next to the stoop. Instruct him to run as fast as he can to Scotland Yard and fetch Inspector Lestrade and tell the Inspector to meet us here immediately. And Watson, give him a couple of pence now and tell him he will get a few pence later in the day depending on how quickly he can run."

Holmes knew how upset I got at times that he used those street urchins as his own personal army, his eyes and ears about London. And now he wants to give a total of five pence to this boy for a simple task. I usually coughed or expelled a deep breath to signal my displeasure, but I could hear the gravity of his tone and thought better of it.

In twenty minutes, my friend had freshened up and dressed. He sat silently in his favorite wing-backed chair, now positioned by the window where he stared down at the street. Upon seeing the police carriage, he sprang to his feet; grabbed his silver-topped, thick cane, his Inverness cape and the deer stalker cap. He walked quickly to the small table, opened the drawer, and withdrew his Webley pistol. It was not often that my companion armed himself to go out.

"Watson, please bring your service revolver."

I returned to my room as quickly as I could, grabbed my coat and bowler hat, and retrieved my Mark III from the dressing table. I paused to pick up my umbrella. Stepping out of my room, I found the detective had already exited the front door.

Before getting into the police wagon, Holmes told the officer our destination. The detective eschewed the usual appellation of greeting as he was self-absorbed in thought as we pulled away. It was Lestrade who broke the silence.

"And where might we be going this dreary morning?" said Lestrade. "I pray it isn't to start a ruckus in a posh gentleman's club or a row in another brothel in the East End, as we seem to be headed that way. I don't need any more trouble out of you this early in the morning, as my reputation will surely begin to take a tumble."

"No, Inspector, we are about to solve the unsolvable crime. It will add to your dauntless reputation." Holmes turned his head to stare out the wagon window and again cloaked himself in silence.

Approximately twenty minutes later, we had crossed the bridge over the Thames, going past the spot where the murders had taken place, and ended up on the other side of the river. Our wagon stopped in front of the six-foot gate and columns that held the familiar sign, Her Majesty's Royal Naval Port Of London Office Of The Harbor Master.

"Good God, Holmes, what do you have in mind coming here? If you are planning to make a scene I'll have no part of it."

"Patience, Inspector, all will be revealed in time," the detective said.

After disembarking, I said to my friend, "We have already been here and been escorted out. Although they were most discourteous, they had nothing to say that would help us with this case."

"At the time, no, but I think they will be most helpful this time."

Holmes approached the front gate, a wrought-iron fence with ornamental spears protruding along its top railing that completely surrounded the two-story, wood-slat building. He grabbed the gate and shook it, only to find that it was locked. I saw a look of frustration on my friend's face, then one of the burly sailors who'd accosted us the day before exited the building.

"Hey, you there, go away. This is Navy property," said the man as he started towards us.

"Watson, this is our key."

The navy man stopped just short of where we all stood.

"Marston, isn't it?" said Holmes. "Could I trouble you to come over here a moment?" I could see the detective staring intently at the man's coat. But Marston hesitated and his hand went to a large ring of keys suspended from his belt.

"What are you talking about?" he said with a sneer. "Why should I be doing anything for the likes of you?"

"I assure you that I will make it very worth your while," Holmes added.

Unnoticed to anyone else, he reached behind his back and took my umbrella from my hand and slipped his cane into my other hand. "Watson, would you please be kind enough to hand me all of the money in your wallet?"

Reluctantly, I removed my wallet from my inner jacket pocket and gave all my pound notes to my companion; though for the life of me I didn't know why. Holmes clenched the money tightly.

"Good sir, I will give you all of this if I can be allowed in to see the Harbor Master immediately."

Holmes held the notes several inches outside the gate, just beyond Marston's reach. The First Mate cautiously moved closer, eyeing the three of us and the handful of money. Slowly, he leaned forward and reached through the bars to take hold of the money. It was then that Holmes thrust the crook of the bumbershoot through the bars, hooking the man's neck and pulled him forward violently. Marston's head smashed solidly against the iron bars. The First Mate slumped to the ground. My companion knelt down, repositioned the umbrella and hooked the ring of keys off the man's belt, pulling them towards us and through the bars to gain entrance. My companion handed my pounds back to me.

"See here, Holmes," Lestrade said, stepping forward. "What do you think you're doing?"

My friend ignored him and unlocked the gate.

Holmes clenched the money tightly.

As we entered, Marston began to stir. Holmes then handed my umbrella back to me, retrieved his cane, raised it up and smashed it down hard across the man's head.

"What the bloody hell," said Lestrade. "He's a Naval First Mate, for Queen's sake."

"I care little for his so-called rank, Inspector," Holmes said. "Did you notice his peculiar gait? Look down at his boots. The soles are heavily worn on the insides of his shoes just as the ones that I observed at the banks of the Thames." He stooped and picked up the man's left arm. "And this, no doubt, is his dominant hand, as demonstrated by his wearing his revolver holstered on his left leg. The keys were on that side as well."

Lestrade's mouth worked in apparent frustration. "But it's no crime being left handed."

Holmes eyed the Inspector for several seconds, then said, "If you recall, I pointed out when we were down at the scene of the murders that the killer of Barney delivered the blows with his left hand, as did one of the mysterious men who attacked Watson and myself yesterday on our way to see you. Now, please be so kind as to slap the derbies on him."

Lestrade stood there silently assessing the situation, his lower lip jutting outward in contemplation.

"Be quick about it, man," Holmes said. "There's work to be done; murderers to catch."

After a few seconds more, Lestrade heaved a sigh, bent down, and handcuffed Marston. "All I can say is you had better be right about this, Holmes, or we will all be in a pickle."

"Quite right, Inspector," Holmes said. "But to quote Cervantes, 'let us not throw the rope in after the bucket.'"

Lestrade stood up and appeared befuddled. "What in blazes are you talking about?"

Holmes peered at the man and then said, "If you want to apprehend those responsible for the murders of Dead Fish Barney and Pete the Greek, as well as untold crimes against Queen and country, you must do exactly as I direct. Otherwise, all will be lost."

Lestrade's mouth again worked nervously.

Holmes waited a few moments more, then said, "Might I suggest that you summon your man to stand guard over this prisoner."

"Listen, Holmes, if you think I'm going to let you go charging into the Harbor Master's office, then you're sadly mistaken."

"Inspector," the tone of the detective's voice clearly signaled that there would be no further argument. Their eyes met, locked in an intense stare. "For Queen and country."

Lestrade's lips drew up into a confused frown and he whistled to summon the driver of the police carriage over, instructing him keep watch on Marston, who was still unconscious.

Holmes nodded in approval. "Now, Inspector, I need you to stand by that doorway and wait for exactly eight minutes. Once those eight minutes has elapsed, and not one minute before, I want you to enter through that door and announce your presence in a very loud and authorative voice. Do you understand?"

"What in the blooming hell..."

"Do you understand?" Holmes said forcefully.

Lestrade swallowed, glanced around, and then nodded. The three of us made our way up the short path to the building.

"Eight minutes," Holmes reiterated. "And not one moment before."

Lestrade nodded, took out his pocket watch, and positioned himself by the door to the two-story building.

Holmes nodded once again and we went inside.

"Holmes," I said. "What are we doing?"

"Not now, Watson."

We climbed the stairs to the second floor in silence. As we reached the cluttered second floor room, Jenkins, the other First Mate, was walking towards the stairs. We all stopped abruptly.

"Watson, we have found our second killer. Notice that he is missing a gold crown and anchor button from his right sleeve and that he has a fresh wound on his cheek. He lost the button on the shore of the Thames, obviously wrestling with Pete, and he received the injury from me when I struck him with the whip."

Jenkins touched the scratch and frowned. "I owe you for that one." He quickly drew a pistol and pointed it at us. "Empty your pockets and throw anything you have down the stairway. And be very careful how you do it."

I slowly removed my service revolver from my coat pocket, held it between two fingers, and threw it down the stairway behind me.

"You too, Mister Holmes." He waved his Navy Colt at us. "And put down that fancy walking stick."

My companion bent down slowly and set his cane on the floor. Raising himself up, he put his left hand in his coat pocket and began to fumble around. "My pistol is in here somewhere." This distraction allowed him to slip his right hand into his other pocket, grip his revolver, and fire off a shot through his coat. The bullet hit the First Mate square in the chest. He slumped to the floor.

Holmes rushed over to the bleeding man, knelt, and cradled his head. Jenkins was having trouble breathing and was gurgling blood.

"Watson, come here," Holmes said.

I joined my friend, bending over to inspect the wound. Standing, I could only shake my head.

Holmes looked down at the dying man. "I suggest that you might want to confess your sins, Jenkins. It appears that you don't have much time."

The First Mate continued to gasp for breath as his eyes began to flutter and roll upwards.

"Focus on me, man," Holmes demanded. "I want to hear you utter his name. You know to whom I refer." Those last words seemed to have been dragged from Hades itself.

Jenkins' head dropped to one side, his vacant stare resembled the bulging eyes of a river trout that would now never close.

Holmes picked up his cane and stood, gesturing toward the office in the far corner. "Come, Watson, we still have one more quarry to bring to ground."

"Who?" I asked. Then a familiar voice rang out.

"That's far enough, gents," Captain Payne said as he stepped into the room holding a long-barreled revolver.

"Your two cohorts are either in custody or dead, Captain," Holmes said. "And you'll be joining them soon enough with an appointment at the gallows."

The Harbor Master's face took on a mirthful expression. "I think not. It'll look so clean and easy to figure out. You two came up here and got in a tussle with Jenkins. Shot him dead, and then threatened to kill me. So, I had to shoot you both in self-defense."

Holmes continued to march across the room. "And what fool do you think will believe that story?" He was only a few meters from the other man when Payne lifted the revolver and cocked back the hammer.

"That's far enough." He jiggled his revolver at Holmes. "Now, pull that pistol carefully out of your pocket; real slow with your other hand so you don't try the same trick on me that you did on Jenkins."

With his gloved left hand, Holmes reached across his body and gently removed his Webley from out of his right pocket.

"Now, throw it into the corner over there." He motioned to the far wall behind him which held the stacked life preservers. "And drop that bloody stick." My companion let his heavy cane fall from his hand."

Payne's face twisted into a leering grin. "Now you two walk nice and slow over to that wall there."

As Holmes and I walked, he indicated to the two wooden crates piled on top of each other. "Are these ready to go to storage? Too much traffic on the other side of the Thames last night to get them to Mullberry's warehouse?"

I saw that the boxes were marked Destination Johannesburg South Africa.

There was a look of surprise on Payne's face. "You know a bit too much about naval business, Mister Holmes." He emitted a sonorous breath, then asked, "And who else have you been talking to besides your bedfellow here?"

"See here, man," I said.

"Shut up," Payne said. He gestured with the pistol again. "Who else knows?"

"Who else knows about your insidious scheme that included the tragic death of my two friends, correct?" Holmes said with disdain. "And about your shipping gun powder from China to the rebels in the second Boer War, contained in these crates."

"Answer my question now," the Harbor Master said. "Or I'll put a bullet in the good doctor here."

Suddenly from below we heard a scuffling sound, accompanied by the stentorian announcement, "this is Inspector Lestrade of Scotland Yard."

It was just enough to shock Payne, who began to turn toward the stairway. Holmes, planting his feet solidly on the wood floor, reached back with both arms, grabbed the top crate and shoved it forward. It tumbled to the floor, splitting open, but not far enough to reach Payne. As the crate cracked open, porcelain vases came crashing to the floor, breaking into many pieces, scattering about the floor like a jigsaw puzzle, revealing mounds of black gun powder.

Payne whirled back toward us, discharging the revolver as he turned. The round shot by me, missing my head by scant inches.

It was then that Holmes made his move. My companion pounced like a jungle cat at the Captain. Holmes' unleashed a powerful, chopping blow to the Harbor Master's wrist, causing the gun to drop from his hand. Payne stumbled back against the small table. Without hesitation, he reached up and grabbed the Midshipman's sword hanging on the pegs on the wall. He began swinging it wildly, flaying the air in front of my friend. Holmes shuffled backwards, always keeping his eyes on the blade. The sword came inches from his face. The next swing cut the right side of his open over-coat. Holmes began to circle the room, always keeping both feet on the floor in case he had to change directions quickly. He was now standing over his discarded cane.

Suddenly, he reached up and threw his deerstalker cap at Payne. The Navy man instinctively ducked. My companion quickly retrieved his cane from the floor.

"You think that walking stick's going to help you?" Payne said.

The Captain lashed out, but his blade was blocked by the detective. The sharp sword sliced thin slivers of wood from the cane. I knew that Holmes' weapon was more than an ordinary walking stick. His heavy cane was made of a circular brass tube which was then wrapped in oak. It was now the detectives' turn to parry and thrust. My friend was gaining the upper hand, although Payne was steadily whittling down the wooden shell on his cane. The duel was fierce with neither man giving quarter. Still moving in a circular path, Holmes positioned himself in front of the eastern window where the sun had risen above the London skyline.

Unexpectedly, my companion gripped his long coat with his left hand, holding it out to his side like the wing of a giant bat. Even though he was squinting into the sun, the Harbor Master saw this as his opportunity and charged at Holmes. As the Captain lunged, the detective swirled, stepping aside with the grace of a matador, avoiding the straight forward attack. Payne missed and smashed through the glass pane. His scream accompanied him all the way down, ending with a ghastly abruptness.

I hurried to the window. Leaning out over the sill, my eyes were greeted with a most disturbing sight. Payne was suspended six-feet above the ground, skewered on the spikes of the metal perimeter fence

"My God, the man is impaled on the fence," I said.

Just then we heard the blustering sound of Lestrade running up the stairs. He emerged at the top, glanced down at the dead man on the landing, and then back to us, a look of sheer panic frozen on his face.

"What in the devil happened?" he asked.

Holmes reached down and picked up his hat, taking the time to brush it off before replacing it on his head.

"The killers of Dead Fish Barney and Pete the Greek have been brought to justice, Inspector," Holmes said. "And a treacherous traitor of England has met his just fate as well." He gestured toward the window. "I'm sure that the man you have in custody, Marston, will give you the full details once he's interrogated."

"Now just a blooming minute," Lestrade said.

Holmes smiled ruefully. "In the absence of his forthcoming confession, allow me to elucidate."

"Please do," I said.

Holmes took a deep breath. "Harbor Master Payne, obviously in a bit of a snit for being placed in such an ignominious duty assignment, soon saw the possibility of pilfering supplies of military grade gunpowder, bound for the Royal Navy's ships and cannons, to sell it on the black market to aid the South African Republic rebels in the latest Anglo-Boer War."

Lestrade's eyebrows rose like twin caterpillars. "But, that'd be treason."

Holmes nodded. "Certainly, it was not a very patriotic move for a Royal Navy captain, but ingenious just the same. Who would suspect the Harbor Master of being a smuggler, when he was the one entrusted to stop such activities?"

Lestrade frowned. "But how did those two buggers under the bridge fit into this?"

"May I remind you that those 'two buggers' were my friends." Holmes paused and Lestrade muttered something akin to an apology. Holmes continued. "It was Payne's two First Mates who murdered my friends under the bridge while he watched. It was also they who rousted the patrons of that East End tavern looking for Pete and Barney. To aid in his scheme, Payne made certain that all the lights were extinguished along the Thames, so that the activity of the crates of gunpowder being unloaded from the ships anchored in the middle of the river would go unnoticed. The crates were brought over to the warehouse of his accomplice, Mullberry. He'd been hiring itenerant workers to unload the stolen goods. Payne was using light barges with no running lights in the dead of night to ferret his unregistered and purloined goods. The heavy mist and fog gave him more cover."

"Criminey," Lestrade said. "A brilliant scheme."

"And a traitorous one as well," I added.

Holmes got a distant look in his eye. "Pete and Barney must have heard the barges, or possibly seen them, as they sailed down to Mullberry's warehouse. Most importantly, they found a crate that was lost overboard and washed up to shore where they were camped for the night. My two friends evidently went down to the warehouse to see if there would be a reward. Mullberry began to panic, knowing that if the word of the pilfered gunpowder spread, the whole smuggling operation might be exposed. He contacted Payne, who sent his two brutes, Marston and Jenkins, out to find the displaced men who had the crate."

Holmes paused again, his expression taking on a pained cast.

"The men at the bar agreed that the two brutes who'd come in had an official looking bearing about themselves. But they were not police. It was their Navel training. In their ham-handed search for Pete and Barney, they evidently murdered the first homeless man they found, but not before undoubtedly forcing him to tell of any other men usually camped along that embankment."

"But how did you connect all this to Payne?" Lestrade asked.

I had the same question burning in my mind.

"Elementary. If you recall, when I visited the scene of the murders, I observed some relatively fresh black powder… gun powder. It was obviously not from a pistol. It was from the crate found by Pete and Barney. At first, I assumed the pieces of porcelain were just part of the debris that had washed up on shore. But the mound of gun powder still interested me.

"Upon the night I revisited the Thames, the scheme unfolded like a Chinese parasol. First, I recalled seeing a few half-hidden billets on Payne's desk from Africa. The smashed plank I found upon my return visit to the scene of the crime confirmed my suspicions when I deciphered 'OUTH—RICA' burnt into the wood as its final destination to be 'South Africa'." He shook his head sadly. "Hail Britannia. A man in the service of his Queen and country ultimately betraying both, feeling, no doubt, from his warped and evil perspective, forgotten. Stuck behind a desk in this smelly port, passed over for promotion. Undoubtably, he and Mullberry had been in business for quite a spell. Who knows what other goods they might have been pilfering for their own gain?"

"Bloody traitors," muttered Lestrade. "I'm going to send a detachment to grab Mullberry as soon as I get back to the Yard. We'll grab that bloody bugger and I'll squeeze him and this Marston bloke until one of them cracks."

"As I'm certain they will, Inspector," Holmes said. He turned to me. "Watson, I do believe our work here is done." He began walking toward the door and I fell into step next to him. He appeared more somber than I had ever seen him.

"At the very least," I said in way of amelioration, "you were able to bring to justice those responsible for killing your friends."

"They got off easy, Watson," he said, the words sounding as if it were the first relaxed breath of a once drowning man.

We walked slowly to the doorway, and then stopped abruptly at the landing. Holmes stared down at the supine body of Jenkins.

"It is times like this that I wished I believed in the afterlife, Watson, so that Payne and his cohorts would burn for all eternity in the fires of Hell."

He then turned and began walking down the stairs.

THE END

THE STORY BEHIND THE STORY

This is my second visit to Victorian England with Sherlock Holmes and Doctor John Watson. This time, instead of the usual trope of someone appearing at 221 B Baker Street either entrapped in a dire situation or embroiled in a mystery, this story begins with one of Holmes' Baker Street Irregulars bursting through the detective's door with news of a double murder by the Thames. The victims are two derelicts, associates and long time confidants of Holmes that he had befriended, while in disguise, as he traversed the seedy underbelly of London's East End. Now the game was afoot. This is the portrait of an extremely intense Sherlock Holmes. He could not let this murder go unsolved. This time it was personal.

In retrospect, I learned everything about life through comic books, TV, movies, and Ace pulp fiction novels. Now, along with my lifelong friend, Michael Black, we have both had the honor of writing two Sherlock Holmes' stories for Airship 27. Plus, together, we created the adventurer, Doc Atlas. Doc has appeared in four novellas, Mike's novel *Melody of Vengeance* and the co-authored *The Incredible Adventures of Doc Atlas*, an omnibus of five novellas that begins in the Yucatan peninsula in 1947 and concludes in Washington, D.C. in 1951 at the McCarthy hearings.

For more information on Doc Atlas go to www.doc-atlas.com. All credit for that unique site goes to the master of the webs, Kurt Wahlner.

Airship 27 has recently announced that it will be the exclusive home of Doc Atlas. Mike and I are currently working on a new Doc novel and are extremely excited to be working with Ron Fortier on the new adventures of the Golden Avenger.

Lastly, I wish to acknowledge Ron Fortier, publisher of Airship 27, for allowing me to travel, once again, with the Great Detective. Ron's encouragement and exceptional editing skills have made me a better writer.

I would be remiss if I didn't thank Brian Hester, DC., Danica Oparnica, ANP. PMHNP., and Keith Sutton, MS. FNP. APRN-BC. who have kept me on the path to good health and sanity. But it has been written that to be truly sane, you must embrace your insanity.

I have to thank Carl Wayne Ensminger for research that placed me walking the streets of Victorian London.

My eternal gratitude goes out to Michael A. Black, my best friend since we met as youths at the top of a dirt hill. The adventures that we shared and Mike's prolific body of work producing thirty novels, dozens of short stories and numerous articles prompted me to pursue my dreams of writing. No man could ever have a greater friend for life.

None of this would be possible without the unconditional love of my lovely wife, Susan Marie Koss Lovato. She allows me to indulge in my fantasy worlds while being a beacon always showing me the way home.

And thank you to Elaine Mary Michels Lovato, my mom, who started this whole thing.

RAYMOND LOUIS JAMES LOVATO loves writing pulp fiction with his lifelong friend author Michael A. Black. Ray also enjoys traveling the world with his lovely wife, Susan. Years ago, on a five-hour flight to Sint Maarten, he was inspired to draft an homage to Doc Savage, the Man of Bronze. After presenting the first chapter as a serial birthday gift to his best friend, the Adventures of Doc Atlas was born. Black wrote the first Doc Atlas novel, A Melody of Vengeance, as a tribute to the Pulp Age of Heroes.

Sherlock Holmes

in

"The Adventure of the Apologetic Assassin"

By
David Friend

f the many sketches I have placed before the public concerning my friend Mr Sherlock Holmes, several have involved happenings which many casual observers would doubtless consider impossible. From the matter of Mr Grimesby Roylott and his curious menagerie, to the Thor Bridge incident, these have been solved by the only man, in my belief, who was equal to the challenge. Holmes, with his formidable faculties for deduction and logical synthesis, and penchant for the original and outré, had made such occurrences his speciality.

A mystery of a similarly peculiar import—and one I have meant to relate for some time—was the Erasmus Brew case. Even now, as I write this, I am chilled by the seemingly preternatural phenomenon which confronted Holmes and I on that day in 1889. A man found alone and stabbed in his study, the door locked and barricaded by chairs and a table, while several men vigilantly guarded the room from outside. With both murder and suicide ruled out, it could only have been an act of a disturbing and otherworldly provenance.

The case presented itself in the middle of August. I had not seen Holmes since the Leander Forge case some weeks earlier and had been dividing my time exclusively between my professional duties and my wife. After a particularly arduous morning of paperwork, I was relieved to find my afternoon to be free of any further engagements. I bid farewell to my colleague Dr Jackson, took the train from Paddington to Marylebone and returned swiftly to Baker Street. It felt strange, walking such familiar steps yet knowing they would no longer lead me home.

From the moment the dear Mrs Hudson admitted me within, I heard the sorrowful strains of Holmes at play on his recently purchased Stradivari. I found him in his rooms upstairs, standing by the fireplace, his back to me. He was apparently oblivious to my presence, his tall thin figure clad in a silk dressing gown. I listened quietly as I knew how severely he looked upon interruptions but, to my surprise, the whining ceased as abruptly as any disturbance I could myself have made.

Without so much as a glance over the shoulder, he said, "It has been some time, my dear Watson. I trust only good reasons have kept you away."

I recoiled in surprise. "Holmes!" I said, aghast. "How did you know I was here? You could not have heard my footsteps above the music!"

"Unquestionably not," he said, turning to face me at last. "Do you have a hypothesis?"

I was at a loss to explain it.

His mouth twitched into a smile of amusement—one of those fleeting jerks which only happened when he was properly pleased. "My good-natured Boswell, I was standing by the window a few moments ago and saw you outside."

With a familiar resignation, I took my usual place in an armchair. I was used to being outdone by my friend, though there were times when I managed to impress him by applying his methods myself. Having witnessed his efforts at such close quarters, I would be a fool not to have picked up a few of his tricks along the way.

"How is your lady wife?" he asked, but his voice did not hold any interest and I knew he was only asking to be polite. Since my marriage to Mary, whom I had met during the episode of the parcelled pearls, I had detected a quiet sort of irritability from my friend. It was almost as if he was not at all pleased that my new life of matrimony was keeping me occupied elsewhere. I had read of cases in the papers with which he had himself been engaged and I had, I admit, felt a stir of envy upon contemplating the adventures which he was enjoying alone.

I can report now that I was to accompany him further—the spectral hound case was only three months hence—but, at the time, I had every reason to believe that whatever collaboration we had shared was over. I was not aggrieved, however. In marriage, I had experienced something which I considered more than the pursuits Holmes and I had enjoyed. I had a wife who relied upon me and that felt satisfying. I had become used to a sense of pride and position. There would be no more adventures, I decided, with my friend Sherlock Holmes.

A knock at the door broke into my thoughts. It was the page boy.

"Please sir," he said in a reedy voice, "but there's a visitor for you."

"Show him in, Billy."

"He's outside, sir, in a cab. He wants you to see him there."

Holmes's brow folded into a frown. He was not amused but was, I think, intrigued. "Unorthodox, but very well," he murmured, standing. He drew off his gown, beneath which was a suit, then unhooked his coat and top hat.

Outside, the wind had arisen and I was happy to shelter within the cab. The man waiting there was spindly and middle-aged, perhaps undernourished, with an ashen face and thinning, matted hair. Although well-dressed, his coat-sleeves were jagged and his shoes were clearly worn.

Holmes gave our visitor—or perhaps we were his—a cursory glance and had barely taken his seat before he said, "You have never been married and you live alone. Despite your dishevelled appearance, you are, in fact, exceedingly wealthy, though do not rely upon many servants. You are unaccustomed to travelling, highly impatient, and are presently in fear for your life."

I looked at the man opposite but, to my amusement, he looked decidedly unimpressed, with not a flicker of surprise across his thin face. His brows then beetled together as though conferring with the other and seemed to decide it was time to speak.

"Your conclusions are correct, Mr Holmes, though you do convey them a little melodramatically. Your reasoning is also rather obvious." I glanced back at Holmes and saw his eyes flash with irritation. "If I had been married or had servants," our client went on, "and was used to people seeing me, I would care about my appearance. And though my clothes are rumpled and I wear them inelegantly, they are of good, expensive cloth, which means I must be wealthy. I have a pallid countenance and therefore do not often leave my home. The fact I have this morning indicates that my concerns are urgent, the reason I did not summon you by telegram is because I hate waiting for an answer, and I am fearful for my life as I have not left this hansom, even though your residence is a mere yard away. Now we have that tiresome business behind us, perhaps you can finally help me."

Holmes had recovered himself, but was clearly still put out. He enjoyed his piece of theatre as any veteran *primo uomo*. "If the matter that so concerns you is sufficiently interesting, I may just do so," said Holmes with no little hauteur.

As the cab moved on, the man looked without, his eyes searching the strangers as we passed them. "I do not want to stay in one place too long," he told us. He levelled his gaze at Holmes and his expression was one of a man who was truly desperate. "My name is Erasmus Brew. This morning, I received a letter." He fished out a piece of paper from his breast pocket and handed it across to my friend. "It was apparently penned by an assassin." His voice was calm, despite his fantastic words. "In it, he apologises to me, his next target."

Holmes read it and then passed it to me. Even after so many years, I can vividly recall the menacing message as though I had received it myself this very morning. The sense of purpose, in such a few bitterly blunt words, was in itself unnerving. I read the letter aloud, as though to prove to myself that I was not seeing things and it was actually true.

"*I am terribly sorry to tell you this, but I am going to kill you. It will happen very soon, so do not plan too far ahead. Best wishes, Your Killer.*"

Holmes's head was tilted back and his features looked more hawk-like than ever. "This assassin has a perverted sense of etiquette," he said. "It is singularly unconventional. Did this arrive with—?"

"There was an envelope, yes," said Brew, anticipating his question. Holmes pursed his lips and I could tell he was not amused. "It was typed," Brew went on, "not handwritten, and it was also hand-delivered. I have no enemies to speak of and this is the first threat I have received. I hope that has answered your next few questions."

Holmes gave him a cool stare. "Perhaps," he said suavely, "you would feel better served handling this affair yourself."

Erasmus Brew looked as though he had anticipated this also. "I have come to you for deductions I cannot make on my own, Mr Holmes."

It occurred to me that he was a churlish, undiplomatic and disputatious man and I was not surprised that somebody wanted him dead.

The afternoon sun was paling as we turned a corner into a quiet salubrious district of large Georgian houses and the cab drew to a halt. Holmes lurched out. I have always thought him strangely feline in his movements. His smirks and quirks and sudden jerks made it seem as though he could do anything of any sort at any moment.

Brew clambered out. As I did the same, I noticed he was staring fretfully at the horses.

"What's the matter?" I asked.

A shadow had crossed his face. "There was an incident," he said, "about six years ago. I was nearly run over by one of these things." He nodded weakly to the horses. "I was dawdling in the road and before I realised what was happening, the beasts were hurtling towards me. I was close enough to feel their breath."

"What did you do?" I asked.

His eyes were dimmed with recollection, as though he could see the scene just as clearly now. "My man, Cotter, quickly pulled me away."

"You were lucky," I agreed.

Brew did not seem so sure. "I've rarely left the house since," he said sadly.

Holmes was looking at him with interest, but a moment later Brew recovered himself. "I mustn't be out here too long," he murmured and showed us indoors. We found several men of a considerably lower class waiting in the hallway. "My guards," said Brew. "Courtesy of the road-house. They shall keep watch as I stay in here." He moved to a door and opened it. "This study will be locked and barricaded with my desk and anything else I can push against the door. With these men on sentry too, no one can reach me."

I thought this a little excessive but wanted to be polite. "'One who is wise is cautious'," I said, quoting Proverbs, as I often did when a patient was distressed.

He disappeared within and I heard the lock slide across and then the heavy movement of furniture. The guardsmen stared curiously at the door as chairs and other items were pushed against it.

"He's certainly being careful," I remarked.

One of the guardsmen laughed raspingly. He was a gaunt, dark beard-ed man with an angular jaw. His teeth were few, his mouth a thin line and strands of unkempt hair dangled over his forehead.

"I suppose you're wondering what the deuce is going on," I said to him. He shrugged as though he did not care to be told. "Have you met Mr Brew before, Mr …?"

"Spriggs," he said. "'E gets us to bring 'im beer. Too lazy to come down the road himself. He never likes to leave the house."

I nodded. It seemed Brew had been telling the truth. He really did re-main indoors.

I looked at the other men. A couple were sitting on the steps of the stairs, staring sullenly at their shoes, while the other four were leaning against the wall.

Just then, an elderly, diminutive woman with a pale, sagging face ap-peared. Holmes introduced himself and she explained she was Mr Brew's landlady, Mrs Haggerty. With a diffident rap on the study door, she called, "Mr Brew? Would you like a brew?"

No sound, from what I could hear, greeted her offer. She knocked again and then returned to us, her brow knotted with confusion.

"There's no answer."

Holmes twisted around to the study door. He knocked heavily and waited a few moments. His face tightened in a way I had not seen for some time. "Mr Brew!" He balled his fist and beat the door until the lumber rattled. It took a great deal of effort to burst the lock and even more to push the furniture aside. Even then, the door only opened a little and I am sure only someone of Holmes's slenderness could slide through.

A chest, a desk and a couple of chairs had been pushed against the door. It was not a large room and there were no windows. The wallpaper was brown and stained with smoke and the fireplace was empty, with handfuls of coal scattered about as though dropped there carelessly. A bookcase was leaning crookedly against the wall, its narrow shelves packed tight with many heavy tomes. A small armchair was placed in the corner, mottled and hunched, as though embarrassed to be there. There was one striking feature, however, which drew all eyes and sank every heart.

Erasmus Brew was in the middle of the room, slumped on the floor, a knife in his back.

Holmes stood stock still, staring down, his gaunt face an utter blank.

Earnestly, I stepped towards the body and bent over it. Brew's face was a pale mask of panic. His sightless, startled eyes were wide and alert, the lips twisted grimly in a silent scream. He looked as shocked as we felt.

"It must be suicide," said I. "Yet why would a man frightened of dying kill himself?"

Holmes remained wordless. His eyes rolled across the man's body as he inspected each inch in turn.

I ordered one of the men to summon the constabulary. Staring at the corpse, I felt the urge to close Brew's eyes, such was the horror which haunted them, but fought the impulse. "Perhaps," I said, "with his murder inevitable, he thought he should do it himself."

Holmes shook his head. "It wasn't suicide, Watson. He could not reach his back that way." He pointed and I followed his finger. It was true. The knife had been placed between the shoulder blades and was far too straight.

"Then how did he die?" I asked. "Nobody could have got to him—not unless they could walk through walls!"

I turned my head and eyed the walls cautiously. We would not be confronted by an apparent phantom until a little later that year, but my mind was recoiling even then. I like to think of myself as a pragmatic man, but I knew what science could not answer.

As he so often did, Holmes seemed to hear my thoughts. "I have told you before, Watson: once you eliminate the impossible, whatever remains, however improbable, must be the truth."

He withdrew into silence again and remained that way until an official arrived in the corpulent shape of Inspector Bradstreet. We had already met him twice in the past couple of months and he was again wearing a frogged coat and peaked cap.

I took the liberty of furnishing him with the facts and the Inspector's mouth pursed in puzzlement. "It's impossible," he said. "Nobody could have got into the room. With the door locked and barricaded and watched from without, there is no way in which this man could have been murdered."

"And yet, Inspector," said Holmes tersely, "since that is evidently the case, perhaps you would be so kind as to cease your twittering and allow me to focus on how it *did* happen."

Bradstreet looked like he was about to protest and I did not blame him. Holmes did not suffer fools gladly and he could be most impatient at times, particularly if people did not follow the same thoughts as he. I suggested we go to the kitchen.

Mrs Haggerty was weeping quietly as we entered it. I distracted her by asking for tea. We sat at a wooden, rickety table and I rubbed my hands together briskly. It was cold and the fire was not lighted. I glanced about the place. The walls were a pasty white and I detected a glimmer of rising damp crawling along the one before us. A stove, black and grimy and caked with coal dust, took up most of the space opposite, and the muddy mark of boots stained the floorboards beneath. The Inspector took his cup appreciatively, but Holmes did not seem to notice his at all. He was staring at the floor, as though inspecting the dirt which had fallen there.

"I'm so sorry," I said to the old lady. "How long have you worked for Mr Brew?"

Her brow crumpled as she crossed the years. "Since '86," she said.

Holmes had taken off his hat and had put it under his chair—a gesture, I believed, designed to make our listener forget about his higher status and to treat him as an equal. Deference, he had explained to me before, could conceivably cause a person to suppress information or to even forget it altogether due to anxiety. I have never met anyone who could put people at such ease—or, for that matter, rile so many others—than my friend and in this instance he was graciousness itself. Other than those who tried his patience, Holmes respected everyone, whatever class or age or sex. From the young boys he enlisted to uncover information to the common man on the cobbles and even to royalty.

"Any other staff?" he asked, but the old woman shook her head. "Are you not lonely?"

Mrs Haggerty shrugged. "Since Levi passed, I stay here a lot, where I have Mr Brew." She handed Holmes a china cup.

"Indeed," I said. "What took your husband, if I may ask?"

"I'm so sorry. How long have you worked for Mr Brew?"

The landlady suddenly looked grim. She had been reaching for my cup but now paused. "Scurvy," she said with regret. "I wanted to take him back to Altnaharra in Sutherland, where he was born."

I nodded understandingly. "My father was from Spinningdale." She did not seem to have heard me, lost as she was in her memories.

"He'd always wanted to see it again. If Levi had to die anywhere, it should have been there. But," she said on a sigh, "he was too stubborn. Didn't want to leave Mr Brew in the lurch, he said. Saw it as his duty to stay on, even at the very end. That was just like Levi, that was. I was very grateful to Mr Brew for letting him stay on." Her eyes filled with tears. "So very grateful."

I stood up and patted her on the shoulder consolingly. Holmes, who did not approve of emotion at the best of times, decided to leave the rest to Inspector Bradstreet.

"Why send a letter to someone you are about to kill, apologising for the very deed?" he said as we walked down the street. "Surely, all that would do is warn them!"

He hailed a cab and I wondered where we were to go. I was surprised, though a little disappointed, to discover it was Baker Street. I had hoped for something less leisurely but Holmes, it seemed, wanted nothing more than to seat himself in his armchair, lift his knees to his chest and cogitate. I stood at the window, the wind picking up as the night fell across the city. Deep, dull fog pressed against the glass as though it wanted to be let in.

I left my friend filling his pipe, went home to my wife and did not return again until morning. Upon entering, around eleven of the clock, I thought the fog had indeed intruded upon the rooms as I couldn't see for greyness. The whole place seemed caught in a heavy cloud of acrid smoke. It only began to clear when I threw open the windows and waved a Bradshaw at it.

"I thought you only had three!" I complained as the last of the tobacco smoke reluctantly drifted without.

Holmes was sitting, languid as ever, in his chair. His clothes were unchanged, his expression just as abstract, and his hand was clutching the briar as though he were determined to die with it.

"I do not mind admitting," he said casually, "that this particular case is proving altogether more taxing than I anticipated."

I moved out into the hall and collected the papers which Mrs Hudson had left there. "Let us see what the press has made of it," I suggested.

Holmes threw back his head and barked with laughter. It had a cynical hardness to it, though no doubt he was genuinely amused that I should be seeking guidance from such dubious quarters.

"My dear Watson," he said jovially, his mouth still twisted with mirth. "I beg you to desist. No doubt I will already have to suffer an account of this case in one of your colourful chronicles."

I returned with the papers and, also, the post. My friend was often inundated with requests for help. I offered an envelope to Holmes but he dismissed it with a wave. I was used to opening such correspondence myself and sat down on the opposite chair to do so. The letter staring back at me, however, was nothing like the kind we had received before.

"Holmes," I rasped. "This is …"

I unhooked my eyes from the dreadful note and turned to him. He was looking at me most keenly, having detected from my voice that something was wrong and even suspecting, I believe, the cause of my consternation. I handed the letter to him wordlessly. The letter had come from the apologetic assassin.

"Dear Mr Holmes," it read. *"Your interference has made it difficult for me to contemplate any other course than this. I shall be taking your life at the earliest opportunity. I am greatly sorry for the inconvenience of your death, as I am sure you would otherwise have been able to continue your impressive career. As you will no doubt appreciate, I cannot risk anyone uncovering my identity, particularly someone such as yourself. Kind Regards, Your Killer."*

Holmes cast the note aside and stood up. "If you would, cable Inspector Bradstreet and inform him that I will not be troubling with the case any longer. Ask him also to convey my apologies to Mrs Haggerty. And then tell the press."

I stared at him, perplexed. "You are saying—" The words stuck in my craw. "You are giving up?"

Without a further word, Holmes strode over to the table on the far side of the room and began setting up his laboratory. I watched him curiously and, I must admit, a little disbelievingly. Yet there was something about him which made me know he was speaking the truth. His movements were languid, with none of the tension and high energy which came when his mind was occupied with a problem.

I departed for the post office, my head heavy with wistful thoughts, the morning fog dissipating around me. My friend's reaction to the letter concerned me greatly. Rarely had Holmes exhibited such feelings as fear. Or maybe, I considered, it was remorse. As would be the case with Mr John Openshaw and Mr Hilton Cubitt of Ridling Thorpe Manor, Brew was a client whom my friend had failed. It also concerned me that a whole night of continued cogitation had apparently yielded no results. Could it be that his abilities were beginning to desert him? Perhaps Holmes had found all answers to the case so elusive that he had used the letter as an excuse to abandon his investigation.

The days which followed gave me no reason to believe otherwise. Holmes occupied himself with his scientific pursuits, beginning a monograph on the polyphonic motets of Lassus, and I was kept busy with my practice. The newspapers quickly forgot about the perplexing death of Erasmus Brew and turned their attention to other sensational matters.

The next time I visited Holmes, two Saturdays hence, he was without another case. I was so concerned that I decided to confront him on the issue.

"Holmes," I said, as he was bent over his chemistry set, "failure is not necessarily a negative occurrence. For instance, Newton failed at school. One mustn't be disheartened by such a thing."

My friend continued applying his instruments in silence and, for a moment, I did not think he would answer. "What are you waffling about, Watson?" he asked mildly.

I sighed. "I'm merely pointing out that your inability to solve the Erasmus Brew case is not—"

He looked up at once, his eyes aflame. I realised I had made a *faux pas*. It is not permissible to refer to an embarrassment, after all. He stood straight and a thin smile curved into place. "You believe I failed," he said. "My dear Watson, you do gravitate towards the most ridiculous conclusions." I looked on confusedly as he fetched his hat and stick from the stand. "We are due to be elsewhere."

I was as baffled by his behaviour as I was by the sealed room which had played such a devilish trick on our late client. You may countenance my astonishment as I realised it was to this very house that Holmes now led me. With a timorous chill, I clambered out of the dogcart and watched, perplexed, as he knocked on the door. It was soon opened by Inspector Bradstreet, tall and triumphant, and clearly eager to see my friend.

Holmes led us both into the study, where I stood nervously and eyed the old and withered armchair, stippled with dust and loosened threads, and the rickety table which Brew had pushed against the door for his own pitiful protection. Holmes called for the landlady and the poor woman looked shocked when she saw him, as though it were a distressing reminder of her employer's death.

"Mrs Haggerty, thank you for permitting us," he said graciously. "Inspector, arrest her."

Bradstreet stared widely at my friend as though he had cried out a curse. "What do you mean?" he said. "This dear lady is—"

"A cold-blooded killer, yes," said Holmes.

The old lady was staring at Holmes herself but it was through a prism of cold and clear calm.

"Mrs Haggerty, you told us your husband, Levi, had grown ill with scurvy and that you had wanted him to return to his birthplace of Altnaharra, Northumberland, to die but that he would not leave his employer. I am afraid that was a lie. I had an associate of mine, Langdale Pike, go there and search the parish records and determine whether a man named Levi Haggerty had been born in the hamlet between sixty and seventy years ago. According to my correspondence, there was no man by the name of Haggerty born there during that time. There was, however, a man named Levi. Levi Cotter."

"Cotter!" I ejaculated. "That was the name of Brew's man who had saved him all those years ago."

"I believe that man and this lady's husband were one and the same," said Holmes. "I researched Levi Cotter. He left Scotland in his twenties to find work in London, had married Beryl Haggerty and lived with her in Bethnal Green."

I turned and looked at the old lady with some shock. Her brows were knitted, her eyelids heavy and she was staring dreamily at the floor.

"He worked as Brew's man for many years," continued Holmes, "even as he became ill. It is my belief that Mr Cotter had asked Brew if he could retire and receive a small amount of money which would allow him to return to his birthplace and see out his final weeks. He even reminded Brew of the time he saved his life and would consider it a debt discharged. But Brew was an arrogant, heartless miser of a man whose parsimony can still be witnessed in this very room. He refused, not wanting to let a servant go and certainly not wanting to pay for services he would not receive.

"After Mr Cotter died, his wife," he gestured to the old lady lamely, "was not only bereaved but hungry for revenge." He stared at her squarely and her head lifted, the dull eyes meeting his. "You worked up some references and offered yourself as his replacement. Someone to cook and clean and fetch him tea. You had never met Brew, so he did not know you, though you still gave only your maiden name to avoid any connection to your husband—though, as all landladies, you still employed the appellation 'Mrs'. As the months turned into years, you dreamed of killing Brew. You just did not know how to do it. Ideally, you wanted him to know he would soon die. To look at his life and fear his death. Just as your husband had.

"The letter was the only way to do this. The apology was a conceit; an excuse to let Brew know that his end was near. Like all murderers, you needed an alibi. It was necessary for the murder to be committed after you had left the house. But how could this be achieved?"

I looked at Holmes curiously, keen to know whether he had truly uncovered the truth. His eyes shone with the excitement of all grand revelations, his stance erect and surging with energy.

"If one takes everything but the body out of the equation—the guards outside, the lock, the barricades—then the murder must have happened in precisely the same way. All the lock tells us is that no one could have entered. The only logical explanation is that Brew did it himself."

"But you said it wasn't suicide," I pointed out.

Holmes nodded calmly. "That's correct," he said. "Brew presumably wished to stay in the room for a long time and did what anyone else would do upon entering a room. He sat down." With a bony finger, he indicated the threadbare armchair in the corner. "In this chair, in fact, and sliced his back on the sharp knife placed there." He jerked the chair around so the back was exposed. Like the rest of it, the material was withered and weak. He poked a finger through a hole and it appeared at the other side, where he wiggled it playfully. "The blade was slid through," he explained, "balanced on the threads. The pressure of his body against it caused it to move upwards slightly, free of those threads, and when he stood up the knife came with him."

I shook my head in wonderment. "Holmes, that's remarkable," I said.

My friend lifted a hand to silence me. "That is not all," he added. "Panicking, Brew tried to reach the door and get help, but he couldn't make it through the barricades that he himself had placed there. Defeated, he died slumped in the middle of the room."

I registered this bleak information in silence. "How perfectly terrible," I said hollowly. "I presume this lady also sent you that letter. The one apparently penned by the assassin, apologising for making *you* the next target."

"Mrs Cotter was worried I would solve the case and wanted to scare me from it," he said. "I needed her to believe she had done so. I rather feared she would try and distract me by killing another to give more credibility to her fictitious assassin."

I frowned. "Why not just have her arrested?"

"I did not yet have the proof," he said with a shrug. "I only have it now because I instructed Spriggs and his friends to visit Brew's solicitor and offer their help to clear out his belongings. I knew from what I had seen in here that Brew was not only a miser but an inveterate hoarder who never turned out any of his possessions. Not even letters, which he would pile up in a small room upstairs. They sifted through them and discovered one from Beryl Cotter in which she begged Brew on her husband's behalf. Spriggs wired me about it earlier this afternoon and I arranged for the Inspector to meet us here."

Inspector Bradstreet chuckled. "If you ever want to join the Yard, Mr Holmes, there will be a place for you."

Holmes looked appalled. "I am sure that will never happen."

I suppressed a wry smile, but Bradstreet did not seem to have perceived the slight. "You are better than you give yourself credit for," he said waggishly.

He called in his sergeant, who took Mrs Cotter née Haggerty tenderly by the wrist.

"Treat her kindly, sergeant," said Holmes. "This lady may suffer for her crime, but she has already suffered something far worse."

I left the house a lot less nervously than I had entered it. The shadows and walls of that windowless room had seemed so menacing before, but it had no hold now. We clambered back into the dogcart, and as the horse began to trot us away, I reflected with amusement on how my friend had worried me so. I also considered my own feelings about joining him on a case once more. It is true that it had seemed strange, initially, particularly as I had become used to such a quiet domestic existence. But, I now decided, there was always room in my life for two things which so often meant the very same.

Glorious adventure and Sherlock Holmes.

The End

STORY NOTES

I've always been a big fan of the Jeremy Brett series. It expanded, and often even improved upon, the original stories while Brett will always be the definitive Sherlock Holmes as written by Doyle. Indeed, it's Brett I have in mind whenever I read or write Holmes. The first story I did, 'The Adventure of the Apologetic Assassin', had been inspired by its own unlikely title and involved an impossible crime. And I love impossible crimes—which means, of course, I'm into *Jonathan Creek*, one of British television's best mystery series. Uniquely, every episode of the show, all written by genius David Renwick, revolves around an impossible crime and the unassuming designer of magic tricks who solves them. It's certainly a strong influence on my scribbles and got me in the frame of mind to tackle another such mystery in my second pastiche.

And what can be more impossible than someone walking on water? Working out the trick, though, is—well, tricky. When it came to the client, I wanted to bring back Violet Hunter, as one of my favourite Holmes stories is 'The Adventure of the Copper Beeches'. Since she later became a headmistress, that set my story at a school, but I didn't want it to be too similar to 'The Adventure of the Priory School', so I didn't go deep into the culture of the place. The stuff about the secretarial college involved a bit of research, and the places mentioned were real institutions.

I wanted to show a little of Watson's life and the effect that Holmes has on it ('The Adventure of the Yellow Face', by the way, is mentioned because it's a good story with a bad rep), and also the effect he has on the police. I didn't want to wheel out Lestrade, so I used Inspector Bradstreet, and tried to fit him with a bit of character while I was at it. As ever, there's an 'unseen adventure' that is referenced, which here involves Brigadier Benjamin Horrigan, who gets a mention in each of my pastiches. Holmes knows he's a fraud, but the man is so popular he has become dangerously influential. Also, I wanted Holmes to consult a psychologist for a case, as he always was a little ahead of his time when it came to criminal investigation. In fact, I think he still is...

Made in the USA
Monee, IL
27 December 2019